I Was, Am Will Be Alice

Elise Abram

http://emsapublishing.com

Also by Elise Abram

Phase Shift

The Mummy Wore Combat Boots

Throwaway Child

The Revenant

Acknowledgments

I set out to write this book after reading a column by Chuck Sambuchino on the Writer's Digest website, listing new agents looking for clients. One of the agents said that she'd love to read a young adult *Time Traveler's Wife*. I loved *Time Traveler's Wife,* and accepted the challenge. As I wrote, I realized that the topsy-turvy world my Alice was experiencing was a lot like what Alice in Lewis Carroll's *Alice's Adventures in Wonderland* felt, and I found myself incorporating elements of that into my story as well, mainly in the naming of the characters, which are either based on the names in the book, or in some cases, the names of the actors playing some of the characters in the Tim Burton version (even though I haven't seen it yet).

I was first introduced to Lewis Carroll's *Alice in Wonderland* while taking a university level children's literature course. *Alice's Adventures in Wonderland & Through the Looking-Glass* and *Peter Pan*, were by far my favourites, with *Winnie the Pooh* coming in a close third. I've watched many interpretations of Alice and Peter over the years, but none of them did the originals justice. At least, not until ABC's *Once Upon A Time* tackled the *Peter Pan* story, and it was fabulous. I think this is where calling Alice's friend Pete Flay comes from. There are no boy characters in Alice, so when I needed a name, I chose a synonym for pan, maybe because I was so mired in OUAT at the time, or maybe because Neverland and Wonderland both have that ethereal, unreal feeling that my characters were experiencing in their lives.

I owe a debt of thanks to Chuck Sambuchino, Audrey Niffenegger, Lewis Carroll, Edward Kitsis and Adam Horowitz, and Tim Burton for much of my inspiration.

Thank you also to my colleagues and students at Maple High School who continue to support me in my writing and publishing endeavors. Nothing warms the heart more than when a random student, one whom you have yet to meet, stops you in the hall wanting to talk about one of your books. Thanks also to the many people who will help me by publicizing my book, posting during my blog tour, reviewing, and retweeting and/or reposting. A special thank you goes out to the members of the Clean Indie Reads Facebook page, for their ongoing support and advice and for convincing me that I didn't need to swear in order to pen a realistic teen fiction. A special thanks to Christine Grey and Barb Goss, who continue to support, inspire, and impress me with their work and feedback.

Thank you, also, to my friends and family. I get quite a bit of inspiration from my children, and many of the insults Pete and Alice banter back and forth comes from them. Thanks, especially, to my daughters who help to fill me in on teen popular culture, like the names of actors and singers they're interested in.

Lastly, many thanks to you, dear reader, for picking up this book and for reading it. It is my hope that you will enjoy the time you spend with me and my characters over the course of the remaining pages.

I Was, Am, Will Be Alice

by Elise Abram

"I'm sure I can't be Mabel...she's she, and I'm I, and—oh dear, how puzzling it all is!"
— *Alice in Wonderland* by Lewis Carroll

"I wish for a moment that time would lift me out of this day, and into some more benign one. But then I feel guilty for wanting to avoid the sadness; dead people need us to remember them, even if it eats us, even if all we can do is say, 'I'm sorry' until it is as meaningless air."
— *The Time Traveler's* Wife by Audrey Niffenegger

I Was Alice

1

Alice is 9

The first time it happens, it happens like this:

I'm huddled beside the bench in the grade three cloakroom, head scrunched against my knees, hands clasped behind my head. I hear the shots, three of them, and I swear my heart stops pumping each time. There's a woman next to me, kneeling, whispering in my ear, telling me it's going to be okay. Her hand grips my shoulder firmly, and there's a familiar quality to her voice that's somewhat soothing. The man's heels clack into the cloakroom and the gun cracks as he readies it for the next shot. The woman stands. and I can tell by the air she moves with her that she's taken a step toward him. Her lips make a wet sound as if she's parted them, and she draws in a breath as if to speak, and then the gun booms—it's deafening—and she goes down.

I scream and I go away.

When I come back, the woman is gone. So is the man with the gun. The classroom door opens with a whoosh. My breath catches in my throat and my heart thumps in my chest and I hear shoe clacks again...

2

Alice is 9

"Alice?" a man says when the clacking stops. It's loud enough to snap me from my trance. "You're covered in blood! Are you okay?"

I blink at him. "I don't think it's mine."

The man, Principal Cotton, clucks his tongue and says, "For God's sake, girl, why are you still here?"

I shrug my shoulders. I have no idea.

His shoes click away. When they click back he has a woolen blanket in his hands. I feel the warmth of his body as he nears and the wet warmth of his breath at the back of my neck as he drapes the blanket over me. He's a smoker. I can tell.

The blanket's scratchy, like Daddy's beard on a weekend morning. It starts to slide off me, but I grab as much of it as I can and pull it close.

Mr. Cotton holds his hand out to me. I take it and let him lead me to the office.

It's weird sitting in the Bad Kid Chairs, and I get A Case of the Nerves waiting for my parents to come. I have to breathe deeply and evenly; the last time I got A Case of the Nerves, I went away, and I don't want to do that again. Not here. Not now.

By the time my parents come for me, Mr. Cotton has let me get washed up. My clothes are sticky in places where the blood is still wet and hard where it's dried in others. We sit in his office, the four of us around a small, round table. I try to picture us sitting this way in a coffee shop, waiting for the waitress to take our orders. Mom orders a latte, lactose-free and with three sugars. Dad orders something slushy. Mr. Cotton looks like a tea man to me. I order something fruity and icy with lots of whipped cream.

Mr. Cotton says, "She was curled into a ball when I found her," spoiling the illusion. "She was just glued to the spot, huddled into a ball and holding her breath."

"Where did the blood come from?" Mom sniffles. I hate it when she cries.

"We don't know. She seems physically unharmed." Mr. Cotton shuffles the papers on the table in front of him. "I want to give you this." He hands her a pamphlet. "Grief counsellors will be here for the foreseeable future to talk to the children who need it, but seeing as Alice was so close to...well, to the action, Post-Traumatic Stress is a likely possibility."

Mom gasps. "Oh, God!" Dad reaches for her hand. I sit in my chair taking long, deep breaths, willing myself to grow smaller and smaller until I disappear.

"Call this number, Mrs. Carroll. There are counsellors there to help *you* cope, too. Support groups and the like."

Mom reaches for a tissue from the box on the table. She blows her nose, looks at her lap, and continues to weep.

"Thank you, Mr. Cotton," Dad says. He stands up and shakes the principal's hand. He touches Mom's shoulder and she stands, too. She nods and forces a smile at Mr. Cotton.

"Come, sweetie," Dad says to me. He takes my hand and pulls me from my chair.

The drive home would be silent but for Mom's sniffles and snorts and gasps. When we get there, she announces, "I'm going to lie down for a bit." She smiles at me and says, "You can lie with me if you like, Alice," as an afterthought.

I nod. I don't feel like being comforted by my mother. I feel embarrassed at losing control. Ashamed at being found by Mr. Cotton, of all people, just sitting there, crying like a baby. I want to eat chocolate cake till I puke and crawl into a hole somewhere and die.

"Ice cream sundaes, kiddo?" Dad asks.

I nod and smile in spite of myself and follow him into the kitchen.

3

Alice is 9

Dr. Hatfield is a pretty redhead about Mom's age. She lets me go into her toy room when we arrive. "Pick any toy you like," she tells me. I choose a stuffed, pink and fuzzy unicorn with iridescent horn and wings.

Dr. Hatfield smiles at my choice and says, "She's pretty, isn't she?"

I turn toward her, hold the unicorn at arm's length and say, "It's so fluffy!" in my best *Despicable Me* Agnes voice. Dr. Hatfield smiles, but I don't think she gets it.

We go to the next room. I sit on a worn sofa. Dr. Hatfield sits in a worn, brown leather armchair on the other side of a beat-up, old, wooden coffee table.

"What happened, Alice?" she asks me.

I shrug and pretend to be more interested in the pink unicorn's fur. I think I'll call her Princess Pinkie Pie.

"Do you want to tell me about your last day at school?" Mom pulled me out of school after It happened. I haven't been back in three or four days now. Mom hasn't been to work in that time, either. It's really boring at home with her. We watch a lot of television, bake, and make crafts. Mostly, Mom lies in bed and either watches television or sleeps.

I shrug again. Princess Pinkie Pie's horn looks twisted, but when I try to unravel it I realize it's just a cone of pretty material sewn to look twisted.

"When did you first think you might be in trouble?"

Again, I shrug. I let Princess Pinkie Pie run her fluffy, white tail through the circle that forms when I touch the tip of my thumb to the tip of my forefinger.

This goes on for a while, Dr. Hatfield asking questions, me shrugging as I examine every centimetre, every millimetre of Princess Pinkie Pie's body. At last, she tells me to put the unicorn to sleep for the night and calls Mom into her office.

There's an oversized bed in an oversized dollhouse that's not quite large enough for Princess Pinkie Pie to sleep comfortably, but the room has pretty pink and cream striped wallpaper with pale pink flowers in full bloom. There's a window, and a dresser, too. A picture of thick blades of grass and a happy-faced daisy under a blue sky is hung over the headboard. A fat yellow and black bee wearing a huge grin buzzes over the daisy.

As I lay Princess Pinkie Pie on the plastic bed I imagine myself in a make-believe house, in a make-believe room, lying on a make-believe bed. I am the same as all of the make-believe people who live in the house. I am the perfect doll of a child. I never get into trouble. I am not sick with Post Tra...whatever Syndrome. I never disappear. I never find myself bloody and shaking in the cloakroom at school, make-believe or otherwise.

"...traumatized to the point of..." I hear Dr. Hatfield say. I kiss Princess Pinkie Pie goodnight, lay her on the bed, and sneak to the door. If I stand behind the open door and peek through the crack between the door and the jamb, I can just see Dr. Hatfield and my mom in the next room and hear them as if I were still in the same room as them, as if I were right there, still sitting on the ratty old couch beside my mom.

"What do I do?"

"I can help her. Next time she comes, we'll play a game or two, try to build a rapport."

Whatever that means.

"I'm hoping she'll open up to me once she trusts me."

"What about school? I can't keep her out much longer. I can't miss work much longer, either."

"Take her back to school tomorrow. Stay with her for a while."

Like that's going to happen.

"She needs to begin to feel safe in the school environment again."

When we're alone in the car I tell her, "I think I can handle school tomorrow."

I can tell it takes a lot of effort, but Mom smiles. "Didn't I tell you it's not polite to eavesdrop?" She backs out of the spot in the parking lot. When we're on the road she says, "I can go with you, you know, till you feel safe and all."

"It's just school, Mom."

"But Dr. Hatfield said—"

"I heard what Dr. Hatfield said." Mom looks at me out of the corner of her eyes and presses her lips together in disapproval. "But I think I'm good."

"Really?"

"Uh-huh."

There's one other thing I'm good at apparently—lying to my mom.

4

Alice is 9

I go back to school the next day. They're holding class in the library. The principal has moved us there because it's at the front of the school and none of us would have to pass by the scene of the disaster to get there.

A grief counsellor has moved into the spare room in the front office. I meet her on my first day back. We're sitting in the library watching *Charlotte's Web* (we'd finished reading it the very day...you know...happened) and Pete elbows me. "Next victim," he says.

"What?"

"That's right. You don't know."

"Know what?"

Pete looks over his shoulder. I follow his gaze and feel my face beam. It's Miss Dinah!

"Grief Lady."

"What?" Doesn't he see her standing there? I'm just about to stand and run to her, hug her, hold her, tell her I'm so glad she's okay, but Pete says, "They brought her in to talk to us about Miss Dinah, Michael Barrie, and that kid, Ada, you know, the kids that died.

"Lacey? You know how she's afraid of the ghost she insists she saw in kindergarten in the cloakroom? She had to practically be hospitalized. She kept on saying the ghost was an omen, that she must be psychic or something because she saw the ghost and it was a sign of bad things to come in that room."

I look back at Miss Dinah, but she's gone. This other woman, a pretty brunette about the same age as Miss Dinah, stands in her place.

"Grief Lady's been coming into our class ever since, picking us off one by one. She says it's to talk to us, but some of us don't come back.

"Mr. Heart?" He's our new teacher, an old man who's practically ancient, with his grey hair and paunch belly. "He says some of the kids are too upset to come back after talking about That Day, but I think it's more than that."

The Grief Lady plasters a smile on her face and advances on our class.

"Grief counsellor, my ass! I think there's more to it than a lone psycho going postal on the third-grade class. I think the government was involved, and the kids that don't come back saw something they shouldn't have, and they refuse to keep it quiet, so they off them."

After Pete watched this 9-11 documentary with his dad, he started to believe The Attack on the Twin Towers was a huge conspiracy theory and that the U.S. government was involved. Pete's research didn't stop there, oh, no. Day after day I had to listen to him talking about magic bullets in the J.F.K. assassination and how Marilyn Monroe was killed by the Kennedys because she would hold J.F.K. back. Then there was the whole Area 51 Alien Fiasco. And that was just the first week after watching.

Pete continues to spin his yarn about why the government—of Canada, no less—would want to send a gunman to kill a primary school teacher or two and a few kids and maim or wound a few others, but I'm too busy trying to read the Grief Lady's lips as she talks to the new third-grade teacher. When the conversation ends, Mr.

Heart says, "Alice?" and I look up. He crooks his finger at me in a "come here" motion. When I stand he says, "Go with Miss Duchess, please."

Pete puts a hand on my shoulder and squeezes. "It was nice knowing you, Al," he says.

Miss Duchess offers me a seat at a small round table in the corner of her office and closes the door behind us. She sits in the seat next to me, props her elbows and forearms on the table, and clasps her hands in front of her. "We haven't met yet," she says. She smiles and I'm mesmerized. She could be Miss Dinah's sister. When I blink, she almost morphs into Miss Dinah in the fraction of a second my eyes are veiled by my eyelashes. "I'm Miss Duchess."

"Mr. Heart said."

"So he did." She leans back in her chair and buries her still-clasped hands in her lap.

"First of all, welcome back, dear Alice."

I force a smile. Different teacher, different class, and now this inquisition with a stranger—nothing welcome about it.

"Is there anything you wanted to talk about today?"

I shake my head. "Uh-uh."

She takes a beat then says, "Do you know what happened here the other day?"

Of course I know what happened, stupid, I want to say, but I nod instead.

"Do you miss Miss Dinah?"

Another stupid question. Of course I do. Why do you even care?

I shrug my shoulders.

"Do you want to talk about it?"

The grilling by Dr. Hatfield two days ago, another one tonight, Mom's inability to even look at me without tearing up, Dad's near silence and pitiful stares? The last thing I want to do is talk about it even more. I shake my head.

"How does it make you feel?"

I shrug.

Miss Duchess tries her best to give me a verbal hug, to iron out my wrinkled feelings, but I don't want any of it. One shrink a day is enough. Any more than that and my brain may shrivel up like a raisin or something.

At last she says, "I'm going to be here for the next few weeks, Alice. If there's anything you need, anything I can do—anything from talking to helping you take a time out—you be sure to let me know, okay?" She parts her lips and bares her teeth in a hideous forced smile and I can't believe I ever saw a resemblance between her and my beloved Miss Dinah.

"Can I go now?" I ask, barely able to keep my behind in the chair.

She nods. "Uh-huh."

I bolt for the door.

I can't believe I missed *Charlotte's Web* for this.

5

Alice is 9

Pete lies beside me on the grass, playing with a feather. He holds it over his mouth, lets go, and blows, competing with himself for the best time afloat. I pick out a single blade of grass, examine it, toss it aside, and pull another from the ground.

"My mom took me to a shrink," I say to Pete, my eyes locked on the grass blade between my fingers.

Pete turns his head toward me. The feather, no longer airborne, falls onto his damp lips and sticks. He sits up quickly, sputtering and wiping his mouth clean.

"You're so gay," I tell him, shaking my head.

"You don't mean that," he says in his best Miss-Caulfield-Gym-Teacher voice. "You don't mean, 'he's so homosexual,' you mean 'he's so silly.' What he's doing is stupid, not homosexual." He mimics Miss Caulfield's accent so the word comes out "huh-muh-seckshul". I laugh in spite of myself.

"Goof," I say.

"Dweeb."

I go back to pulling out blades of grass. Pete hugs his knees and watches the little kids in their play area.

"You want to talk about it?" he asks.

"Nope," I tell him. "You?"

"I don't know." Pete's fingers slowly crawl toward mine. When they touch, my heart skips a beat. Our fingers feel comfortable that way, entwined with each other and with the grass. "Where were you when it all went down?"

"Near the bench. My brain short circuited. I found the closest thing and tried to make myself as small as possible next to it. You?"

"In the classroom. Under Miss Dinah's desk."

I nod. For the first time, I look up from the grass into his eyes. They are dark brown, almost black. His eyelashes are dark and thick. The only time I've ever seen lashes that long was when my parents went to their friend's annual Halloween party and Mom wore false ones, only hers were silver, not black.

"You see anything?" Pete asks.

I shake my head before I even speak. I saw plenty. I saw the man with the noisy shoes point a large, black gun at me. I saw a woman I didn't know appear in front of me. I saw the outside of the school. I saw the cloakroom and my shoes in a puddle of blood beneath me. "Uh-uh," I tell Pete. "You?"

"Not much. I was hiding and all. I saw gun flashes. It wasn't as cool as they make it seem on TV."

Pete looks up at me. He squeezes my hand. A grin grows on his face. "Race ya," he says. He's up and running before my brain has the chance to register what he's said. I pop up and follow him to the fence.

"No fair," I say. "You had a head start."

"Your legs are longer," Pete says. It's true. I'm a few inches taller than Pete, though technically he's older by a few months. Dad calls my legs coltish, like a horse. I think he means it to be a compliment.

Pete bends over, rests his hands on his knees, and pants. "My parents are sending me to a shrink, too," he says without looking up at me.

The school bell rings, or chimes, or however they describe the noise schools make to measure time. Pete straightens, punches me on the shoulder and says, "Later, gater." He runs toward the school.

6

Alice is 9

Dr. Hatfield talks to me alone at first. I ask for Princess Pinkie Pie before we begin. She lets me get her and hold her while we play this game. It's a card game. Each card has a picture of either a slather of peanut butter or a slather of jam or a slice of white bread. Another set of cards has instructions for making a sandwich. The game is sort of like Go-Fish because we ask each other if we have any jam, any peanut butter, or any bread. If we have it, we must give it up, and then we can build the sandwich on the card we picked. When we're done, we pick another recipe card. The winner is whoever has made the most sandwiches when the cards run out.

Afterward, Dr. Hatfield wants to talk to Mom alone, but Mom asks that I be there with her. "She's only going to be wherever we leave her with her ear to the door," Mom says.

Dr. Hatfield explains that we played the game as a getting-to-know-you exercise. Her goal is to build a rapport with me so I will open up to her later.

She asks Mom how I've been, and Mom says I've been the same. I wish she'd ask me so I can tell her. About the Grief Lady. About the new teacher. About the new classroom. About Mom and Dad handling me like an already cracked egg, and if they're not careful, my insides may run out and I'll die, or something. About how I'm freaked out at what happened the other day. About how I don't know how I got to where I was for those minutes I was gone. About the woman who was shot instead of me. About missing Miss Dinah. About feeling bad about the other people who got hurt or worse.

"Is she still having nightmares?"

Mom answers that she doesn't think so, but she doesn't know. Just like Mom's worried about me, I'm worried about her. I've never seen her eyes so puffy from crying, never seen such dark shadows under her eyes from lack of sleep. You'd have to be stupid to think that's because of anything but me. Of course I'm still having nightmares, but because I don't cry out, and I don't want to burden her with it any more than she already is, I just don't tell her about them anymore.

"That's a good sign, right?"

"I suppose," Mom says.

"*Is* it a good sign, Alice?" Dr. Hatfield asks. Not wanting to contradict Mom, not wanting to set her off again, I nod. It's freaky enough seeing your Mom cry. It's torture knowing you're the one that made her do it.

"Regardless, she's not herself," Mom says. I prick up my ears. "I know she's not sleeping. She's certainly more withdrawn than usual. She's afraid," Mom's breath hitches here, "she's afraid it could happen again."

Dr. Hatfield nods, writes something on her pad of paper, and says, "I'd like to try pharmacological intervention. Not for the long term, mind, but just until she's feeling better. More like herself."

Mom nods. I don't know that word, but I do know it doesn't sound good. I watch the commercials for the shows on television so I know what "intervention" means, it means stepping in to stop a bad behaviour. My heart starts to beat a little faster when I say, "What's that?" and I clutch Princess Pinkie Pie a little tighter.

"It means taking medicine to help you feel better, dear," Mom says. To Dr. Hatfield, she says, "What do you recommend?"

"There's been some work around SSRIs and children suffering from post-traumatic stress."

"SSRIs?" Mom asks.

"Selective Serotonin Reuptake Inhibitors. Anti-depressants."

"I'm not depressed," I say, defending myself. I'm not freaked out because of the shooting, either–I realize the chances of that ever happening again are minuscule. I'm freaked out because I disappeared. One second I was there, and the next I wasn't. For the whole shooting, *I wasn't in the room*! Then I was, and I was covered in blood, and I was crying and *mortified*! That's what scares me the most. That I might do *that* again. Disappear. I've told no one about it, not Mom, not Dad, and certainly not Dr. Hatfield.

I haven't even told Pete. If I did, he might think I was abducted by aliens or something, in order to account for my missing time.

Dr. Hatfield smiles. "People who are depressed rarely think they are, Alice. I'd like to try the treatment all the same." She reaches for a prescription tablet on the table at her side. "I'm recommending Imipramine, a small dose, five milligrams to start, one a day until I see you next. We'll see how Alice is faring and if we need to adjust the dose at that time."

Mom smiles and says, "Thank you, doctor." She tells me to put Pinkie Pie to bed in the next room.

Dr. Hatfield whispers her next words. Neither she nor Mom know I hear her say, "SSRIs are often contraindicated where children are concerned. Watch her for increased thoughts of suicide—"

"Suicide? Alice doesn't—"

"Call me if you have any concerns, Mrs. Carroll."

When I come out of the toy room, Dr. Hatfield is writing something on the back of a card. Mom takes it from her, nods, and says, "Come along, Alice." She holds her hand out to me and I take it.

7

Alice is 9

Mom wakes me with a shake. "Oh, for heaven's sake, Alice, get up!"

The world is hazy at first. I hear the whirr of the floor fan, the tap-tap of the window blinds when the air hits it, and Mom huff in frustration. I say, "What time is it?" but what comes out of my mouth sounds more like a series of groans.

"I woke you up more than half an hour ago!"

"You didn't," I say, sounding a bit clearer. I roll over and see a shadow figure at my bedside. Mom. Dressed for work and ready to go.

"Oh, I most certainly did, young lady." She takes a breath and says, "Honestly, Alice, if you can't get out of bed in time for school maybe we need to rethink your bedtime hour."

My foggy brain takes another step toward clarity. Seriously? I went to bed at eight-thirty last night. How much earlier can I be expected to fall asleep? I hold a hand up in a stop signal. "I'm fine. I'm up, see?"

"Your body's up, but your brain's still asleep."

"No." I clear my throat and force my eyes wide open. The sun is bright through the blind slats. "No, I'm good." I scooch to the edge of the bed and force myself to stand. I'm a little shaky at first and my head is kind of loopy, but it soon clears, and I eventually see clearly. Mom's not wearing her happy face. Trouble is, she's not wearing her sympathetic face either.

"I need to go to work, Alice. *Promise* me you won't crawl back under the covers?"

"I'm up, Mom. I promise. I *swear!*"

"Uh-huh," Mom says, and I can tell she's not convinced.

Trouble is, neither am I. I envision myself as a cartoon character, rooting around in the kitchen for the toothpicks in order to prop my eyelids open.

Cold water. That's what I need. But even after I splash my face with it and brush my teeth, my odds of climbing back into bed are pretty good, I have to say.

Back in my room I grab my iPod and text Pete, *call on me. ring bell til I answer.*

u okay al, he texts back while I'm pouring milk on my cereal.

ttyl, I text.

After breakfast, the fresh air, and Pete's gabfest on how the government plotted to prevent electric cars from being sold because they were worried that if they weren't selling gas then they weren't making money, I was pretty awake. But after History and Math, sitting in the cafeteria at lunch, and lounging under one of the shady trees in the schoolyard after eating, I'm spent. I just can't face Daily Physical Activity—DPA. Not the way I'm feeling.

The Grief Lady welcomes me with open arms when I knock on her office door. I think I disappoint her when I tell her I'm overwhelmed at being back in school and need to lie down. I go into the back room, lie on the cot, and sleep until Pete comes to fetch me after school.

The Grief Lady actually looks worried for me, but she lets me go with Pete after making him swear he'll stay with me till my parents get home, which he does.

8

Alice is 9

The next time I go to see Dr. Hatfield and she asks how I am, Mom complains, "She sleeps all day."

"That's not unusual for someone suffering from depression—"

"I thought she had PTSD?"

"Depression is one of the ways PTSD manifests."

If that were true, then why did the D in PTSD stand for "disorder" and not "depression"?

"It's the drugs you prescribed."

"It may very well be."

For the first time since we've arrived, Dr. Hatfield turns to me and asks, "How do *you* feel, Alice?"

I shrug. "Okay, I guess."

"Do you feel drugged?"

I shrug my shoulders again. What does *that* feel like? "I don't know."

"Do you feel sleepy, like to the point of not being able to keep your eyes open?"

"Sorta."

"Are you sleeping through the night?"

"Through the night and half into the day," Mom says.

"Are you still having nightmares?"

Both sets of eyes are on me, Mom's and Dr. Hatfield's, and I feel like a bug under a microscope. I nod gently.

"What are they about?"

I look from Mom to Dr. Hatfield and feel like I'm wearing my insides on the outside, where they both can see. I don't want to talk about this, so instead of answering, I yawn. It lasts really long. My mouth opens so wide I think the joint in my jaw might pop. When it's over, I say, "Can I go get Princess Pinkie Pie?"

"Do you need her help with this?" Dr. Hatfield asks.

I nod again.

"Very well, then." She purses her lips at Mom and I can feel their eyes following me into the toy room. When I return with Pinkie Pie, I hear them whispering. It sounds like grilled cheese sizzling in a frying pan.

"Is Princess Pinkie Pie ready?" Dr. Hatfield asks.

I nod.

"Good. Can the two of you tell me what your dreams are about?"

I nod and tell them all about them. How I dream I'm the one who was shot. How I dream I was outside of the school when the shooting was going on. How I imagine myself running through the school halls to the third-grade classroom and see everyone dead, bodies lying in a heap on the floor, silent and unmoving. How I turn and look into the face of the shooter, but I don't see more than his silhouette, because his big gun is pointing straight between my eyes, and all my brain can do is force them cross-eyed to look straight down the barrel. The more I talk, the tighter I grip Pinkie Pie.

Halfway through my story, Mom gasps and reaches for the Kleenex. Dr. Hatfield writes practically every word I say in her notepad.

When I'm done, Dr. Hatfield turns to Mom and says, "The medication isn't working."

"If she takes it a bit longer? A smaller dose?"

Dr. Hatfield shakes her head. "It's helping her sleep, but it's not helping her forget. One of the symptoms of PTSD is the inability to stop thinking about the traumatic event that caused it. Because Alice is groggy all day, it's not on her mind. But if she's sublimating during the day and it's manifesting itself at night? Well, that's not our intention in prescribing the meds in the first place."

"So stop the medication?" Mom says. She reaches over and gives my hand a squeeze.

"Stop the medication," Dr. Hatfield confirms.

"Then what?"

"Then we try to get her to talk about it during the day. If she talks about it, gets it off her chest, so to speak, the theory is that it won't fester inside."

In the car after the session, Mom turns the key in the ignition and puts the car into drive. She checks her mirrors, shifts the car back into park, and then turns the engine off. "Talk to me, Alice," she says.

"What should we talk about?"

"Not we. *You.*"

"Okay," I say, stretching the second syllable out because I can't figure out what she's up to. "What about?"

"What Dr. Hatfield said."

"I didn't understand a lot of what she said. Words were too big."

"She said you need to talk about what happened in order to let go of it."

"I don't want to," I tell her.

"I'm worried that if you don't you won't get better, my love."

"I *want* to get better." Tears begin to form in my eyes.

"Then tell me what's going on."

I want to tell her, but she won't believe me. I want her to know, but she'll say I'm making it up. Before I can stop, the words fall from my mouth: "I disappeared when the shooting started," I say.

Mom swallows loudly. "Disappeared? What do you mean, disappeared?"

"I mean, I left the room."

"You walked out?"

I shake my head.

"You hid?"

I shake my head again.

"Alice, you're not making any sense."

"I left the room during the shooting. One minute I was there and the next I wasn't. When I realized I was back, it was all over."

"Oh, dear God! And you've just decided to tell me this now? *After* the session with Dr. Hatfield is over?" Now I do cry, big heaving sobs that I can't stop. Mom undoes her seatbelt and reaches over to me. She holds me until I'm all cried out.

"I didn't mean that, Alice. I know this is difficult for you—for all of us. I just...what *happened* in that cloakroom?"

I don't answer her. In fact, I don't do anything, no nods, no shrugs, nothing. When we get home, I go straight up to bed and cry myself to sleep. Allie the Alley Cat, my favourite stuffed animal's there for me, but I want Pinkie Pie. Something about her being a doctor's stuffie makes it much easier to talk to her than any of my other pets.

9

Alice is 9

"Alice! Bedtime!" Mom calls. There is one last clatter of dishes followed by the click of the dishwasher latch and then the swoosh of water being sucked up and sprayed inside the machine.

"Almost done, Ma," I holler back.

"Not almost—*now*." She's snuck up behind me, so close it startles me when she speaks.

"Okay," I say, squeezing in a few more keystrokes.

Mom pinches my lower lip. "Don't you stick that lip out at me, young lady." She smiles. "I'll pull it off." She gives an exaggerated sigh of defeat and says, "Five minutes to finish up, okay?"

Her fingers leave a dry patch on the inside of my lip, so I lick it till it feels normal again. "Bedtime, Allie," I say. Allie the Alley Cat stares back at me with glazed black eyes from on top of the computer monitor. I log off the site, shut the computer down, grab Allie, and go to say goodnight to Mom who's settled into her love seat to watch television. The love seat is the most comfortable chair in the house. It's also at an angle that only one of the two pillows is far enough from the TV in the room, so it's the best place to sit when you want to be alone or to lie down. Only problem is, if Mom finds you there and she wants to sit, she makes you move. "I'm being Sheldon," she says when she does, talking about the guy on that comedy show about *Star Trek* and science, who never lets anyone sit in his spot on the couch.

I climb on top of her, sliding into the crack between her body and the back of the couch. My head rests on her chest. Dad jokes that I like to lie this way because Mommy has built-in pillows and he doesn't. When he does, I tell him to stop—I don't like sex-talk like that.

"Hey, sweetie," Mom says. She smoothes my hair against the back of my head and kisses my forehead.

"Mommy, am I broken somehow?"

"What? Of course not. You, my love, are perfect." She squeezes me until I can no longer breathe. When I'm about to scream for mercy she lets go. "Why would you ask such a thing?"

"I don't know." I feel tears begin to burn my eyes, so I close them. A tear falls onto my cheek, but I ignore it.

"You are the best thing I've ever done with my life. Do you know what I had to do just to have you?" I do know. She tells me every year on my birthday and a few times in between, just for good measure. "Daddy and I thought we'd never have children. And then I got pregnant. I spent nearly two months in the hospital before you were born, just so that if anything happened we'd be close to a doctor to have it taken care of. When you finally came, you spent another month in intensive care because you were so early and so small. The doctors didn't think you'd make it."

Hearing my origin story doesn't help me at all. Just because I was born perfect doesn't mean I still am. Knowing that I could've died when I was that small, or before I was born, doesn't help me deal with the fact that I could've died a few days ago, or sometime in the future, or anytime between now and then.

"Then why the doctors? Principal Cotton said—"

I feel Mom's body jerk beneath me as she cranes her neck to look at me eye-to-eye. "What did he say to you?"

"Nothing—"

"But you just said—"

"In his office. Right after. What he said to *you*."

"That's just...grown-up talk, sweetie. That's not for you to—"

"And again in Dr. Hatfield's office—"

"You heard what she said to me?"

"Uh-huh."

"You heard...everything?"

"Pretty much."

"Don't worry about that. You just worry about getting better, you hear?"

I nod. I don't ask why, if I'm perfect, I need to get better.

"Good. It's bedtime, then." She kisses me on my forehead again, and I kiss her back on the cheek. "Off to bed with you."

I stand beside the love seat and offer up Allie's head for her to kiss. "I'm not touching that thing with my lips, kiddo." She smiles again. "Go on. I'll come to check on you later." I start up the stairs and hear her call, "And don't forget to brush your teeth!"

Teeth brushed and face washed, I fill my water cup and take it to my room where it sits on my nightstand in case I need it at night. Allie is silent witness to the care I take to brush each and every tooth and scrub each and every millimetre of my face. I arrange her beside my pillow when we're back in my room. My other stuffies shoot jealous daggers at her. "Don't be that way. Tomorrow night might be *your* night," I tell them. I turn them so their backs are to us and they can't make Allie uncomfortable with their glares.

I don't like to dream lately. Before...you know...I had some good ones. Unicorns with multicoloured manes of daisies taking to the air on the backs of ginormous blue birds, finding a pot of Polly Pockets at the end of the rainbow. Since...you know...most of my dreams are the same.

The man enters the cloakroom, the soles of his shoes clacking, each step sounding like a kind of junior gunfire. I look up at him, but can't see his face. I try to scrunch down until I'm no bigger than a mouse, a ladybug, on the ground. I see my reflection in the chrome plating of the bench beside me, looking like it's made of rubber and someone's stretched it, first this way and then that, and I tightly squinch my eyes so I don't have to look at it. I hear a click, and then a deafening boom. Blood splatters, blood that's not mine, on me, on my clothes, on the floor in front of me, and then I'm outside of the school, beneath the cloakroom window, shivering. The only sounds I hear are my breath and my heart beating loudly in my ears, and then I wake up.

Other times, there's the boom and then I wake, but not before the realization that it's *me* who's been shot.

That's the dream I have tonight. I think I scream when I wake because Mom comes rushing into my bedroom. "You okay?" she asks.

"Oh, Mommy!" I burst into tears. "I may not be broken, but my dreams certainly are!"

"Shhh, shhh, shhh," she says as she climbs into bed beside me. She slings a heavy arm over my belly and squeezes lightly. "It's just a dream." It sounds like she's trying to convince herself of this fact more than me. Trouble is, today it was a dream; the other day it was reality. My reality.

"It's just a dream," Mom repeats. I close my eyes, sniffle, and pray that's all it was, a stupid dream. But no matter how hard I try, I cannot purge the events from my memory.

10

Alice is 12 and 4

I'm having that dream again.

Footfalls tick in the hall, the beat slow and regular, counting down the seconds left in my normal life.

Click. Clack. Click. Clack.

A momentary pause outside of the grade three classroom.

Shuffle. Spin.

The door knob explodes with what sounds like a clap of thunder directly overhead.

Click. Clack. Click. Clack.

The funhouse mirror image in the chrome of the bench leg.

The muzzle of the gun, shaft pointed directly at me, staring, like a dark, unblinking eye.

The flash after the trigger is pulled.

I wake up and run to the bathroom to splash cold water on my face, my breathing still heavy, my heart still beating double-time. I look up into the bathroom mirror, half expecting to see the contorted image of my face, the same one I saw on the bench leg in the cloakroom on That Day...

"Hey!" A man calls, his voice distant and meek as if heard through the watery ripple of a dream.

"Hey, you," he calls again, louder, clearer than at first.

I open my eyes. The night air is humid, the ground beneath me moist against the soles of my feet.

"Hey, kid, are you okay?" I blink to clear my vision. It's not the man with the gun. It's Mr. Cheshire, the night-time custodian at my school. I remember him helping us fold the volleyball net after our school was skunked in the last tournament.

"I want my mommy," I say and burst into tears, both of which make me seem like a pouty little baby instead of a pre-teen ready for high school next year.

Mr. Cheshire holds his forefinger up and I nod, as my body collapses onto itself until I'm crouched into a small ball on the pavement. Mr. Cheshire returns moments later with a heavy, gray, woolen blanket, with red and white stripes on each end. The colours remind me of the sock monkeys we made in Art earlier in the year.

He helps me inside and offers me a cup of tea with honey, and two arrowroot cookies from the caretaker's pantry while we wait for my ride.

I'm horrified to learn he's called the police instead of my parents.

The ride home is silent. The officer in the passenger's seat keeps looking back at me, either to make sure I'm okay or that I'm still there. I wouldn't put money on either if I were him.

I get out of the car. The passenger officer puts his arm around my shoulder and leads me up the front walk. Dad's car is in the driveway, so at least I know someone's home. What will I say to them when they open the door?

Dad's the first to respond to the doorbell.

"We found your daughter, Mr. Carroll," one of the policemen says.

Dad says nothing, but runs a hand across his forehead, as if his brain hurts to think about the situation.

Mom wanders over to stand just beside and a little behind him. She gasps when she sees me. "What is this?" she asks.

The policemen stand behind me. One of them says, "The custodian at your daughter's school reported he found her wandering in the garden at the front of the school."

Mom gasps again. "In the garden?" she says.

"What was she doing in the garden?" Dad asks the policeman and then he repeats the question to me. I shrug my shoulders. I don't know what I was doing in the garden. Last thing I remember, I went to bed in my room, upstairs, in this house. Last thing I remember, I was about to be shot in my dream and got up to splash water on my face.

"Mommy?" a small voice comes from high above us where a little girl, no more than four years old, is standing on the stairs, holding onto the railing. She's wearing a pink romper with turquoise piping and tie, and a Barbie picture on the tank. The outfit looks distantly familiar.

"Sweetie," Dad says to her, "take..." He pauses as if unsure what to call me. "Take Mabel upstairs, will you? See if you can't find her some clean clothes, something of Mom's, to wear."

Daddy pulls me over the threshold and hugs me tightly. He kisses the top of my forehead, which sets off the waterworks.

"I don't know what happened, Dad. One minute I was in the bathroom and the next I was at school."

Dad shushes me and tells me to go get dressed. "My daughter sleepwalks," I hear him say to the police. "She must've been napping and I forgot to lock the door. I promise it won't happen again."

How can he be sure of that when I can't even be sure of it myself?

The little girl goes into my parents' walk-in closet and looks for a t-shirt hanging up on Mom's side of the cupboard. I could probably find something a little more to my liking—I've become an expert at swiping Mom's clothes and convincing her they're mine—but I think I'm still a little in shock. Mom and Dad didn't exactly look like themselves. And who is this little girl staying here?

She hands me a t-shirt and a pair of yoga pants. "You name Mabel?" she asks.

"It's my middle name," I tell her. Just then it strikes me as odd that it was what Dad had called me—he never uses my middle name unless he's mad, and then he calls me by all my names, last name included.

"Mabel my name, too." Crazy kid. She's gotta be only...what? Three? Four? Little kids get so confused at times.

"Why you here?"

"I...I don't know."

"Where you mommy and daddy?"

"Downstairs."

I pull the t-shirt over my head. It smells like Mom's perfume. She must've worn it before and hung it back up when she was done. The yoga pants are a little baggy, but they'll do.

"My mommy and daddy downstairs, too," the girl says.

"Thanks, kiddo." I ruffle her hair and go down the hall toward my bedroom. It's Pepto-Bismol pink. There's a junior bed and a Barbie Princess comforter and sheets instead of my cast iron daybed and the One Direction comforter I bought last summer. Instead of Selena, Taylor, and Harry on my wall, there's an arrangement of framed Disney Princess portraits.

"What the...?" I say.

"This Allie's room," the girl says, following me in.

"Tell me about it."

"I a princess."

I hear the front door close and Mom and Dad talking in hushed tones in the front foyer. "Shh," I tell the girl, holding my forefinger to my lips. She repeats the sound and gesture and I wonder if it looks as silly on me as it does on her.

She follows me into the upstairs hallway where we listen to the conversation through the railing.

"She can't stay," Mom says.

"Where else can she go?" asks Dad.

"Home."

"This *is* her home."

"That prepubescent girl is *not* my baby."

"I'm telling you it is."

"No," Mom says curtly. I imagine her shaking her head for emphasis.

"Wendy," Dad says softly, "she *is*." He sighs heavily. "I don't know how, I just know she is."

Mom gasps. She sniffles, and I can tell she's crying. I feel terrible—worse than the agony of missing out on 1D tickets, worse than finding out there isn't a single pair of Taylor Swift Red Keds left in the entire city in my size—knowing it's because of me. The pit in my stomach, the one that's been there since this whole ordeal began with Mr. Cheshire in the school garden, like the Grinch's heart, grows three sizes at that soft, seemingly insignificant sound. "She is, isn't she?" I hear Mom say.

Now I imagine both of them nodding.

We sit around the kitchen table. Mom scoops Heavenly Hash ice cream from a tub on the counter into small bowls. Every once in a while, she sneaks a look at me above the frame of her glasses. Mom places a bowl of ice cream in front of each of us and the girl begins to chant "Whip cream! Whip cream!" Mom goes to the fridge and gives her an aerosol bottle of Cool Whip. The girl takes it, sprays a generous helping into her bowl, and then holds the nozzle to her mouth and sprays directly into it.

"Alice, please!" Mom says.

Both myself and the girl look at her and say, "What?" though the girl's word is muffled by the layers of whipped cream she's crammed into her mouth.

"Okay," I say after a beat, "what's going on here?"

"We were hoping *you* could tell us," Dad says.

"I don't know. I mean...I don't know."

"What do you remember?"

I shrug and study the moisture collecting on the outside of my bowl, watch as the flecks of chocolate in the luscious, brown, creamy scoop begin to perspire. "Like I said before, one minute I was in the bathroom, and the next, Cheshire's calling to me like I'm some kind of a freak."

"How did you get there?"

I shrug in response, pick up my spoon and start mashing the ice cream against the side of the bowl with it.

"I'm scared, Dad," I say.

"I know, sweetie."

"Not your daddy. Mine," the girl says. She shoves another spoonful of whipped cream into her mouth and chants, "Mine! Mine! Mine!" over and over again.

"Okay, what's with her?"

"Out of the mouth of babes, huh?" Dad says to no one in particular. "Technically, I'm not your dad, not yet."

"What?" The word squeaks out of my mouth, quashed by the waterworks starting up again.

"There has got to be a logical explanation for this," he says.

"Mom?" Mom squishes her lips tightly together and shakes her head. She pushes her ice cream bowl away and clasps her hands in front of her on the table.

"I know you're my daughter, I mean, you look so much like Alice there's no way you're not related, but...I don't know."

"More!" Alice begins to chant. "More! More! More!"

"Was I really that annoying when I was her age?"

"Honey, you don't know the half of it."

I look over at the kid. She's formed her hands into fists and is banging them on the table, punctuating each word as she says it.

"You, young lady, have had enough garbage food for one day. Time to brush your teeth and wash your face," Dad tells her.

"No! No! No!" Alice continues.

"Yes! Yes! Yes!" Dad says over her. He stands up, scoops her up out of her chair, and over his shoulder. I used to love it when he did that. It made me feel like I was flying. Unfortunately, it also made me feel like I had to pee something bad as he'd always land my bladder square on his shoulder bone.

Dad turns around so the girl can face Mom. "Kiss your mother goodnight." He bends his knees slightly so she can reach without Mom standing, and takes her to wash up for bed, leaving Mom and me at the kitchen table, alone.

"Are you okay?" she asks me. "Are you well?"

I nod. She looks so beautiful. She's slimmer than I remember. She wears her hair with bangs which she let grow out a few years ago. The lines around her nose and mouth are much softer, too. Other than that, she looks exactly like my mom.

If she really is my mom, who's this other kid that appears to be living with them in my house, in my room, with my name? It can't be me. It can't be. I'm me. And I'm here. And the girl is there...upstairs with Dad, getting ready for bed.

Mom reaches over and pins a lock of hair behind my ear. "You've grown," she says. "How old are you?"

"Twelve."

"Do you have any boyfriends yet?"

"Mom..."

"Have you gotten your period yet?"

"Mom!"

"I just...I'm trying to come to terms with this. You look so much like my daughter, but my daughter's upstairs with my husband."

"I know." I chance a glance at her, then look away, shamed by the weight of her stare. "Freaky, huh?"

"Freaky deaky," she says. Professor Farnsworth from *Futurama* says that. Mom heard it one night and it stuck. She says she likes the sound of it.

We laugh softly and shortly together. It feels good to laugh, to feel happy, rather than scared out of my flippin' mind.

"So..." she says.

"So..." I repeat.

Our eyes meet and she smiles a smile that seems forced. I've freaked her out. I was right before: something *is* wrong with me. Something is *very* wrong with me.

"Do you have anywhere to go tonight?"

"Mom?"

"Right. This is your home. This is where you need to be.

"I can set up a sleeping bag in Alice's room. Just be aware: she's a chatty little monkey and she'll talk your ear off thinking it's a slumber party if you answer her."

I smile to myself.

"What?"

"You used to call me that all the time. A chatty little monkey."

"Well, you were, as you've probably already noticed."

I nod and say, "Uh-huh."

"Okay. I should have a spare toothbrush in my room. You know where everything is?"

I nod once.

"Right," Mom says, "Of course you do."

We both stand. She tucks some more hair behind my ear and then gives me a hug. "My Little Alley Cat." She takes my face in her hands and holds it far enough from her face so that our eyes lock. "Do you remember that? My Little Alley Cat?"

"Of course I do."

Mom nods, lets go of me and walks out of the kitchen. She turns at the arch leading to the front hall. "I don't know what's going on here, Allie, but one day we'll find out. I promise you."

"I know," I say, but this time it's *my* smile that feels forced.

11

Alice is 12

Mom's assembling her lunch when I get to the kitchen the next morning. Dad's sitting at the table eating Honey Nut Cheerios. "You used to have more hair," I tell him, hugging him around the neck from behind.

"Thank you, Captain Obvious," Dad says. I can't help but giggle.

"It used to be so soft and curly." My hand bounces lightly on the coils of hair, still thick around the back of his head and on the sides. When I'm done, I kiss his growing forehead.

"She's right, you know," Mom says. "That's one of the reasons I fell in love with you."

"Gross, Mom."

Dad passes the Cheerios to me. I pour a heaping bowlful and drown it with milk. "And now?" he asks.

"Well," she says. She shrugs and says, sort of nonchalant, "I've found other things to love."

Dad blows her a kiss.

"Again," I tell them, "gross." I crunch on a spoonful of Cheerios.

"Since when do you care about my hair?" Dad asks.

"I don't. It's just the first thing I noticed when I came down this morning. I looked at you and thought that the last time I saw you, you had more hair."

"The last time? You saw me just last night, Alice."

"I know. And the last time I saw you, you had more hair."

"Last night?"

"Yep."

"Where were you last night, Alice?" Dad asks. He holds onto his spoon, still dipped in the cereal bowl. He hasn't raised it to his mouth since I mentioned his hair.

"Here. In the house."

"You went back, didn't you?" this from Mom who abandons her lunch prep on the counter and sits at the table beside me. She reaches for my hand, and I let her take it.

"I don't know what you mean." And I don't. I mean, I had a wicked dream last night, one that seemed really real, but I woke up in my own room, in my wrought iron daybed, in my One Direction bedding, and okay, so I was wearing an old t-shirt of Mom's and her yoga pants when I woke up and I don't remember going to sleep in them, but I was dreaming last night. I had to have been.

"Last night was the night you travelled back in time." Mom says this as if it all makes sense to her, that it doesn't sound as cray-cray to her as it does to me. I look at Dad thinking I'll see confusion on his face. Instead, his features are lax and he's nodding in agreement.

"Six years ago," Dad says.

"No," I whisper.

"When the police showed up at my door, I nearly freaked," Mom says. "I mean, the girl they brought to me looked so much like my baby, but she—you—were so much older, you couldn't be. I didn't know what to do."

"So we told the officers you were sleepwalking and that I forgot to lock the front door," Dad continues. "They seemed okay with that. They warned us to be more careful next time and they left. You were upstairs with— well, with yourself—getting ready for bed, so Mom and I decided to let it play itself out, and we'd resolve it in the morning."

"No," I say, a little louder than before.

"I mean, if you were who you claimed to be, then the only people who would miss you were us, and you were already with us, so we figured no harm, no foul," Mom explains.

"No!" I clamp my hands over my ears and shake my head back and forth repeating the word. Fireworks explode in my brain, and my heart begins to pound, alternating beats between my temples and my chest. It couldn't have happened. It couldn't have *actually* happened. But if it didn't, how could they know what I'd dreamed of last night when I hadn't told them yet?

The anxiety continues to build in my chest. Wake up, I tell myself, Alice Mabel Carroll, you wake up this instant! My eyes squeeze shut tightly enough to make my forehead ache.

Mom's cool hand reaches toward my forearm, and I open my eyes. Mom presses her lips together and the corners raise into a grin. "Yes, my love. Yes." With my hands over my ears, it sounds as if she is speaking under water.

I look toward my dad. He nods once, firmly. "It's true," he says.

Mom puts pressure on my forearm and I lower my hands from my ears.

"But it can't be," I protest.

"I know," Mom says, softly. "But it is."

"But how? *How* could that have happened?"

"I don't know," Mom says. "*We*," she looks toward Dad, "don't know."

"But we're going to find out, Alice, we promise you that," Dad says.

"This is a joke, right? Any second now, Ashton Kutcher's going to pop his head into the room and tell me I'm being punked."

"I wish that were true, honey, but it's no joke."

I look from my mom's face to my dad's and then at my cereal bowl. Though they look unchanged, they would have soaked up so much milk by now they'd have the consistency of mush. Mom would quote Sheldon from *The Big Bang Theory* and say they'd lost all molecular integrity. On a normal day, I'd tell her I couldn't believe she'd actually said that. Mom would ask why, and I'd shrug, and then she'd shrug. When I finally saw the episode the quote came from, I told Mom that Sheldon had said the same thing she does about her cereal. She asked where I thought she'd gotten it from. I was convinced it was a chicken or egg scenario. Which came first, Sheldon saying it or Mom?

"I'm a freak, then. Is that it?" I ask.

"No, not a freak, just...different," Mom says.

We're all quiet for a moment, and then I say, "So I'm a time traveller?"

Dad's shoulders seem to deflate. He even makes a noise like all the air is escaping from him. "It certainly looks that way," he says.

"Yay, me," I say sarcastically.

"Oh, don't be that way," Dad says.

"Yeah, I mean, how many people can say they've met their own selves as a toddler?" Mom asks.

"Met and been annoyed at her—" Dad says.

"Right," Mom says.

"So this is a *good* thing?"

"It's a...*different*...thing, right, John?" Mom asks Dad.

"Absolutely right," he says.

I think back to the day of the shooting, how I disappeared from the building, how I found myself under the classroom window and then back inside the cloakroom, and wonder if I did it then, if I'd time travelled then.

Maybe this freakish—different—ability isn't so bad after all. If I had time travelled that day, then maybe being broken wasn't so bad. On at least one occasion so far it'd saved my life.

Mom pops out of her chair and goes for the wall phone. "Who are you calling?" I ask.

"Your doctor, and then my work, and then your school. We're going to nip this thing in the bud and set the ball rolling to figure out what's going on inside your body to make this happen to you."

12

Alice is 12

The doctor's office is full of old women with walkers, coughing and gnashing their ill-fitting dentures. I will myself to grow small until I'm so insignificant I disappear, and all this time travel nonsense is forgotten.

Eighties music is piped into the office through hidden speakers. Mom starts singing along with the tune playing. "Stop," I tell her quietly.

"What?"

"Just stop, okay?"

"But it's Culture Club. *Clock of the Heart*. How can you *not* sing to a song like that."

"Mom..." Her name comes out whiney, like "moh-ohm" and she smiles, like she's accomplished her personal mission to embarrass me in public.

"You know, I saw The Culture Club once, at the old Exhibition Stadium, before they tore it down. It was the last day of summer vacation before I was supposed to go away to university." Mom's always talking about university and the concerts she saw when she was a teenager. I wish I could go to concerts. She keeps telling me how concerts were so much cheaper when she was a kid, how at some places—like the Ontario Place Forum—concerts were free with admission, or how Canada's

Wonderland used to have a whole series of seven dollar concerts.

Lucky.

"I bought a souvenir of some kind, a t-shirt, or a program, probably a program because they could be preserved better than t-shirts. Anyway, I bought a souvenir, and when I went for my wallet later, I noticed it was gone. My purse didn't have a zipper on it, so either I put it back and someone pick-pocketed it, or it fell out, or something, but I had to go to university without ID, which was hard because you needed ID to open bank accounts and get student cards and get into bars and stuff."

"How was the concert?"

"Hum? Oh, it was okay, I guess. Honestly, I don't remember. I guess the memory of the concert has been overshadowed by the memory of the lost wallet."

Mom is full of these stories. She tells them often. Usually more than once. They always have some kind of moral. I think she does it so she can have a reason to tell me about growing up. You know, do as I say, not as I do, or learn from my mistakes because my whole life is a cautionary tale or something. Will that be me twenty years from now, spinning yarns to children of my own? I wonder what I'll tell my kids about *my* life? Would they think I'm crazy listening to my story about the time I met myself when I was four? I'm sure what's about to unfold in the doctor's office will be a hoot and a half. Maybe one day I'll tell my kids about *that*. If I ever bump into my older self, I'll be sure to ask if I do.

The nurse calls my name. Mom whispers, "Remember: let me do the talking, okay?"

I don't answer her. My stomach feels about to explode, and my bladder seems suddenly full. I wipe some sweat from my upper lip.

"Allie? I said, *okay*?"

"Fine, Mom. Whatever."

"Not whatever."

"Whatever. *Okay*?"

Mom sighs. It's the best I can do, given the circumstance.

Dr. Rickman knocks on the door before she enters the examination room. "Is it safe to come in?" she asks. Dr. Rickman was my mom's doctor before she was mine. About two years ago I got tired of seeing a man paediatrician and asked Mom if I could see an adult doctor. A *lady* adult doctor. Mom laughed. She said how lucky young women were nowadays that they had a choice of doctors. Dr. Rickman's her first lady doctor. Not because she preferred her doctors to be men, but because lady doctors have been few and far between for most of her life.

Dr. Rickman's young. The diplomas on the wall say she graduated as a doctor only four years ago. Mom must've been one of her first patients. She's the same height as me, which is to say, short, has dark skin, shoulder length, curly hair, and brown eyes. She wears her lab coat unbuttoned over jeans and a golf shirt coloured a pretty shade of purple that's almost blue. "How are we today?" she asks. She sits at the computer desk in the corner and logs into the Mac on the desk.

Mom and I murmur some form of "good" in reply and then Dr. Rickman says, "So what brings us here today?" like that: not "you" but "us" as if, somehow we're in on my defect together. I guess we are, in a way. Dr. Rickman, get ready to rock your world.

"It's Alice, doctor."

"Okay. What seems to be the problem?"

"She's...not herself, lately."

"Oh?"

"No. She's..." Mom, Dad and I had a pow-wow after breakfast this morning and we discussed how we might broach the subject of my...ability, for lack of a better term, with the doctor. They fabricated all these symptoms that were similar to what I was experiencing, with the hope they could convince the doctor to give me the tests they thought I needed, which was basically a full body work-up. "She's been having headaches."

Not before this morning, when I tried too hard to shut my parents out. It was my fault, really. I hadn't wanted to know that what I'd convinced myself was a dream was for real.

"When did they start?"

"After the incident at school." That wasn't so much of a lie—that incident was a game-changer on so many different levels.

"How many years ago was that, now?"

"Three."

Dr. Rickman types it into the computer, her fingers moving faster than the speed of light. "You haven't said anything in any of our previous visits."

"No," Mom says, "because until now they've been few and far between. They're happening more frequently now."

"And how do you feel when you have a headache, Alice?"

I shrug. I'm supposed to let Mom do the talking, after all. Besides, I wouldn't know what to say. Our mission today is to get a head-to-toe exploration of my body. I wouldn't want to screw that up for us.

"Nausea?"

"Uh-huh."

"Dizziness?"

"Uh-huh."

"Do you see lights?"

"I guess."

She types some more. "What else?"

"She's begun to sleepwalk."

"How often?"

"Most nights."

Way to lay it on thick, Mom. At best it was one night. Eight years ago...or was it last night?

"She's opened doors and left the house on occasion."

Besides, I think we're pretty sure it wasn't an episode of sleepwalking. Mom and Dad are convinced I was time travelling. Either that, or we have some sort of psychic link that caused us all to have the same dream last night, and then some sort of group hallucination that led us to believe it was real, like those people who gather at Lourdes to stare into the sun, and then claim to all have seen the Virgin Mary in the sky.

"What you describe is not unusual for PTSD." Post-traumatic stress disorder, for which I, apparently, have become the poster child. Three years in therapy, and becoming unstuck in time.

"But if it were...PTSD...why would the headaches and things manifest now? Why not three years ago?"

The doctor shrugs. "We're still trying to unlock the finer points of the brain. Even today, no one quite knows how it works for sure. Maybe it didn't happen three years ago because Alice hadn't hit puberty yet. Maybe it has something to do with her hormones, maybe not. Maybe she's just developed a new coping mechanism."

"How can a coping mechanism be debilitating?" I ask. She's making me mad. I don't understand how all of this could be related to stress. I mean, most kids in my class went through the same thing I did and none of *them* are reacting this way.

Dr. Rickman shrugs again.

"What about the blackouts?" I ask. If our goal is to get me a CAT-scan or MRI or whatever, that would be a good symptom to have, wouldn't it?

"You experience blackouts?" asks the doctor.

Mom looks worried. This wasn't the plan. Mom likes plans. She's always making lists and checking off To Dos on the list. She says she feels a sense of accomplishment when she finishes one of her lists. Crumpling the paper and throwing it in the trash is more satisfying than a cigarette after sex, I overheard her tell Dad once when he asked about her lists. Okay, first: ew! and second: TMI, Mom! (I wonder how Mom even knows how that feels, considering she brags how she's never smoked even a puff of anything in her life.)

I nod to answer the doctor's question.

"How often?"

"It's happened a couple times, now." That's not even a lie. It happened during the Incident three years ago and again last night.

"Have you noticed any triggers? Something that happens before you black out?"

I shake my head.

The doctor opens a desk drawer, flips through the folders in it, and withdraws a form. "I'm ordering a fasting blood test, echocardiogram, CT, EEG, and MRI. I'll get the secretary to call the hospital and schedule them on the same day to speed things up a bit."

Score!

"It's serious?" my mom asks. I don't know why she looks so concerned. We've won the medical lottery. She and Dad are getting exactly what they wanted.

"We'll know better after the tests." I look at Mom. Her eyes are tearing. I take her hand in mine and squeeze.

When the doctor finishes typing, she says, "Hop up on the exam table and we'll take your pressure." She pronounces my blood pressure normal. She listens to my heart and dubs that normal, too.

"My office will call you after we've made testing arrangements."

Mom manages a nod. She brushes a tear from her cheek.

"We'll call you either way, even if the tests are negative."

"I appreciate that, Doctor," Mom says. She thanks the doctor on the way out.

"I don't know about you," Mom says once we step from the office into the sweltering pre-summer heat (I'm not even joking—the weather's been anything but normal this last year), "but I could go for a huge helping of ice cream." She doesn't mean ice cream, she means frozen yogurt. There is this amazing froyo place not too far from us that offers about a dozen self-serve flavours and a gajillion toppings. Froyo's never been so unhealthy. I like it because you get to taste as many flavours as you want before you settle on the ones you like best.

"I'm with you, Mom," I tell her, and I can't imagine a situation or time in which I wouldn't be with her.

13

Alice is 12

It's the night of the meteor shower in the fall of my twelfth year. Mom and Dad insist on going to watch in a park in North Toronto where the CBC says is the best, darkest place in the city to see the spectacle. They tell me I should ask Pete and so I do. To my surprise, he accepts my invitation.

We pack old comforters into the trunk including the Barbie Princess one, a Styrofoam cooler of ice, bottled water and pop cans, and four Rubbermaid containers, two of Mom's homemade party sandwiches, and two of her World Famous Cookies 'N' Cream Brownies (an amazingly decadent, over-the-top concoction of chocolate chip cookie crust, Oreo cookies, and brownies), get Pete at his house, and we're off.

The ride to the park isn't nearly as long as the time taken to find a parking spot. Dad hands Pete the Barbie Princess comforter. Mom dips into the cooler and fishes out two bottles of water, two cans of pop, a container of sandwiches, and one of brownies, packages them all in a plastic grocery bag, and sends Pete and me on our way.

"Meet back here, at the car, at ten-thirty," Mom says.

"Text us if you need anything," Dad tells Pete.

"Yes, sir, Mr. Carroll," Pete says.

"Way to lay it on thick, dude," I whisper to him and play-punch him in the arm.

"John's fine, Pete."

"Yes, Mr. Carroll, I mean, John."

"Well, you two go and have some fun now," Mom tells us. She grabs Dad's hand and giggles like a school girl.

Dad nods. "But not too much fun," he adds, sternly.

I roll my eyes at him. "Come on, Pete," I say. I grab Pete's hand and lead him away from my parents who are mooning like a bunch of high school kids on a first date.

"Don't do anything I wouldn't do," Dad hollers after us.

"Oh, God," I say rolling my eyes again. Trying to forget my parents' sugary sweet and syrupy courting ritual, I tug at Pete's hand. "Come on," I say.

We find a spot on an incline where we can lie on an angle on the comforter and we're near vertical. We look up to the stars, but nothing's out of the ordinary yet. "You hungry?" I ask Pete.

"Those some of your mom's amazing brownies?"

"Uh-huh," I say. I take the container from the bag, open it, and wipe the melted ice from my hands on the comforter beside me. "I helped, too."

Pete takes a piece from the container and maws down. "That's why they taste extra special tonight," he says through the mouthful. His teeth are ringed with dark chocolate from the brownie. Crumbs from the cookie crust fall to his lap.

"Gross," I say.

He covers his mouth with his hand till he can swallow, then cracks the lid of one of the water bottles and rinses. He swallows, shows me his teeth and says, "Better?"

"Better," I say. We pack the food away and lay side-by-side on the comforter. It isn't long before Pete takes my hand in his. The electric current our skin generates when we touch shivers all the way up my arm, down my torso, and into my stomach.

"This is nice," I say, looking up at the sky. I want to take a peek at Pete, to see the expression on his face, but I can't bring myself to. Instead, I close my eyes and imagine what it might look like if the two of us were to walk hand-in-hand this way forever.

"Did you see that?" Pete says loudly a moment or two later. His outburst is followed by oohs and ahhs from the people around us.

"Damn, I missed it. My eyes were closed."

"Well open them."

"I will." We watch the sky in silence. A bright silver streak crawls across the stratosphere and everyone around us gasps. "I saw that one," I tell him.

The silence resumes, and not just for us, it seems, but for everyone in the park, as they wait with baited breath for the next rock to shoot into the atmosphere.

"Alice?" Pete asks.

"Uh-huh?"

"Why were your eyes closed?"

"I was dreaming."

"About what?"

About us, dummy. What else does a girl dream about when a boy, who also happens to be her only friend in the whole wide world, takes her hand? "Nothing." More streaks light up the sky, some of them flickering like light bulbs turning on and off, others with tails leaving trails like fireworks. We watch for a while, cheering and clapping with the crowd. When there's a lull in nature's show I say, "Pete?"

"Yeah," he answers, dreamily.

"What do you think of time travel?"

"Do you mean like in fiction, or in reality?"

"In reality."

"I think it could be neat."

"Yeah?"

"Yeah."

"But what if you couldn't control it? What if it happened and you had no say in where or when it did?"

"Bummer."

"Yeah."

Pete rolls over onto his side to face me. "Where would I go when it happened?" he asks. "Could I see, like, dinosaurs, or travel to see how mankind evolves a couple a thousand years from now?"

"I don't know. Say you can only travel in your own lifetime."

"So I could see my future?"

"Yeah, I guess. But mostly your past."

"Lame."

"I know, right?" I let go of his hand and roll onto my side so I'm facing him with my head propped on my hand, ignoring the gross factor that it's full of my sweat and Pete's mixed together. "And you can't tell yourself anything—"

"Because of a paradox, right?"

"And because you kind of like your life the way it is, and you'd be scared to death you might change it up somehow, and not necessarily for the better."

"Could I make contact with people I know?" Pete asks.

"You wouldn't have a choice. I mean, being a kid and all, where else would you go when it happens but to be with your parents?"

"You could memorize things," he says, brightening, "like winning lottery numbers, or ball teams, or horse races, and tell *that* to your parents. There's no way *that* wouldn't make your life better."

"Unless your parents get obsessed with things like that. You know, say your dad has a hidden gambling addiction that he's fighting and he doesn't want anyone to know. If you give him the winning horses and he places the bet, it could rekindle the addiction. He could even use the money on other bets that lose. *That* wouldn't help your family. Actually, it would probably destroy it."

"And there's no guarantee the same numbers or horses would win in different timelines," Pete says, taking up the argument.

"Exactly my point."

He takes a beat and then says, "Al? Your dad doesn't have a hidden gambling addiction that he's fighting, does he?"

"*God*, you are *such* a dweeb," I tell him, and roll over onto my back.

Pete takes another beat before saying, "You're right, Al. Being able to time travel only in your lifetime and only in your own city would be an extremely lame ability to develop. Especially if you're a kid."

My heart sinks. Pete, my only friend in the world besides my parents and doctors, thinks I'm lame.

Hold on, Alice. He didn't say *you* were lame, he said your *ability* was lame. And he didn't even say that. He said *an* ability with those lame limits would be lame. He has no idea we're even talking about you.

My train of thought's interrupted by Pete's lips hitting mine so hard our teeth clank together. His mouth is closed as he mashes it against mine for about a ten-count. That crazy lub-dub thunking rematerializes in my torso and my stomach lurches.

Pete kissed me.

Peter Flay kissed *me*.

My first kiss.

From Pete Flay.

I open my eyes and focus on his worried face, his nose suspended inches from mine, so close that if we took simultaneous deep breaths they might touch.

"I'm sorry, Alice," he says. He sits up, knees bent, elbows on his knees, face buried in his hands. "I am so sorry."

"No, Pete, it's okay." I sit up, too. I put an arm around his back, rest a hand on the shoulder farthest from me, and nestle my cheek on the shoulder closest.

He takes his hands away from his face. "You just...you were staring, and you looked...God, how you looked—"

"Pete?" I say. He stops babbling. "It's okay." And then I do something I've only ever seen in the movies and on television. I crook a finger under his chin, lift and turn his face a little, and bring my lips to his. We sit like that for a few seconds and then our lips part and then come together and then separate.

"Ten out of ten," I say. "Not too wet. Not too dry. Just enough pucker. All in all, the perfect kiss."

Pete smiles awkwardly. Though it is hard to tell given the darkness, I think he's blushing.

People around us applaud and for a stupid second I think they're weighing in on the effectiveness of the kiss as well, but then Pete says, "We're missing the show."

I nod and lie back on the comforter. Pete follows. It isn't long before Pete takes my hand in his again and squeezes.

14

Alice is 12

The call about the tests from Dr. Rickman's office came in a few days ago. Mom and I are sitting in a corner of her office, trying not to look grossed out by the older gray-hairs shaking or hacking up a lung, or annoyed at the babies crying as we wait.

u there, Pete texts. I would have thought things would have been awkward between us after the meteor shower, but they kinda sorta went back to normal. We're still best friends, only now we're best friends who sometimes hold hands or steal a quick kiss when no one else is around.

ya, I text back. *prw.* Parents are watching. Pete needs to know to can the wishy-washy stuff when one of my parents is around. I haven't let them in on our secret yet. Mom's too stressed by the suspense of waiting for Dr. Rickman to make sense of it all to even care about me and Pete's first kiss. She sits trying to read her latest eBook, biting at her cuticles as she does.

wan2 g2 park, he asks. Before we were…you know, Pete and I used to hang at the park regularly, usually with other guys from our class. We'd play Tag, or Marco Polo, or Tag Football, or just swing on the swings, or lounge and talk. Well, Pete mostly talked to the others and I mostly listened. Lately, the park is where Pete and I hang out when we need some alone time. We can lie for hours on the grass, picking out shapes in clouds, or having swing races, or just swaying in sync, holding hands.

idk, I text. *Drs apptmt*

uok

checkup

Outside of that convo we had watching the meteors, I haven't brought up time travel with Pete. If there's one person on the face of this earth—outside of my mom and dad, that is—that would believe what's happening to me, I think Pete would be it. Still, no sense testing that theory before its time.

18r, he asks.

maybe

pcm Please call me. Wow. I never considered that Pete may have it bad for *me*, I mean, worse for me than I do for him. The thought of that makes the muscles around my heart tighten. I sigh and shift my weight to my other butt cheek.

"Won't be long now, hon," Mom says, interpreting my newly discovered revelation about Pete as Waiting Room Restlessness. I grin at her and she grins back.

can't. not now. sry. ttyl?

maybe :-7 His smirky smiley makes me laugh.

"What's so funny?" Mom asks.

"Pete's text."

"What's he say?"

"Nothing."

"Fine," she says jokingly, "don't tell me."

"Every girl needs her secrets, Mom."

Mom plasters another grin on her face, shakes her head at me a few times, then returns to her eBook.

If Dr. Rickman keeps us waiting in the waiting room for forever, she keeps us waiting in the exam room for forever and a day. When she comes in, she closes the door behind her, washes her hands in the small sink in the corner, and logs into the Mac on her desk. "Sorry to keep you waiting so long," she says as she completes this ritual. "One of the partners called in sick this morning and it's all the rest of us can do to pick up the slack."

"That's okay," Mom tells her.

Dr. Rickman smiles a closed-mouthed smile at us. She clicks opens PDFs of my test results, taking a moment to quickly glance at each before moving on to the next. "You're here for test results, correct?"

"Yes," says Mom.

"Negative."

"What?"

"All of the tests were negative."

"But how can that be?" Mom asks.

"The blackouts are most concerning. No abnormalities of circulation means no syncope due to poor circulation. No epilepsy..." she clicks a few more times. "Heart normal, no arrhythmia. Blood panel normal.

"Mrs. Carroll, you have a healthy twelve-year-old on your hands here."

That can't be, my brain screams. Something's wrong with me. I wanted the tests to come back showing something, anything, was wrong with me. I never thought about how we'd proceed if the tests were negative. All of them. Tears begin to burn in my eyes and I sniffle. Dr. Rickman anticipates the waterworks and hands me a box of tissues.

"So what now?" Mom asks. Her voice catches a little and I know she's holding back tears of her own.

"Nothing now. She's perfectly healthy."

"I'm sorry...what did you say?" Mom says slightly louder than normal.

"There's nothing more to do. The tests came back negative. According to the paperwork, she's perfectly healthy."

"Excuse me, Doctor, but my daughter is anything but healthy."

"There's still the PTSD to consider—"

"I'm sorry," she says, pressing her lips into a hard line and shaking her head. "I don't believe that."

"Mom," I tell her in a low voice, hoping to get her to lower her voice a couple of octaves in the process, "it's okay."

"It's not okay. *You're* not okay." To the doctor, she says, "What if one of these days she steps off a curb and into a bus while sleepwalking?" I decide not to remind her that I wasn't actually sleepwalking the night I showed up on her doorstep, wrapped in a police blanket, and flanked by a pair of officers.

"There are precautions you can take," says Dr. Rickman, and I wonder how she can remain so calm when my mother's on the verge of losing it.

"Precautions," Mom says, sort of challenging.

"Installing an alarm system, for example."

"We *have* an alarm system. And Alice knows the code."

"Use a different code when you lock up at night, one she doesn't know. If she tries to open the door, the alarm will wake you.

"Does Alice still see her psychologist? Dr..." she clicks the mouse a few times, "Hatfield, was it?"

"Regularly. Ever since the incident occurred almost three years ago now. With all due respect, Doctor, I don't see how this could be explained away by post-traumatic stress."

"Children's brains react differently to stress than adults' do, but there will come a time in the near future when PTSD will no longer be a part of Alice's life."

That's what *she* thinks. What about the traumatic stress brought about by having to watch a younger version of yourself gorge on ice cream topped with whipped cream and sprinkles?

"We could always try medication again," Dr. Rickman suggests.

"Medication?" Mom asks. I glance at the door to make sure it's shut so we have our privacy. I'm not looking forward to walking through that waiting room after this knock-down-drag-out. "You just said nothing's wrong with her—why would you medicate someone who's perfectly healthy, according to you?"

"Mom, please," I plead. I hate that she's speaking to Dr. Rickman that way, petite, friendly, calm Dr. Rickman. I need her to stop.

"We often find success using benzodiazepines with anxiety-related sleepwalking—"

"Anxiety? That's the equivalent of offering my daughter a Band-Aid while she's sitting here hemorrhaging."

"Mom, stop!" I tell her. My heart starts thumping, clunking in my chest, threatening to leap up and into my throat.

"I will *not* stop, Alice," Mom says, practically hemorrhaging herself. "There's something wrong with you," she tells me. "And if you can't find out what," she tells Dr. Rickman, "then we'll find another doctor."

"If you'll just calm down, Mrs. Carroll—"

"I will *not* calm down." Thunk goes my heart. "Don't you dare tell me to calm down." Thwak. That crazy thunk-thwack beat starts to echo in my temples and the room begins to spin. My reflection, faint and ghost-like in the computer monitor over Dr. Rickman's shoulder, looks like it's going down for the count.

"I want a second opinion," Mom says.

I'm no longer in the room—or even the same time zone—in order to hear Dr. Rickman's response.

15

Alice is 12

I become aware of my surroundings in sensory layers: the smell of gasoline, propane, rotting garbage; the feel of chilly air biting my skin, breeze whooshing by me, threatening to throw me off balance; the bitter taste of stomach acid backing up in my throat; the sight of cars speeding by, going opposite ways on the road in front of me; the sound of horns blaring, people cat-calling. This is followed by the realization that I'm standing near a busy intersection somewhere downtown, underdressed in crop jeans and a t-shirt, and completely alone.

I sprint to a side street alleyway and hide from the public eye. Once there, hunkered behind a rather smelly dumpster, I scope out my surroundings: dead end to the left of me; unconscious drunk guy down a ways near the dead end; grimy windows and tottering fire escape ironwork stretching upward for miles; bright city lights to the right of me; a store on either side of the alley opening. One of the stores has an outside display of sweatshirts.

Here's the plan: sneak back to the main street, grab a hoodie from the pile, and disappear back into the alleyway. In other words: steal.

What if I get caught?

I could go to jail, wind up in juvie, like on television, featured in my own episode of *Scared Straight*, or something.

But if I don't do it?

If I don't do it I have to hang out in this alleyway, shivering until I go back. That could be any second. Or hours. Or days. And while the last time was the longest I'd ever stayed away at a few hours, who's to say it won't be longer this time? What if the wino wakes up? What if someone looks down from their window and calls the police? I could still wind up in juvie, jail, or worse.

I can't just stand here hiding in plain sight in this freezing weather in only a t-shirt, indefinitely, I finally decide upon—and carry out—The Great Hoodie Heist.

It seems like everything's going to plan. I manage to stay hidden in the shadows between the buildings and then behind the tablecloth on the display in front of the store. I reach up and feel the crisp, clean cotton of a sweatshirt near the centre of the pile closest to me, and yank it from the table. And though I feel bad about the other bright-white clothes falling to the dirty sidewalk, I make a run for it back down the alley.

It's perfect. Men's XL. I'm in the process of pulling it over my head when I hear, "Hey!" from the street. I wheel around to see a group of kids, most a few years older than me, all of them shabbily dressed, wearing ripped jeans with black sweaters, or torn black chinos and dirty white hoodies, and jean or leather jackets. They've formed a wall across the entrance, blocking the fluorescent glare of the streetlamps, and all I can think of is "Shit!" I take stock of my situation: there are more of them than me; they are all bigger than me; and they all seem way more street smart than me. If I was scared before, I'm scared shitless now.

This is it. This is the end of me. There's no way I can get out of this alive.

Unless I go back.

But I have no idea *how* to go back.

How did I even get *here* in the first place?

Mom and Dr. Rickman arguing in the doctor's exam room. Correction: Mom arguing, Dr. Rickman taking the beat down.

I was upset, I mean, really upset. How could Mom have been so rude to her? How could she be so loud? She was embarrassing herself, yelling like that. She was embarrassing *me*. I felt the stress building. I wished I were somewhere, anywhere else but there, and then, poof! I was.

So...stress. If there ever were a time I was stressed to the max, it was now. Moreso than with Mom's tirade at Dr. Rickman.

So why am I still here?

The people at the head of the alley begin to walk slowly toward me. "This is our block," one of the bigger girls tells me.

I close my eyes. I want to go home. I want to go home *now*. I want to be anywhere but here. Any*when* but here.

When I open my eyes, I'm still in the alley and the gang is about a metre closer to where I'm standing. I could run, but the alley dead ends about ten metres from the dumpster. Running would probably hasten their advance on me, which means the same end, only sooner. I take a slow, careful step back and away from the gang.

"That means anything boosted from this block is ours."

I take another step back. "Look," I say in a voice so small I can't believe it's mine. I hold my hands up and out in front of me showing them my palms so they can see I mean them no harm. "I don't want any trouble."

"Well, that's exactly what you found," a boy, slightly shorter than the first girl, says. He pounds his right hand into his left fist as if to emphasize how much trouble I've actually found.

"I just...I'm lost," I say. They step closer. I don't know how, but I've somehow backed myself against the dumpster and have nowhere to go. "I don't know where I am—"

"I done tol' you where you are, *bitch*," the girl who first spoke, whom I assume is the gang's leader, says. "You're on our block!" And they come closer.

"No, that's not what I meant."

"So then why don't you tell us what you meant, then?"

I take another tentative step back and a little sideways, hoping I'll clear the dumpster and put some space between us, but wind up thumping my back, flush against the metal.

"I got separated from my parents," I say, trying a new tack.

"Hey, Lory," one of the smaller girls says to her leader, "what do ya know? She say she got parents."

"I used to have parents...once," the boy says, more threatening than wistful. "I *don't* anymore."

They form a semi-circle around me and part of the dumpster so there's no way out. One of the kids pulls at the sleeve of the shirt I'm wearing and I shrug my shoulder to pull away. One of them tugs at the hem of the shirt just below my hips, threatening to pull it up toward my waist, and I bat his hand away. Another of them pinches the shirt near my belly button and gets a wad of flesh with it. I hit that hand away, too, hard.

"Hold up!" the leader shouts. "Hold up, hold up, hold up." She holds her hand up like a cop directing traffic to stop. "What I mean to say is, your hoodie. You pinched it from my beat. That means it's mine, and I want it back."

"You know I'll probably freeze to death overnight without it?" I ask her.

"*That* is *not* my concern."

"I mean, I have nowhere to go to get out of the cold."

She points to her chin. "Does this look like a face that cares?"

I don't want to get beat up.

I also don't want to roam the streets of the city until I become a human Popsicle. "No," I say. The girl's face drops the second I say it, like she's shocked I would dare challenge her, and I regret saying it the moment the word leaves my mouth.

"What did you say? Because it sounded like you said no, and no one, *no...one...*says no to me. Ever!"

"Sounds like someone just did now," one of the boys snickered.

"Shut up, Duck," the leader says.

"Ooooh, you just been tol'," another girl says, but whether to mock Duck or Lory is unclear.

"I'm gonna ask you one more time, 'cause I think I must'a heard you wrong the first time. Give me my hoodie back!"

"It's not yours," I tell her. I feel my bladder threaten to give way, and consider crossing my legs to make sure the pee stays where it belongs. "I stole it, fair and square."

Lory shoves me with her open hand against my sternum, and the wind is knocked from me as my back thumps against the dumpster.

Then I see it. A hand. Poking out from behind and through the gang, opening and closing at me, beckoning me to grab it. So I do. I reach for it. The hand locks with mine and pulls me toward Lory. Rather than sidestep her, my shoulder brushes hers. She must take this as a sign of aggression because she grabs for the shoulder. There's pressure from the tips of her fingers and then her nails rake against the skin, but through the fabric of the shirt, so it's not really painful, and then she's left holding nothing but fabric that stretches more and more the further I get from her, and then rebounds as she loses her grip on me altogether.

There's enough time for me to give the kid gang a backward, over-the-shoulder glance. I see the gang leader standing with her hands on her hips, confused look on her face as if asking what just happened. The other kids look at me as if dumbstruck by this totally random event. I shrug my shoulder to try to right the shirt on my body.

"Get her," Lory commands, and I know that, Prince Charming-like saviour or not, I...*we*...are in for it.

16

Alice is 12

"Run!" the man shouts. He squeezes my hand and drags me along behind him. We run for about a block before I see the glass building façade jutting out toward the sidewalk like gems from the earth, and recognize where we are. "Down here," the man shouts, and pulls me between the glass-fronted wing of The Royal Ontario Museum, and the buildings beside it. We skirt the perimeter of the building through the park behind it, come up on the other side, and stop in front of the employee entrance. The man looks back, wipes sweat from his forehead, and manages to say, "I think we lost them," between pants.

"What the hell?" I ask. My mind is racing. Who is this guy? Some Good Samaritan who saw I needed help as he just happened to be strolling by the alley, and decided to take on a gang of some half-dozen crazed kids to save little ol' me? Did people like that even exist? The thought that he's an innocent in this predicament who simply decided he was going to save my ass is heartwarming, and I'd like to believe this is the case. The alternative, that his being there for me wasn't random, meant he somehow knew I'd be there, and I can't even fathom what that scenario might imply.

"No time," he says. "In here." He opens the door to the employee entrance for me and follows me inside. "Sit," he says. He points to a bank of chairs against the wall opposite the security guards' booth.

I watch as he talks to the guard on duty, sheltered behind glass from about four feet from the ground, and up to the ceiling. I wonder if it's bullet proof. Do people even plan museum heists anymore?

Eventually, he slips a duo-tang through a slot at the bottom of the glass, which My Saviour signs and hands back to him.

My Saviour turns. He's holding two visitor's passes on chains. "Wear this," he says. "Come with me." Whoever he is, he's a man of little words, that's for sure.

He goes to a door on the wall opposite the entrance, and slides his pass through the reader. The LED on the panel goes from red to green, and the door lock clicks. He opens the door and ushers me through to a lighted corridor, much brighter than the room we've just left, and I get a good look at him. His hair is dark and cropped short. His eyes are dark brown, almost black. He's taller than me by more than a foot, and has a slim build. He looks vaguely familiar.

"Do I know you?" I ask him.

"Not now," he says. "Not here." He walks a few feet ahead of me without looking back when he talks. "This way."

"Do you work here?" I ask.

"No. I mean, I can't tell you that."

"Why not? Are you some kind of secret agent? Have you been stalking me?"

He doesn't answer.

"The security guard knows you. He signed you in, and if you don't work here, and your tag is a visitor's tag just like mine, then *he* must know you. I mean, we're like, in the basement of the Museum, right? The employees' area? They don't let just anyone in here. Not unless they're *employees*, right?"

Now he does stop. He turns to face me and says, "Christ, Mabel, I've forgotten what a pain you can be."

Mabel? He called me Mabel! My dad's the only one who's ever called me Mabel when I was out of time. How does he know to call me Mabel and not Alice?

I ask him, and he says, "Just...drop it, okay?" He continues walking down the plainly painted, bright corridor, past door after uniform door. Some of the doors open onto offices, dedicated workers in them, still plugging away. Others remain closed.

"I never told you my name."

He stops in front of the door marked "Staff Room", turns to face me again, and says, "I said, drop it, okay?" voice raised.

"Okay," I say, knowing it's a lie before I even say it.

He uses his keycard to open the door, holds it for me, and says, "Inside," but I stare him down. I know I know him from somewhere, and I know he knows me, and I need to know how. "Not before you tell me how you know me."

"Damn it, Mabel, get inside," he sort of whines, and pushes me through the doorway into another brightly lit room. There are some tables for communal lunches and a few more intimate areas set up with easy chairs, or wooden chairs facing each other with a small table between them. "Sit," he tells me, and because I see he's growing impatient with me, and because I need him to answer my questions, I do. He goes to a bank of lockers against the far wall, opens one with a combination lock, and takes out a t-shirt, yoga pants, and flip flops, which he crumples into a wad in his arms. "Here are some clean clothes."

"I'm fine," I tell him.

"Are you cold?" he asks. "'Cause there's a sweater in here, too."

I shake my head.

He shrugs his shoulders, closes up the locker, and drops himself into the chair on the opposite side of the table. "Washrooms are over there." He points somewhere behind me. I size him up for a moment to see if I can't figure out whom in the hell he is, but come up empty, sigh, and take a washroom break.

When I come back, he's on the phone. I hear him say, "Yeah, I've got her." Pause. "She's fine." Pause. "No, really, she's fine." He turns to see me emerge from the washroom and says to the phone, "Look, she's here now. I gotta go." Another pause. "Okay. Same here." He disconnects and says to me, "Feel better?"

I toss the hot hoodie at him and say, "For you. Consider it a token of my appreciation for being my Prince Charming. In fact, if you won't tell me your name, maybe I'll call you that. What if I call you Prince from now on?"

He rolls his eyes. "Please don't."

"Charming, then?"

"You...are...incorrigible."

"Definitely Charming." We sit for an awkward moment in complete silence, neither of us trying to look at the other. "So do you do stuff like this often?" I finally ask.

"What stuff?"

"Save damsels in distress."

"No. Never. Under ordinary circumstances, I'd have to be crazy to intervene in a situation like that."

"But these circumstances aren't ordinary?"

"Crap, Mabel! Stop asking so many damn questions," he says, sort of whiney again. My brain begins making mental connections, trying to figure out how I know this guy.

"So, if you didn't save me on a whim, then you were there because you knew I'd need saving at that particular point in time, which means you must know me somehow."

He starts shaking his head. "No, I don't."

"You do. You know me."

"No," he says. He gets up and pretends to study the paintings on the wall adjacent to the lockers.

"You know me. The only question is...how?" Charming ignores me and moves on to the next painting.

"When in time are we?" I ask, testing the waters to see his reaction. I get nothing, so I continue pushing buttons hoping to eventually push the right one and get him to slip. "Are you a friend of my parents?" Charming moves on to the next frame, this one holding a map of historic Toronto. "Are you *my* friend? Of course, if you were, that would mean I'm in the future, seeing as I'm not in the habit of befriending forty year old men."

Charming clucks his tongue at this and I know I've scored. "Too old? I know, dumb kids, think everyone over twenty is old. Thirty-something, then?" Charming shakes his head and I know I've pushed another correct button. "So that would mean you're probably friends with me, I mean, Alice me, older me." Nothing from Charming. "Are you my boyfriend?" Nothing. "My lover?" Still nothing. "My husband?"

"Are you hungry, May?" he says, turning. Finally. Another correct button.

"We're married?"

"Mabel, please!" He looks sick, like he's crossed ghostbusting streams or something, and brought about the end of the world as we know it.

"I could go for food," I say, taking pity on him.

Charming leads me to the cafeteria where we wait in line holding plastic trays, and he says, "So what'll it be? Green Jell-O? Red? Splurge with some whipped cream?"

"Forget that. I want one of those huge sandwiches they're whipping up."

"Keep dreaming, Mabel. You know you can't have that now."

"I do?"

"You've never eaten in a situation like this before?"

I wrack my brain trying to recall. I remember having ice cream with myself when I was four.

"You can't eat anything heavy," he tells me. "If you do, you'll sick it up on the other end, and you hate that."

"I do?"

"Yes," he says.

"How do you know that?"

He laughs. "What, like anyone *likes* throwing up?"

He's got a point. "So what *can* I have? Besides Jell-O, I mean."

"You could try a bagel with butter. Hard cheese, if you're ambitious."

"Joy."

"Or have one of those sandwiches if you like. God, Mabel, I've forgotten how aggravating you used to be."

"So you *do* know me!"

"Order," he tells me.

"I knew it."

"Just order, Mabel, okay?" The woman stares at me from across the counter. I take a moment to consider. Charming knows me in the future, so I must've sent him here to save my ass. I also gave him strict instructions not to let me eat anything more substantial than a bagel and cheese, so I'm not sick when I go home. "I'll just have the Jell-O," I tell her.

"Wise choice," Charming says. He takes two dishes of red Jell-O, a bottle of water and one of orange juice from the fridge further down the counter, pays, and then finds a two-seater table in the most remote corner of the room.

"The orange juice is for you," he tells me. He picks it up, cracks the seal, and hands me the bottle. "Drink up."

"Why?"

"Keeps the potassium levels high." He takes off his glasses and blinks, and then I know how I know him.

"Pete?"

"No," he says. He scoops a Jell-O cube into his mouth.

"Is that you?"

"No," He shakes his head frantically. "It's not."

"Why can't you just tell me?"

"Because I don't want to affect the timeline. I kind of like who I am, who you are, and I don't want to change any of it, so can't we please just eat our Jell-O, and wait in silence until you go back?"

Since when did Pete, the dumb, immature geek who used to ask me if I wanted seafood and open his mouth to show me the food inside Pete, become my dad? I remember our talk the night of the meteor shower, and tell him, "Pete?"

He looks up at me, not an ironclad acknowledgment that's his name, but pretty damn close.

"You were right. Time travel *is* lame."

17

Alice is 12

Mom's waiting for me in Dr. Rickman's exam room when I return to the present. I take a moment to catch my breath and orient myself. A moment's all I get, because before I know it, Mom grabs my arm from behind, spins me around to face her, and encloses me in the bear hug to end all bear hugs.

"You're back," she says. She kisses the top of my head. "I was so worried."

"Uh...Mom?" I manage, though my face is pressed against her breast.

"Yes, sweetheart?"

"I can't breathe."

"Right." She lets go of me, takes a breath, and then her face lights up. "I have to call Rebecca," she says excitedly, as if in the time I've been gone they've become BFFs. She draws the curtain around the exam table, and I hear her open the door. She pokes her head through, hails the first nurse she sees, and says, "Tell Dr. Rickman we need her, please?"

"Yes, Mrs. Carroll," says a voice in the hall. How embarrassing. They know her by name already. Now every time we come into this office we'll forever be dubbed The Woman Who Yelled and The Daughter Who Disappeared.

Dr. Rickman knocks on the door less than a second later.

"That was quite the show, young lady," she tells me. I smile nervously in response. "I wouldn't have believed that, not in a million years, if I hadn't seen it with my own two eyes. Kudos to your mom." She washes her hands again and sits back at her desk.

"How often does that happen?"

"That's...ummm..." I count: once during The Incident at school when I was nine, once when I saw myself when I was four, and now. "Three times."

"A day? A week? A month?"

"Ummm...in my life?"

"So it's still a relatively new trick, huh, Wendy?"

"We've...uh...known for quite a while."

"Oh?" Dr. Rickman's fingers fly a mile a minute over the keyboard—she wants to make sure she gets every subtle nuance of my issue down.

"The night before we came to you a few weeks ago, she'd travelled back in time about eight years."

Dr. Rickman stops typing. "Really?"

"The police brought twelve-year-old Mabel to our house. We told them she'd been sleepwalking."

"Four-year-old me was jealous."

"Mabel?" Dr. Rickman asks.

"Alice's middle name. We decided to call the Alice out of time Mabel. To differentiate," Mom tells her.

"Amazing." She glares at me, as if she stares long and hard enough she'll be able to see into my soul and discover the secret to my defect somewhere in there. At last, she remembers herself, shakes her head as if coming out of a trance, and asks, "And so that was which time? One, two or three?"

"Two," I say.

"Time three was here, just now in my office, correct?"

Mom nods.

"And the first time?"

I look down at my feet. "During the shooting."

"Alice!" Mom says. "You never told us."

"What was I supposed to say? That I disappeared and then came back? You would've thought me crazy."

"We wouldn't have. Your dad and I have been waiting for this since you were four, remember?"

"Let me get this straight," Dr. Rickman says. "You disappeared from your classroom *when* that day?"

"When the gunman pointed his gun at me. After he shot."

"You disappeared in front of him?"

I nod.

"Where did you go?"

"I don't remember."

"And just now, where did you go?"

"Just like then, I suppose. Some...when...else."

"But you don't remember where?"

"Uh-uh," I say, shaking my head, lying. I always remember where I've been. Time is linear for me like it is for everyone else.

Dr. Rickman types some more. "I'm ordering a blood test and DNA sample for genome sequencing. With your permission, I'd like to contact a colleague—a geneticist—at the University of Toronto to help read the results. I'd also like to call Dr. Hatfield and have a frank conversation with her about our conversation today.

"You'll forgive me, Wendy, but I firmly believe your daughter has PTSD stemming from the school shooting, which is compounded by this newfound ability of hers. I'm going to recommend antipsychotics as a course of treatment."

Dr. Rickman looks at me and then at Mom. I look at Mom. She looks worried. Dr. Rickman must pick up on this, because she says, "That sounds scary, but it's not to imply Alice is anywhere near psychotic. Antipsychotics are frequently prescribed for severe anxiety that may interfere with sleep patterns. If she's in agreement, we can get started on this course of treatment, asap." She finds a test requisition form in her desk drawer, puts her stamp on the top right corner of the paper, ticks a few checkboxes, and hands it to my mother who folds it into quarters and slides it into the front pocket of her purse.

"The sooner you take care of this, the sooner we can get the ball rolling," Dr. Rickman tells us.

18

Alice is 13

The rest of the year was fairly uneventful, though I was on those nasty meds Dr. Rickman prescribed, so I wouldn't know if something eventful *had* happened unless it jumped up and bit me on the nose, and even then...I was so drugged I slept most of the next few weeks after the doctor's visit away. Then the headaches and dizziness started. When weighing the lesser of two evils—sleeping my life away, feeling topsy-turvy and in danger of falling over, my head pounding, heavy as a bowling ball on my shoulders, or the rare odyssey of a Magical Mystery Tour Through Time—it was a no-brainer. I stopped taking the meds.

I had a party on my thirteenth birthday, if you can call what went on a party. In attendance were my parents, my grandmother, and my mom's single, free-spirited sister that usually has nothing to do with the family except on birthdays and holidays, which is okay by Mom, though she wouldn't actually come right out and say so. Dad's an only child and his parents died before I was born, so I have no family to speak of on his side, save a few of his cousins he sometimes bumps into at the mall or sees at things like christenings and engagements and such. Dad's parents were the youngest on both sides and he was born late in their lives. Most of his cousins are old enough to actually *be* his parents, so he never really got close to them, or so he tells me every time we bump into one of them.

Pete was there, too, of course. Between dinner and cake, we went for a walk to our park. He held my hand and gave me a ring with my birthstone in it, one that I'd admired in front of him in Claire's at the mall. I opened the box and he took the ring out, placed it on my finger, and then kissed me softly on the lips. I imagined this was what it would be like to have someone ask me to marry him, except when the time came, Pete would have stubble on his cheeks that would scrape mine when we kissed, and the kiss would last longer, and be open-mouthed, and with tongue, like on television or in the movies, which I don't understand, because why would you want someone else's tongue in your mouth, let alone accept it willingly and think it's sexy? Maybe it's an acquired taste, like Mom says with her lattes that are so bitter and leave a disgusting aftertaste that I imagine would be the same taste left behind in your mouth after licking an ashtray.

Anyway, I got my period (joy!) and I met a friend, an *actual* friend. A girl named Tina. She's the smallest kid in the class, and she just transferred in this year, so she knows nothing about what happened when I was nine, and I have no intention of telling her. I made sure Pete doesn't either. Tina has a beagle she calls Snoopy and an older brother she hates. I think it's cool. I mean, if I didn't have Pete, having an older brother would be a cool way to meet guys. Tina shakes her head every time I tell her this. The last time she told me her brother was a loner and didn't have but a few friends, and if I saw what they looked like, I'd never say anything like that ever again if I wanted to stay friends with her, so I stopped saying it. I still thought that, as her brother gets older, he'll have different friends, and some of them might be cute, but I keep that thought to myself.

What I really mean when I say the months following the appointment with Dr. Rickman were uneventful, is that I didn't time travel at all. Not even once.

Then we got the phone call. Dr. Rickman's secretary. The genetic sequencing was done, and she needed to see us. Pronto.

Mom and Dad and I go in the next day and the nurse gives us the VIP treatment, taking us directly into the exam room without waiting. Dr. Rickman comes in no longer than a heartbeat later. "Hello, Alice," she says. She smiles and nods at me. I'm sitting on the exam table, and Mom and Dad are sitting in the chairs beside her desk.

"Wendy," she says to Mom with another smile and nod. "And you must be Mr. Carroll," she says to Dad.

"John," Dad says. He stands and offers her his hand.

"I don't believe we've met before."

"We haven't," Dad confirms.

"Please sit." She sits herself and logs into the computer.

"We have the results of the genetic sequencing," she says, looking at her monitor, pulling up my file. "My colleague at U. of T. has analysed the results, and made his recommendations."

"What did you find?" Mom, ever impatient, says. Dad grabs her hand and wraps it inside his hands, as if her fist was a pearl and his hands were clamshells.

"Nothing, really," Dr. Rickman says. Mom gasps and I brace myself for another scene starring Mom the Hysterical. "Everything is normal for the most part. As I said before, Alice is a normal, healthy, teenage girl."

Mom opens her mouth and takes in air as if to speak, but Dr. Rickman continues, making her hold her thought. "There was one thing, however."

"Oh?" Mom says, finally finding her voice.

"Yes. Are you familiar with telomeres?"

"They have something to do with aging, don't they?" Dad asks.

"Sort of, yes. You see, as cells divide and replicate, telomeres act like a cap on the end of the DNA protecting the information stored there, preventing it from being lost. Kind of like how those little pieces of plastic on the end of your shoelaces prevent them from being unravelled. They're necessary because they prevent chromosomes from fusing together or changing, which could lead to a whole host of problems, including cancer.

"As a person ages, the telomeres get smaller. There's an enzyme the body produces called Telomerase Reverse Transcriptase that helps preserve the telomeres as the cell divides, but each cell is programmed to divide only a certain number of times in a person's lifetime. We think they're related to aging, but on a cellular level.

"Genetic sequencing shows Alice's body produces too much of this enzyme, like a dripping faucet, always in production, not just when cells divide, but on a small scale, and all the time. When she's under extreme stress—like the shooting incident, during a nightmare, or even her reaction to your agitation the last time you were in my office—the faucet opens wide, her cells are bathed with the enzyme, and she...well...travels through time."

"But how can that be?" Dad asks. "I mean, *time travel*?"

"You don't think I'm telling the truth?" I ask.

"No, sweetie, that's not what I meant. I meant, time travel of *all* things. What makes her react *that* way?"

"We don't know. Other kinds of chemical imbalances, hyperthyroidism, for example—when your thyroid works overtime to produce hormones associated with body metabolism and growth—could manifest itself as an increase in facial hair or height, something visible and detectable through blood testing. But this? We're flying through uncharted territory with this."

"So what do we do now?" Mom asks.

"There's nothing we know *to* do in a case like this because it's the first case of its kind. My U. of T. colleague likens it to the next phase in human evolution."

"You're joking, right?" Dad says.

"Sort of. But if we can go with that analogy for a bit—think back to Neanderthal man. The first of them to have a baby with a smooth, upright and straight skull, no brow ridges, dainty bone structure, *et cetera*, must have thought the baby sickly, indeed. I'm sure his—or her—mother worried about it, too. But then more of them started popping up, and before long, the ones *with* brow ridges would have been in the minority."

"So you're saying this is a good thing?" I ask.

"So long as you stay calm and stress-free."

I think about this for a moment, and then tell her, "Good luck to that."

"There *is* one thing we could prescribe."

"What's that?" Mom asks.

"We could try sedatives."

"No." This from Dad. "I don't want her walking around in a haze for the rest of her life."

"Anti-anxiety medication?"

"We already went down that road with the antipsychotics, remember? No more drugs. She's only thirteen, for Christ's sake," Dad says.

"There *is* one other thing, a more natural approach. Let's try..." she hunts around for a prescription pad. She continues to talk once she's located the pad of paper. "Let's try a cocktail of zinc, choline, selenium, and vitamins A, E, and B12."

"What does that do?" Mom asks.

"They've all been known to reduce stress. If we can keep Alice's temperament even-keel, maybe we can prevent her from travelling." She hands Mom the list.

"Thank you, Doctor," Mom says. I hop down from the examination table, and Mom and Dad get up.

"There's one more thing," Dr. Rickman tells us. "If what you say is true, that you materialize somewhere in some random time, without warning, I suggest you find a way to protect yourself."

"How do you mean?" Mom says.

"Get Alice into some kind of self-defence class. Make sure she has the tools for survival in case she needs them."

"Will do. Thanks, Rebecca," Mom says.

I leave her office with a renewed sense of power. I am the new *homo sapiens*, the first of my kind. In years to come, my children's children will seek me out as the mother of humankind and put my face on the cover of *National Geographic*. I'm going to learn self-defence, so the next time I'm swarmed by a gang of thugs I'm going to take them out, ninja-style, ten at a time, and then all of history will read about the girl superhero whose mission is to keep the city safe for the future of humankind.

"You coming?" Mom asks. She holds her hand out for me. I take it, and she leads me out of the office. On the way to the car, I realize the gang of thugs I imagined taking down are probably just infants somewhere in the city now. Half of them aren't even born yet. Rather than focusing on my cool ninja skills, I should be thinking about how and where I can stash some of those breadcrumbs, like the clothes in the locker at the ROM, just in case.

When we get home I record the dates, approximate times, and locations of my excursions through time on a piece of stationary, which I fold in half, and slide into my keepsake box.

19

Alice is 14

"Okay, your turn," Tina says. We're in my room having an impromptu sleepover. I called her earlier. She was bored, and I was bored, and we decided to have a private party, stuff our faces with chips and popcorn, order-in pizza, and drink cola until our guts exploded and our skin erupted like fault lines or tiny volcanoes. "Truth or dare?" Tina asks. I'm kneeling on my carpet with my back to her, leaning against the frame of my bed. Tina's braiding my hair, fastening each lock with a tiny, primary-coloured elastic. I finished hers first. Every time she shakes her head I hear the dull snap of the elastics slapping against her cheek and each other. The idea is to sleep in wet braids and let them out in the morning, making our hair look like it was crimped. With any luck, it'll hold at least until it's time for school on Monday.

"Truth," I say after a beat. Truth is I'm afraid of what Tina might tell me to do if I choose Dare. Call up Pete and profess my undying love for him, no doubt. Or worse, call up one of the goofballs in homeroom and profess my undying love for *him,* instead.

"Wuss."

"Don't go all judgy on me."

"Chicken."

"This game is supposed to be safe. No judgment, right?"

"I don't recall seeing a rulebook for Truth or Dare anywhere."

I turn my head to the side. I like to look people in the eye when I talk to them—all the better to gauge their reaction with. Tina uses the braid she's plaiting to pull my head back to centre. "It has to be a hard and fast rule if we're going to play, Tina."

"No need to get all touchy on me, Al." Tina's like this free spirit. She's loose with the guys and finds it hard to keep girls as friends, probably as a result of it. She's outgoing. She speaks freely, always, exactly what's on her mind. It's refreshing sometimes. Other times it's downright tiring, and sometimes hurtful, but what can I do? She's my only friend besides Pete, and I count myself lucky as a result.

Tina finishes the thin braid, ties it off with an elastic, and measures out another lock of hair. She pulls the strands so tightly as she plaits, it's borderline painful. "I still choose truth," I remind her.

"Fine. Truth." She stops braiding and I feel her tug on my hair as she leans to the side. I hear her slurping Dr. Pepper from the can. It clinks as she puts it back on my side table. She resumes braiding afterward.

"Is it on the coaster?" I ask. My dresser and side table set is this antique, ornate one, carved from blonde wood, and edged with gold paint. Mom would have a conniption fit if she came in and saw water rings or dings on any of the furniture, even though, technically, my room, my furniture.

"Hell, yeah. I'm not going to do anything to incur the wrath of your mom." I made the mistake of telling Tina how Mom treated Dr. Rickman that time in her office, though I didn't tell her the truth about why. Ever since then, Mom's sort of attained badass status in Tina's mind, which is good—it keeps Tina in line whenever she's over.

"So...truth," Tina says. She ties off another braid. "Have you and Pete ever—"

"Tina!" I say before she can even finish the question.

"What?"

"Really? Your chance to learn anything in the world about me, and you ask about Pete?" Part of me is relieved. This is normal, right? Asking each other about their sex lives? Curious teenage stuff. Part of me was frightened she'd ask me about my condition. Part of me is disappointed she didn't.

"I love you like a sister, girlfriend, but I can also read you like a book, and right now there's nothing else I can think of asking, so spill it."

"No!" I'm horrified. Pete and I have never even talked about this before. How can I talk about it with Tina? How can I share *Pete's* secrets with Tina?

"No, you're not going to spill it, or no, you and Pete have never done it?"

"What about you?"

"What *about* me? This is *your* truth, Al, not mine." And chances are, after my answer, Tina will either pick Dare every turn that's hers from here on in or say she's tired of the game to avoid sharing *her* truth on the subject.

I hesitate. I hate this. It feels like I'm betraying Pete's confidence if I say anything more. Tina starts in on another braid. "Well?" she asks.

"Pete and I...we...haven't, not yet."

"There, that wasn't so bad now, was it?"

It was. It was horrible.

"Why not?"

"Huh?" I try to turn to face her again, but her fingers are twisted too tightly in my hair to let my head swivel as much as it needs to.

"Why haven't you done The Dirty with Pete yet?"

"I don't know. I guess we're not there yet."

Tina shrugs. "Maybe he's just not that into you." That's what I mean when I say that sometimes Tina's lack of a filter on her brain-mouth connection is exactly the opposite of refreshing.

"He is. Into me." That sounded a whole lot less stupid in my head than it does out loud.

"How do you know?"

"He tells me."

"Oh, honey," Tina says, like she's my mom about to teach me a life lesson or something. "They *all* say that. They figure it's the quickest route to your pants. Sad to say, it's usually true."

I bat Tina's hand from the back of my head, turn around to sit cross-legged on the carpet, and look up at her on the bed. "Have *you* ever done it?"

"Of course," she says proudly.

"With Nat?"

"Who else?"

"And before him?"

"A few times."

"With who?"

"I don't remember." Something *that* intimate and she doesn't remember? I don't believe her. I wish *she'd* have called Truth instead of me. That way I could force her to do a really embarrassing Double Dare as punishment for lying.

I look away from Tina for a moment, and quietly ask her, "What was it like?"

Tina shrugs. "It was okay."

"Just okay?" Now I'm sure she's lying.

"I don't know." She picks at the thermal blanket folded beside her on the comforter. "It was okay, I guess. I mean, I don't have a lot of grounds for comparison, now, do I?"

"Okay. Don't get testy with me."

She looks up at me with a huge grin on her face. "If I were a guy you could tell me not to get *testes* with you. Get it? *Testes*?"

I roll my eyes at her. She somehow thinks my reaction makes her crude pun even funnier and before long, she's prostrate on my bed, laughing so hard she's crying.

Prostrate. Sounds like prostate. I don't dare share that one with her, or she'd probably laugh so hard she'd need medical attention or something.

I reach for the chip bag on the floor next to me, and take out a big one. Salt and vinegar. The smell of the vinegar creeps up my nose and my eyes threaten to water. Tina calms down as I chomp on the chip. I ask, "Is that bad?"

"Huh?" She motions for the bag of chips using a gimme-gimme opening and closing of her fist with both hands motion, like a toddler reaching for something she wants, and says, "Is what bad?"

"That Pete and I haven't...you know."

"Bumped uglies?"

Okay: gross. I choose to nod rather than tell her so.

"Just with Pete?" she asks. She takes a handful of chips and passes the bag back to me.

"At all," I say, sheepishly.

"Truth?" she asks between mouthfuls.

"That's the name of the game, isn't it?" I say.

"It's not. Bad. Truth is, I wish *I* hadn't yet."

I reach into the bag of chips and pull one out that's folded over onto itself. Wish chip. I close my eyes and pray that Pete and I haven't...you know, because neither of us is ready yet, and not because he doesn't want to because he doesn't like me that much because he's just not that into me.

20

Alice is 14

I go to bed feeling defective, not because of my habit of jumping back and forth through my life, but because I'm still a virgin. I always believed fourteen too young to get involved in things like that. I always thought Pete and I were copacetic with this, that he was happy kissing and cuddling and snuggling and stuff, that the thought of someone else messing around with our privates was gross. Apparently, I was wrong.

Maybe he's just not that into you.

He tells me he loves me every time he sees me.

Maybe he's just not that into you.

He took care of me that time at the ROM, got me out of a bad situation, took me to safety, offered me warm, clean clothes, and fed me.

Maybe...

My air mattress squeaks under me when I roll over, deliberately showing Tina my back. Tina, in bed and snoring away, doesn't notice the snub. I don't know who I hate more—Tina for making me feel abnormal for not jumping Pete like a dog in heat when I see him or me for listening to her.

"He's just not that into you" plays like an earworm in my head.

Dad says I should watch out for boys, that he was a teenage boy once, and he knows what's on their minds because it was the only thing on *his* mind at the time.

So what if boys think about sex? It's one thing to *think* about it; it's a totally different thing to actually *want* to do it, to actually seek it out with a flesh and blood girl.

What if Pete and I haven't done it yet, not because he's afraid to with a real live girl, but because he's really just not that into me.

I open my eyes. The light from the streetlamp streams into my room from beneath the blinds.

*He's just not that into you, he's just not that into you, he's just not...*over and over again, is all I can think of.

I reach for my cell to take a peek at the time, catch a glimpse of my reflection in the darkened screen in the beam of the streetlight, and then everything begins to spin, the air drains from the room until I can't breathe, and then I hear a pop, like a balloon bursting.

21

Alice is 14

When I open my eyes I'm in an alleyway somewhere, the walls on either side of me scaffolded with rusty fire escape ladders. I think, *oh, no,* sit up, and look at the mouth of the alley expecting the same gang of kids. Then I realize it isn't the same alley. Instead of dumpsters, there are really smelly plastic garbage cans, tan-coloured, and with screw on lids. Most of the cans are overstuffed with black-green bags, and lopsided lids, as if each of the bags were Oscar the Grouch wearing a tam. I remind myself that it could still be the same alley, but in a different time, so I look around. The other one dead-ended with more buildings. This one opens to a street at the other end.

I get to my feet and a warm, sweaty hand grabs my breast (such as it is) from behind. I turn to see a man dressed in dirty, tattered clothing with grimy skin and grimy hands and boozy breath and it's too much for me to handle. The scene spins again and part of me is glad because it's the first sign I'm going home, but I bend over and wretch instead. Half-digested pizza, cola, potato chips, and a good helping of stomach acid are dropped onto the man's shoes. He swears at me something vile. I feel for him, you know, because I can appreciate what he must go through to get and keep a decent pair of shoes on his feet so he doesn't lose anything to frostbite, but really, he's brought this on himself. If he hadn't decided to cop a feel from a distressed, pyjama-clad girl, he'd still have his toes come this winter.

"Pedo," I retaliate. I turn and walk away, ignoring his filthy taunts. Screw him and his potty mouth.

I get about six feet from the guy when I feel him grab my hand and pull on it, hard. "Not so fast, sister," he slurs. "You owe me a pair of shoes."

I have enough time to notice he's made no move to take off the old, vomit-soaked pair. "Screw off, perv," I say, and pull my hand free. He grabs it again, so I stomp on his foot. The shoe squelches. He howls.

A car screeches to a halt in front of the alley. The door flings open, and a hand, disembodied by the darkness, suddenly materializes. "Come with me if you want to live," says a vaguely familiar voice. I nod and take the hand. I'm half-pulled, half-climb into the car, and slam the door shut, as the wheels peal us away.

"In case you didn't notice, I was doing fine on my own," I say.

The man reaches between the front bucket seats and throws a blanket at me. "You cold?" he asks me. I look over at the driver, see long, spidery, dark lashes, and know who the guy is. "Pete?" I say.

He turns his head toward me, his brown eyes sparkling in the streetlight glare, and smiles. "Hey, kiddo."

"Dweeb." Pete driving a car. That means he'd have to be at least seventeen if he's driving it legally. I take a really hard look at him to check him out. His cheeks and chin are covered with rusty-brown stubble, slightly lighter than his hair. Or maybe that's because his cheeks and chin are taking in more light than the top of his head. His lips stick out full and kissable from the middle of all that growth. It's amazing what three short years can do to a guy.

Pete chuckles and turns his head back to the road.

I lean back in my chair and snuggle under the blanket for warmth.

"How old are you anyway? Twelve? Thirteen?"

"Fourteen and a half."

"So, like, the extra half is supposed to change your jailbait status or something?"

"Or something," I say.

"Buckle up," he tells me. "I'd hate to have to explain to a cop why I have an under-aged girl naked and in my car at this time of night."

"I'm not naked. I'm wearing pajamas."

"Close enough." He looks over at me.

I fasten my seatbelt and Pete asks, "What happened to your hair?" My hand darts to my hair. The braids. I lost some of the elastics in my skirmish with the guy in the alley. Some of it's still coiled into tight plaits but the rest has begun to unravel; I must look a mess.

"What's happened to yours?" I say, for lack of a better comeback. I wish I could say his hair was thinning, but though it's cut short, it looks as thick as ever.

We drive a few minutes in silence, but then I say, "So how old are you, anyway?"

Pete says nothing.

"Hello? I asked you how old you were, Pete. It's not a trick question."

"I'm thinking."

"About your age?"

"About what I can and can't tell you."

Up until now I'd been studying Pete—the curvature of his eyelashes, the bow of his lips, the angle of his jaw, the contours of the muscles on his upper arms and chest, but now I give an exaggerated sigh and look out my window, head propped on my hand, elbow on the windowsill. "Here we go again," I say.

"What?"

"That whole song and dance about changing the

future and paradox and…other…crap."

"We've had this conversation before?" His tone grows upbeat, amused, almost, so I turn to look at him and find him grinning at me.

"Hello? The road?" He does a double take of sorts, turns to look at the road, turns to look at me, then turns back to the road and focuses there. "Not so concerned about paradox now, are we?"

"You know, Al? When you're right, you're right. And you're right about this one. I mean, I've seen enough time travel stuff to know what could happen in cases like this, and you can change things without even knowing it. Take that Bradbury story we did in English class in grade nine, for instance. *Sound of Thunder*, I think. That guy trampled one butterfly, one single butterfly, and the world was converted over to a communist regime—"

I know the story well. Mom and Dad watch reruns of *Ray Bradbury Theatre* on the Space channel, and when I joined them once, they gave me a compilation of his short stories. "A communist regime that sells jaunts through time to tourists, yeah, like that's plausible."

"In *Butterfly Effect*, Ashton Kutcher blew his arms off to save a kid from suffering the same fate—"

"Which he wouldn't have to have done if he hadn't been a loser and set explosives in the mailbox in the first place."

"What about *Bill and Ted*?" he asks me, and I lose it. I mean, *Bill and Ted*? Really? And since when did Pete become an expert on anything except for *Minecraft*?

"I think you're right, Pete. Let's just not talk. I feel a paradoxical headache coming on."

"Really? You feel stuff like that?"

"No. Not really."

He turns a corner too quickly and the tires screech. "What happened to not wanting to explain the naked jailbait in the front seat of your car?" I ask him.

"Almost missed the turn," he says.

"Where are we going?"

"A safehouse. Just...It's my dad's place. My parents busted up a year or two ago and Dad got a condo nearby. He's away on business this week, and I have a key so I can come and go as I please, which is great, 'cause if I ever have a late night on campus, I got a place to go."

"Your parents got divorced?"

"Crap! That's TMI, right?"

"You go to university?"

"Yeah."

"Which one?"

"Ryerson."

"For what?"

"Physics."

"Oh."

"What?"

I look back at him, and my face flushes with pride. "So do we go there together?"

He shakes his head, signals left, and pulls into an underground parking garage. "Look, all I'm saying is that Bill and Ted learned how to work their shit. Maybe you should, too. Take control of it. Don't wait for the butterfly to die, or your arms to blow off, and—

"Wait..." he says, interrupting himself. "Do you think Ashton Kutcher knew about Bradbury's story when he named his movie?" He pulls into a spot and parks the car.

I get out of the car and whisper "Dweeb," as I close the door.

"So, do you?" he asks as we get into the elevator.

"Huh?"

"Think he knew."

I shake my head and chuckle.

"What?"

"I think the script writers probably knew, yeah."

22

Alice is 14

He leads me into a two-bedroom condo done up mostly in black, grey, and red—a guy's pad. Nice, I guess. The main room has a large, square couch, the kind that wraps around a corner. There's a footrest in the corner of it, making it look like a bed. There's also one of those recliners, the kind that you see in movies about ancient Greeks, where they lay back and eat grapes someone else has peeled for them. There's a kitchen off to the right and a bedroom and hall off to my left. "Dad's room's down there. So's the bathroom," Pete says. "This is my room." He gestures to the small room on the left, goes into it, and digs around in the closet. When he comes back, he has a small backpack with him. "Your mom gave me this," he says.

"My mom?" How's she tied up in all this? She knows I come to see you?"

"I kind of told her I had a list and...don't get angry, but she found *your* list, the original one, in your journal. She packed a bag and gave it to me just in case. I'm supposed to take it with me, but you caught me a little off-guard this time."

"How could I catch you off guard if you have, like, my master playlist?"

"I was...busy, and I lost track of time." He looks at me and tousles my hair like I'm his kid sister or something. "Why don'tcha go get dressed? Put on some real clothes? I'll put something on for you to eat. You must be hungry, huh?"

"Anything but pizza and pop and chips, okay?"

"How's chicken noodle soup sound?"

I giggle. When we were kids, Pete would come to my house after school most winter afternoons, because it got dark quick and his parents worked late. Mom would warm us chicken soup with letter noodles, or animal shapes, and we'd dip crackers in it and eat. Somehow the soup always got cold before we'd finish it. "Sounds good," I call down the hall.

Mom packed the standard yoga pants and t-shirt, both still too large for me, a stretchy, cupless sports bra, boyfriend short underwear—also stretchy—and a pair of lime green flip flops. I pad into the kitchen, my feet slapping against the foam shoe. Pete must hear me first, because he says, "My dad's out of saltines. I hope Ritz'll do," before I step from the carpeted living room to the ceramic tile floor of the kitchen.

I see a water cooler in the corner and ask, "Can I have some water?"

"Glasses are over the sink. Help yourself to the cooler."

I find a tall, turquoise glass with a bubble pattern on it, and flash back to Pete's mom bringing us a tray of Oreo cookies and these glasses, half full of milk, in their basement playroom. We used to use the very tips of our fingers to reach into the glass to dip the cookies. We always dropped some in, and by the end of the glass, there was this dark chocolate sludge at the bottom. While it would have been easier if Pete's mom had served the milk in shorter glasses, or filled them up higher, snack time certainly wouldn't have been as much fun. I guess his dad got the drinking glasses in the divorce settlement.

The cooler glugs, even after I've released the tap and started drinking. As I sit at the table, Pete's phone rings, and though it's across the table from me and upside down, I can still see who's calling.

It rings again, two short buzzes followed by a longer one. A picture of Tina illuminates the screen. Her name and phone number—a 437 exchange I don't recognize—appears in large text below the picture. A Muzak *My Girl* starts playing. I guess sometime between last night and now, Tina's gotten herself a new cell phone number. "Why is Tina calling you?" I ask Pete.

"We're friends." He picks up the phone and sends the call to voicemail.

"If you're friends, why didn't you answer the call?"

Pete stares at me like a deer caught in headlights, no fooling. His eyes widen to owl-proportion, and his arachnid eyelashes freeze to his eyebrows. "Look, Al," he says, and there's something in the way he says it, something in how the tone is super apologetic, that tells me everything I need to know. "Friend", in this case, is a euphemism. Euphemism is one of those words of the day notifications Mom gets on her Dictionary.com cell phone app, so I know euphemisms, and this is one if ever there was one.

"I don't believe it," I say, half-stunned, and get up, walk out the front door, and down the hall toward the elevator.

"Don't be like that, Mabel," Pete whines, and then I hear his bare feet thumping on the carpeting of the corridor.

I push the elevator button.

"Come on, Ma—"

"My name...is Alice," I tell him.

"I'm sorry. Alice. From what I was told you're only Alice if you're from this time, so, my bad."

I hate that saying. *My bad.* Like everything you've ever done, everything no matter how horrific, is made better by admitting it was *your bad.* Like Hitler could make six million plus people un-dead by admitting the Holocaust was his bad. I just glare at Pete in response to that asinine statement. I mean, okay, so if things don't work out between us, he's entitled to find another girlfriend, just don't make it my *best friend.* What in the hell was Tina thinking? Maybe that whole baloney about him not being that into me was a plot, some kind of plan to break Pete and me up so she could have him for herself. So she could break him in for herself. Disgusting!

"Look, come back to the condo with me. I promised you and your mom I'd take care of you when this happened, and I think I left the burner on, and I don't want to burn the building down."

The elevator chimes and the door swooshes open, airier and lower in timbre than the *Star Trek* door swoosh, but a swoosh, nevertheless. I look at Pete.

"Think of all the lives you'll save," he says, and I fight back a smirk. I don't want to smile now. I just found out my best friend stole my boyfriend, and they're old enough to be doing things I can't with him in my own time. Whatever it is Pete's old enough to be doing, he should be doing it with me, and not Tina.

"Please?" He holds his hand out to me.

I cross my arms over my chest and say, "Fine, but I'm not holding that," meaning his hand. I don't know where it's been.

Back in Pete's dad's condo, we sit on opposite sides of the table, each of us with a large mug of soup, the box of Ritz in the middle. I hold the mug between my hands and swirl the soup around a bit. "I could get you a spoon, if you prefer?"

"This is fine," I tell him, trying really hard to hold back the tears. My chest feels tight. This is my first break-up, and I don't know how to react, let alone what to do about it.

"You're not eating."

"I'm not hungry."

"Don't be like that, Al."

"Don't be like what, Pete? Don't be depressed because my heart is breaking?"

"Don't be a drama queen, for one."

I look up at him. My mom used to call me that when I was young. Whenever I over-reacted to something. Pete has no right to call me that. Not now. Not under these circumstances. I think the look I give him is enough to get that message across.

"Sorry," he says.

I take a cracker from the box and crumble it into the soup.

"Look," he continues, "I loved you. Still do."

"Then why's Tina calling you?"

Pete shrugs. "Like I told you. We're friends, Tina and me."

"Thank you, Captain Obvious." Like I couldn't figure out who he meant by "we" without the clarification.

I refuse to believe Pete and Tina are just friends. You don't give girls who aren't your girlfriend a ring tone with a title like that.

I don't know what to do. I love Pete. I want to be with him forever. And this guy, this Pete sitting across the table from me, looks so much like *my* Pete...

I think back to what Tina said to me before I travelled, how Pete secretly wanted to be with me, to have...*sex*...with me, and that I would lose him if I didn't give it to him. How if Pete didn't want to...you know...with me, then he wasn't that into me, and I decide to put it to the test. I get up and go around to where Pete is sitting, and slide between him and the table and onto his lap. I put my arms around his neck and nuzzle my cheek into the crook of his neck where it meets his shoulder.

Pete doesn't say anything. Instead, his arms come up and around my back. This is what I need. This is what I want to happen. And while I can't fathom what it might be like to do this naked, with Pete or anyone else, I pull my face from the crook of his neck and kiss him on the lips.

Pete pulls away. "Alice," he says, sort of scolding.

"Shhh," I tell him. I open my lips and put them back on his, but he pulls his head away again. This time he also grabs my hands from behind his neck and uses them to hold me at a distance.

"This is wrong," he says.

"It's not, Pete. We're meant to be together, you know we are." If I can somehow win his heart back now, he'll have to come back to me. He'll have no other choice but to dump Tina and get back together with me.

"Like it or not, this version of you cannot be with this version of me."

His phone starts to buzz again, two shorts and a long. We both look over to it.

Tina's calling again.

"Right on cue," I say. "Impeccable timing."

He lets go of one of my hands, reaches past me for the phone, and sends it to voice mail again.

"You're going to have to answer that eventually, you know."

"I'm eighteen, for Christ's sake, four years older than you—"

"Not quite three years—"

"*Four* years. Even if I wanted to, it's illegal."

I look up into his doe-like browns. HIs impossibly long lashes blink at me. "*Do* you want to?" I say in a whisper.

"Alice," he says, scolding again.

"Well? Do you?"

"That's not the point. The point is that ship's sailed."

His phone starts buzzing again. "Look," he says, "I gotta get this or she's just going to continue calling until I do." He slides his finger across the screen, brings the phone to his ear, and says, "Hey, babe." Babe? He calls Tina *babe*? I can't believe this.

Pete taps me twice on the shoulder to tell me to get off him, and so I do. He continues to talk in low tones to his *girlfriend* on the phone, wandering into the living room as he does, and I can't believe it. Pete and Tina! Tina and Pete! And I can't help but think that somehow this is all *my* fault!

I stand up and inch closer to the archway between the kitchen and the living room, trying to make out what's being said. "Of course I do," Pete reassures. Of course I care for you, Tina. Of course I love you, Tina. Of course I haven't seen Mabel today. Of course I didn't pick her up in a dark alleyway, near naked. Of course she's not sitting in my kitchen as we speak.

My heart begins to work double time and the air grows thin. I look down at the glass-topped kitchen table, in the middle of cursing my sad-looking face, when I hear the all too familiar pop, and then I'm standing on the air mattress in my room.

Tina snorts in a great snout of air. I drop to the mattress and clamour under my blankets as fast as I am able, making as little motion and as little noise—save for the rustle of the sheets and the creak of the air mattress against the carpet beneath it—as possible so as to not wake Tina. When I'm settled, I lie there staring at the ceiling.

I don't want to be here. Anywhere but here. In this room. With *her.* The other woman.

Something pinches me at the nape of my neck. I put a hand there to get whatever it is and come up with a red elastic. I can't resist but smile knowing Pete's going to be finding tiny elastics in his Dad's apartment, little reminders of me, for the next little while.

When I take a look at it in the bathroom mirror in the morning, my hair looks more like a fright wig than a crimping, so I take a shower and wash it before Mom has breakfast on the table.

23

Alice is 14

Usually Mom's banana chocolate chip oatmeal pancakes and fresh squeezed OJ are enough to brighten any morning, but not today. Traitor Tina sits across the table from me, stuffing her big fat face with pancakes. "These are amazing, Mrs. Carroll," she says, sucking up to Mom. "You should call them Breakfast Crack or something, they're that good."

"Thank you, Tina, dear," Mom says. And though my back is to her, I can practically hear her beaming.

"Seriously," she says, washing down another bite with the juice. "At my place? All we get are frozen pancakes. Mix, if we're lucky. I don't think I've ever had scratch-made pancakes except at restaurants." I open my mouth as if to say it's probably not scratch-made at the greasy spoon joints her family frequents, either, but don't. The last thing I want to do is have breakfast conversation, civil or otherwise, with Tramp Tina, of all people.

Mom flips another four or five pancakes from the frying pan onto the serving plate on the table and smiles at me when she's done. "Alice?" she says, like it's a warning. "Are you okay, dear? You've barely touched your pancakes—"

"I'm fine, Mom," I say, warning her back.

"Really?" Mom asks.

"Yeah," Tina chimes in. She pours about a cup of pancake syrup onto her plate. "Because you're awfully quiet this morning."

"I said I was fine!" I snap at them. "God! Why can't anyone just leave it alone?" I pick up a pancake and shove it into my mouth, whole. "See? I'm eating." My voice is muffled by the pancake I'm chewing on. "Happy now?"

Tina concentrates on her plate, cutting her pancakes into dainty, bite-sized pieces before bringing them to her mouth one at a time, dripping with syrup. Mom returns to the stove. I hear the pan sizzle as she drops a ladleful of batter onto it.

The rest of the meal is suffered in silence, as is the time spent watching television between then and when Tina's mom comes to get her. Before she goes, Tina throws her arms around my neck and hugs me. She whispers, "I'm sorry if I upset you last night," into my ear before she lets go.

The front door shuts and I retire to my room, taking the stairs two at a time, making sure my door slams hard enough behind me to shake a few windows, hard enough to let my parents know I'm in a pissy mood and to leave me alone. And for my mother to know I secretly need her.

In my room, I flop onto my bed, take out the journal I keep hidden between my mattress and the box spring, and open it to my list. There are three dates on it so far, and though I have them memorized, I practice reciting them again before taking a pen from my night table and adding last night's date to the list. Not yesterday's actual date, but the date I saw on Pete's phone when it rang, and the location of the alley where he found me.

I practice memorization of the list again, including the date I've just added, and then a few times more for good measure. At some point, I must give the list to Pete, or to my mom, because so far, Pete's come for me twice, and last night he said my mom helped him, so...

I'm in the middle of reciting the list again when the phone rings. I hear my mom's muffled voice through the walls. It sounds something like, "Ello?

"Oh, hi, Eat." Or it could be Neat. Or Seat. Or Pete.

Mom says, "Hold on," and then she calls up to me. I ignore it at first, but she calls again, and then again. At last, she says something more into the phone, too low and too quickly to decipher from behind my bedroom door. The phone jiggles back into the cradle. Then Mom galumph-thumps up the stairs. The floorboard in front of my room creaks—Dad jokes it's his alarm that I'm leaving my room, and if I ever try to sneak out in the middle of the night it'll wake him, but he's such a sound sleeper that nothing, save a full-blown air siren, will ever even get a stir from him. Besides, if last night's any indication, who says I have to leave through my bedroom door in order to sneak out in the middle of the night?

Mom knocks on my door. I go to it, lean against it, slide my butt to the floor, pull my knees as close to my chest as I can get them, and hug them for good measure. Maybe, if I'm quiet enough, she'll leave me alone. Instead, she knocks three times in succession and says my name. Then again. And again. It's her Sheldon Cooper *Big Bang* impersonation again. She loves that show, and never tires reminding me of the fact.

When I don't answer, she says, "Come on, honey, let me in. You know you waaaanah," imitating the Cheez Whiz commercial. So, okay, it makes me laugh. Not because it's funny or anything, but because she's being such a goofball to get my attention. I groan and slide to standing against the door. Rather than open it to let her in, I climb into bed and under the comforter before I tell her she can come in, which she does, but tentatively so.

"Pete called," she tells me.

"I know." I prop my Zayn-face pillow behind my back, hoping the thought of him that close to my heart will soothe my nerves just the tiniest bit, but it doesn't cut it this time.

"Did you guys have a fight?"

"No," I say.

"And what about Tina?"

"What about Tina?" I snap back.

"You were kind of a bitch to her this morning."

"I didn't mean to."

"You didn't mean to give her the cold shoulder?"

"No." I stifle a grin. "I meant to do that."

"Whatever for?"

"It's complicated." I grab Allie the Alley Cat, prop her on my bent knees, and play with her front paws.

"Maybe I can help uncomplicate it for you?"

I look at my mother. She smiles at me, and I start to cry.

"Oh, honey," she says. She helps me maneuver into a position where I'm almost sitting in her lap. She strokes my hair while I cry When I'm done, she says, "Better?"

"Not really."

"What's wrong, Alice? I mean, what's *really* wrong?"

"Time travel sucks."

"How so?"

"You don't think so? You can't tell me you'd rather have a kid that doesn't change time zones like some kids change their clothes."

"I never said that. Of course your situation sucks. I was just wondering why it sucks so much right now.

"And FYI, I can only pray you change your clothes more often than you change time zones."

"Ha, ha," I tell her. I think about how to broach the subject with her. When I was about eight, we had The Sex Talk and it was the most awkward quarter hour of my life.

I can't talk about what's happening between Tina, Pete, and me without another one of those uber-awkward talks. "Remember before, when you asked me if I had a fight with Pete?"

"Uh-huh." I feel her head nodding against mine.

"Well, I think I sort of did. In the future."

"You're upset because Future You had a fight with Future Pete?"

"Present Me had a sort of fight with Future Pete."

"I see."

I pull away from her so I can see her reactions from this point forward face-to-face. "You do?"

Mom smiles, takes a deep breath, and says, "No, not really."

I shake my head and look away from her, find Allie the Alley Cat in the bed, and hug her tightly.

"I'm sorry, dear, but this stuff is as foreign to me as it is to you. Ask me about troubles you have with a boy in *this* time zone and I'm on it, but trouble that can't even be addressed for years? It's not like they offer courses in Parenting the Future Lovelorn in university."

Just then the doorbell rings. I hear Dad turn the lock to open the door. "Al?" he calls up to me, "Pete's here for you."

"I can't face him now, Mom, I just can't," I say, and do a face plant into my pillow.

"I'll get rid of him," Mom says. She leaves the room and I hear her call down to Dad, "Alice isn't feeling well, dear. Tell Pete she'll have to call him later." I hear Dad parrot what Mom just said.

When he's done, I hear pubescent Pete's voice, replete with cracks and high and low modulations say, "I spoke with Tina earlier—"

"I bet you did," I mutter to myself.

"And I'm worried about her. We both are. Tina says Alice wasn't herself this morning, and then she wouldn't take my call, and now she's not coming to the door—"

"'Women: such beautiful creatures to gaze upon, yet complex to figure out,'" Dad quotes.

"I don't understand," Pete says after a pause.

Dad chuckles. "She'll call you later, Pete. Whenever whatever this is blows over. I'll see to it." The door latches and the lock turns. Mom comes back into my room, closing the door behind her. She sits at the foot of my bed and says, "Begin at the beguine."

"Huh?"

"It's a reference to an old Cole Porter song."

"Who?

"Never mind," she says. "Start at the beginning." And so I do, starting with the old man in the alley copping a feel, eighteen-or-so-year-old Pete taking me back to his place, the pass I made at him, Tina on his cell, and Pete calling Tina "babe".

"Oh," Mom says when I'm done.

"That's it? Oh?"

"I don't know what else to say."

"Sage advice much, Mom?"

"Don't get smart," she scolds. "Look," she says after a beat, "Pete's a nice guy. He really likes you—"

"He apparently likes Tina more."

"Not now he doesn't. Now he likes you."

"I don't think so."

"When he found out you were down he dropped everything and ran over here."

"When he found out from *Tina*."

"Yes, from Tina. Tina's a good friend for worrying about you like that."

"Oh, and a good friend steals your boyfriend like that?"

"You don't know what happens between you and Pete over the next four years or so." She looks at me and brushes a lock of hair behind my ear. "For all you know, *you* broke it off with him."

"But to have make-up sex? With Tina?"

"A, you don't know this was make-up sex. For all you know they've been in a loving, committed relationship for a while now. And B, if I can speak frankly..."

I nod and she continues. "Tina's not only a good friend, she's your *only* friend. You can't afford to blow off good friendships over something that may or may not happen years from now. Pete, too. That's like those *Outer Limits* episodes where someone goes into the past to kill a guy for something he'll do in the future.

"And we don't know what's going to happen between now and then, do we? For all we know, forewarned is forearmed. Now that you know, you can see what's happening as it happens, and smooth things over with Pete before it gets to the point of breakup, if you want to. The bottom line is, we still don't know what happens, or who's responsible for the breakup. For all we know, you meet some tall, dark, handsome stranger you like better than Pete—"

"Or the other way around."

"Or...Pete...meets   a   tall...dark...handsome stranger...that could happen, too—"

"Mom!"

"Okay, a *beautiful* stranger. I'm just trying to make a point, here, Allie."

"Oh, Mom," I say, and nuzzle my ear against her breast. She takes up stroking my hair, even before I'm there comfortably.

"My advice, sweetie?"

I nod.

"Call Pete. Talk to him. Enjoy each other—but not too much—in the time you have together. Let's not worry about the future until it's upon us, okay?"

I nod again.

"So you'll call Pete?"

"Maybe later."

"Come on, Al."

"I'll call him, I promise." And I do, later that night. And Pete's still Pete, and everything seems just as I remember.

24

Alice is 14 and 14

I find myself scrunched into a ball. I'm outside. My feet burn. My body shivers, then shakes, and doesn't stop jiving. My teeth chatter like those dentures that pop out of people's mouths, the ones that eat a swath of food and whatever else is in their wake as they jump across the table in the Saturday morning cartoons I used to watch when I was little.

"Alice?" I hear someone say. It's low, barely a whisper, but someone else is here with me. "Is that you?"

My hands are clamped over my head. I slowly turn my head without taking my hands from over my ears. Standing there, wearing a ski jacket, Toronto Maple Leafs toque, dark scarf wrapped around his neck, and clumsy black ski mitts, is Pete.

"Holy shit, Al! Where did you come from?" he asks, voice creaking like a loose floorboard being stepped upon.

Pete? What's he doing here? "You got clothes for me?" I ask, hoping against hope he's more prepared than he seems. The words are difficult to get out. I'm wearing nothing more than a t-shirt and shorts and it's *freezing* out, to the point that my jaw won't stop chattering enough for me to speak without a stutter.

"Have I got *clothes* for you? Why in the hell would I have clothes for someone who wasn't even there ten seconds ago?"

"You came here to meet me, right?"

"So?"

"So didn't you know I'd be here?"

"I came because the list told me to. I had no idea *why* I was coming here." Pete's seen my list?

"Give me your coat."

"What?"

"Give me your coat."

"Then what will I wear?"

"Okay, so give me your clothes and keep your damn coat."

Pete seems to mull this over for a moment. At last, he unzips his coat and holds it out to me.

"Darn, Al," he says.

"Darn? Really?" He tosses the coat at me. I reach out for it, but it almost lands on the floor. "Goof." I wriggle my arms into the coat and zip it up. Luckily, because Pete's about a head taller than me, the jacket's long, and covers my bare legs, almost to the knees.

"Dweeb," Pete says, and he smiles.

"What's so funny?"

"Nothing," he says.

My legs feel like they're on fire, and I can't feel my toes anymore. "Hey," I tell Pete, "give me your socks, too."

"You want my sweaty socks?"

"Give them to me."

"My sweaty, smelly socks?"

I look down at my feet and can't decide if they're hot pink or cherry red. I've heard tell of people who've lost toes because of frostbite with less exposure. "It's either that or carry me around for the rest of my life after my toes turn black and fall off."

Pete looks positively green at the picture I've just painted. He takes a beat, sits himself down, right there, right down on the snow. He takes off first one boot, then the sock, whips it at me, puts the boot back on, and repeats the process with the next one. Thin as the socks are, it doesn't take long before my feet begin to thaw a little and burn a lot.

Sort of secure in my attire—okay, Pete's attire—I take a moment to look around. We're in the schoolyard. It's near dusk, and I materialized under the window of my grade three classroom. Pete found me crouched under the same window I found myself the day of The Incident, when I blipped out of one time and into another. Back then, my problem saved my skin. Right now, it's threatening to flay me of it if I don't get someplace warm, like in the next few seconds or so.

I look back at Pete who's begun to shiver himself. He hugs himself, alternating between patting and rubbing his shoulders for warmth. "So what now?" he asks.

We wind up across the street and down the block from the school in a Tim Hortons doughnut shop. Luckily, Pete's got cash on him, because, well...let's face it: I travel light. Inside, Pete gives me his gloves and toque to wear. which goes a long way to helping get back the feeling in my fingers and ears. He makes me sit in the corner furthest from the register so as not to arouse suspicion. From where I sit, I think the point's moot, as we are two teens, one without a jacket, the other without boots, in the dead of winter. We order large hot chocolates and Boston Creams. The first sip feels great going down, as if the cold's frozen me from the inside out and it's only now begun to thaw. It's so good, I wish I could fill a tub with it to soak my feet. Hell, I wish I could bathe in it.

Pete sits across from me, staring. "So what gives, Al?"

"What do you mean?" I say, trying to play it cool.

"Where'd you come from?"

"You know."

"I have this list," he says.

"I know," I say.

"You do?"

"I know about the list, Brainiac. I wrote it."

"You did?" he says, sounding sort of surprised.

"What I don't know is how *you* got it."

"Someone gave it to me."

"Someone?"

"A woman."

"Who?"

"I don't know...this woman. She looked like she could've been your mother's younger sister, or your older sister, or something."

"When?"

"I don't know, Al—" The high-pitched tweet-tweet of Pete's phone starts playing. Pete just looks at me dumbly.

"Your phone," I tell him. I can feel the vibrations thrum against my thigh through the pocket of the coat I'm wearing.

"Don't you need to get it?"

"You have it," he says.

"Do you want it?"

He holds his hand out to me. I fish through his pocket and get out his cell phone. It's in a red leather case with a hard cover over the monitor, the one he got a few months ago after he cracked the glass, so I don't know who's on the line until he flips the cover open, and looks up at me. "This is weird," he says. He holds the phone toward me so I can see who's calling.

It's me. I'm calling. This time's Alice. Pete's still looking up at me, the colour drained from his cheeks, like he's just seen a ghost, and I suppose, in some respect, he has.

"Where's your phone, Al?"

"At home, I guess."

"Who'd be calling on it?"

"I don't know. My mom, maybe?"

He looks down at the phone.

"Well? Aren't you going to answer it?" I ask, and he does. I can hear a female voice calling "Hello," repeatedly into the receiver, and I'm pretty sure it's not my mom on the other end.

"Who..." Pete says stuttering. He clears his throat and tries again. "Who is this?" he manages.

I hear the girl on the other end answer him. Pete responds, saying, "Look, I don't know who you are or how you got this phone, but you're not Alice. I'm sitting right across from Alice, so you can't possibly be her."

"Pete," I say, trying to calm him.

The girl on the other end sounds like she's going ballistic, and Pete defends his position that whomever she is, she's a fraud, because the real Alice Carroll is sitting right in front of him. I say his name again, and hold a finger up to my mouth to shush him. He tells the girl to hold on and takes the phone down from his ear, but I can still hear her calling his name, asking him where he is. On the one hand, I want him to tell her, so she can bring warm clothes and Mom with her, so I can go home, and be comfy and cozy in my own house, and wearing my own clothes. On the other hand, I don't know if I want to see myself. I mean, I probably know what's going on, so it's not a matter of freaking *myself* out. The real question here is if *Pete* is ready to contend with *two* of me. That's right, I tell myself, I don't want to see myself because *Pete's* not ready for it.

"Tell her you'll call her back," I whisper.

"She wants to know where we are."

"Don't tell her. Just...tell her you'll call her back."

Pete tells the girl on the line he'll call her back. She protests, but I tell Pete to disconnect and turn his phone off, which he does. He watches as the phone's monitor goes dead, and then looks up at me and says, "What the hell, Alice?"

What the hell, indeed.

25

Alice is 14

Pete and I stare at each other dully for a few seconds, and then he says, "You haven't answered my question, Al."

"I thought 'what the hell' was rhetorical."

"Smart ass"

"Turd."

"Seriously, though," he says. He leans forward and continues in a whisper. "You haven't gone all *Orphan Black* on me now, have you?"

Another of Pete's obscure science fiction references, no doubt. I just look at him and blink a few times so he gets the implied "huh?" in my body language.

"You know, like, clones and all."

"You think I'm a clone?"

"How else would you explain it?"

I shake my head as if it might erase everything that's been said between us since this nightmare began and exhale as if to blow away the dust. "Can we just start at the beginning, Pete, okay?"

Pete nods.

"So you mentioned a list, right? You said a list told you to meet me at the schoolyard, right?" Pete nods again. "What list? Where did it come from?"

"It was weird, you know?" He straightens up in his seat and holds both hands up in front of him, like he's telling all traffic to stop or something, and says, "So, okay." He plants both hands on the table and squirms a little in his seat. "So this lady comes to me one day—"

"What lady?"

"I don't know, some lady—"

"What did she look like?"

"That was the first weird thing, you know? She looked a little like...like your mom...or maybe like *you*. So I was like, okay, weird—"

"When did this happen?"

"I don't know. Maybe five or so years ago? Anyway, she's all like Arnold Schwarzenegger in the second *Terminator* movie, and I'm John Connor and she has a mission for me."

"And what was that?"

"She gives me this list and tells me that I need to be where and when the list tells me if I want to help you."

"And then?"

"Miss Primrose—you remember: our third-grade lunch monitor—calls me, and I turn to look at her and the woman kinda disappears."

"Where was I when all this happened?"

Pete shrugs.

"Where's the list now?" I'd like to see it. I want to see if it's the same list on the page I've been keeping in my journal. What if the woman Pete told me about was *me*? It makes sense, after all. I mean, who else but Pete would I trust with my secret? With my well-being? With my life?

Then I remember what happened the last time Pete "saved" me, the last time his phone rang and the caller wasn't me, but Tina on the other end. I remember freaking out because Pete sent her calls to voice mail, and acted all strange because he was trying to do what was right by me, even though he didn't love me anymore.

But what about Way Future Pete? The guy I called Charming, the one who took me to the ROM for food and clothes and kind of hinted he knew me in the future? That means whatever happens to Pete and me to estrange us, something else happens to reunite us sometime in the future future.

I look over at Pete, who sticks his finger into exposed doughnut filling, scoops some out, and licks it off. The bow of his lips arch, and I remember how kissable those full, warm, soft lips are.

Pete shrugs in answer to my question; he doesn't know where the list is.

"What happened to it?"

Pete shrugs again.

"If you don't have it, how did you know to come for me?"

"I copied it into my phone so I'd always have it on me. Programmed the dates into my calendar, too."

"Can I see them?" I ask.

Pete shrugs, turns his cell on, unlocks it, calls the file up, and is about to hand the device to me, when he says, "Wait a minute."

"What?"

"I don't think I'm supposed to show it to you."

"Why not?"

"I don't want to cause a paradox."

I sigh. "This isn't some stupid movie, jerkwad. Paradoxes don't happen in real life."

"That's because people don't time travel in real life."

"Hello? McFly?" I feel like knocking on his head like Biff does when he calls Marty's dad out in the *Back to the Future* movies.

Sudden realization spreads across Pete's face. His eyes seem to glow as if backlit. "So *that's* what happened to you," he says, voice exuding awe. "How did you do it?"

I sigh and shake my head. It's then I notice two uniformed police officers entering the restaurant. They walk up to the cash register, bypassing the line of customers, to speak to the cashier. She calls another woman over. The second woman speaks to the police in a voice so low, I wouldn't know she's saying anything at all if it weren't for her mouth moving, and the officers' heads nodding, almost in unison. I tap Pete twice on his forearm with the back of my hand and nod toward the register. Trouble is, the employee does the same nod in our direction.

"Trouble," I tell him.

"They're not here for us, Al."

"Bet your ass they are."

"But we haven't done anything."

"Two kids, alone without adults, one without a jacket, and the other without pants or boots in this weather? Smells like runaways to me."

The police give the employee an exaggerated nod, turn, and take a few steps toward us. "Time to bolt," I tell Pete. I grab his hand and lead him out of the restaurant. When we reach the sidewalk outside, I tell him to run.

Neither of us looks back to see if the officers are following.

26

Alice is 14 and 14

We run, as seems to be the case whenever I meet Pete out of time, him taking the lead. We wind up back at the school.

"Were we followed?" he asks when we stop.

I shake my head and try to swallow. It feels like the lining of my throat sticks, and I cough.

"Come on," he says, between pants.

"Where?"

"Inside."

"Is it open?"

"The front door usually is. I think it's a security thing or something." We try all of the doors, one by one, until, sure enough, the last one swings open. "Shhhh," Pete tells me and we sneak inside.

My socks, wet from the thaw at Tim's and frozen again against the concrete as we ran, slide on the tile floor. The material feels glued to the soles of my feet, and I wonder if they'll come off without taking too much skin with them.

We walk slowly, mindful of our surroundings, on the lookout for the caretaker, down the hall, past the kindergarten class, and then the first grade. If we keep going in this direction, we'll hit the third-grade classes before long. I whisper, "Hey, Pete," to warn him against that, but he shushes me.

Second grade. Aquamarine door nearly entirely obscured with paper doll cut-outs, one for each child in the class.

"Pete?" I say again, but Pete keeps pulling me toward the next set of doors, closer and closer until the room, The Room, is the next on the right.

I call Pete's name again, but this time stop dead in my tracks. Pete drops my hand and turns toward me. "I can't," I whisper.

"Can't what?"

"Go there."

"Where?"

"There." I nod in the direction of my third-grade class.

"It's just a room, Al."

"Thank you, Dr. Freud."

"Just four walls and a door."

"That what your shrink told you?"

"It's what he told me to tell myself if I was ever afraid of going in."

He turns toward the door, takes my hand, and takes a step forward, so he's in front of the closed door.

"Pete?"

"Yeah?"

"Are you afraid?"

Pete nods. "Are you?"

After the attack, they moved our third-grade class to the library for the remainder of the year, but it's not like it's the first time I've been back since it happened, far from it. I've teleported in before, but always in the middle of the act. I'd never entered the room of my own accord. And never at night. "Terrified," I tell him.

Pete swallows loudly. "We can do this, Al," he says. "There's safety in numbers, right?" He looks at me. "At least, that's what they say."

We stand there, staring at a sign reading, "Welcome to Miss Queen's class," on the door. There are construction paper flowers with a child's name in the centre of each one. Nothing to this, right? Once upon a time, Pete and I crossed this threshold daily—several times a day, in fact. Once, this was our room, our home away from home. Time to erase the echoes of the past from the walls and draw a new story on them, huh?

"Try the knob," I tell Pete.

"*You* try the knob," he tells me.

"Ass wipe," I say.

"Belieber."

Of all the stupid things…

"You take that back," I tell him.

Pete chuckles. "Okay, okay," he says, covering his head as I swat at him.

"Say it."

"Fine, Al, I take it back."

"Okay, then. Just for that, *you* try the knob."

"Women," he says, in mock wonder. He reaches slowly for the doorknob and turns it. The door opens with a click.

"You first," I say.

"Ladies first."

"Age before beauty."

"Wimp."

"Loser," I retort.

Pete pushes the door open. From where I stand I can see the room, divided in two by a concrete block wall. To the left is the classroom proper, to the right, the cloakroom, where It took place. I blink a slow blink, long enough for It to play in a slide show of images on the monitor of my mind. I imagine I hear the gunman's heels click-clacking in the hallway, growing louder as he grows closer. The school is already in lockdown mode, so the classroom door is locked and shut, the lights out, students huddled away from the outside windows, and away from the sightlines of the one in the door (even though it's papered over with someone's artwork). The click-clacking stops right outside our door. There's a moment of extreme and utter silence, and then, BLAM! and the chink of metal as the bullet casing and bits of doorknob and door hit the tile floor. There are a few more click-clacks and then BLAM! BLAM! A whimper escapes from my throat. The gunman pivots. More click-clacks and...

Pop!

I find myself in my bedroom, in my bed, and in spite of the fact I'm still wearing Pete's jacket, shivering. I turn on the bedside lamp and start screaming.

27

Alice is 14

I barely hear Mom's voice over my screaming. She comes in, turns the light on, and turns as pale as my feet. "Oh, my God, Alice," she says, part lament, part question. At my bedside, she says, "You're shivering."

I look down at my feet, white, like a corpse's, swollen as if water-logged, and scream again.

Mom takes my face in her hands and makes shushing noises. "Alice," she says, firmly. "Alice, look at me. Look at me."

Dad comes in and I turn my head toward the noise he makes. "At me, Alice," Mom demands. I nod and look at her. In the commotion, she forgot to put her glasses on and I wonder how much she can actually see, even this close up. Her eyes look greener than I remember.

"Get a blanket, John," she says without breaking our staring match.

A moment or two later there's this weight on my feet, and I scream again, this time in agony, rather than fear, as Dad covers me, first with one comforter, then another, and I realize one of them has taken Pete's jacket off me at some point. I guess it's hard to keep track of time when you're dying of hypothermia.

"Gently!" Mom says.

"Sorry," Dad says. He looks almost as green as Mom's eyes.

"What happened?"

I try to answer, but I'm shivering so hard my jaw won't relinquish control to my tongue and lips long enough for the words to come out.

Mom says, "I'm calling Rebecca." She turns as if to leave, but I grab her arm and say, "Don't go." She smiles and says, "Just for a moment, honey. I need to get my phone. Okay?"

I nod. The bed jostles when she rises, and the comforters rub against my feet, feeling every bit like sandpaper on an open wound. I hiss a deep breath in response. "Who's Rebecca?" I ask Dad when the pain subsides a bit.

"Dr. Rickman, remember?"

"They're on a first-name basis?"

"They talk," Dad says with a shrug.

"About me?"

Dad shrugs. "She has her on speed dial," he offers.

Great.

Mom comes in with her phone to her ear. She's not talking, so I assume it's ringing. I turn my head to my bedside table and see it's 2:47. "It's the middle of the night," I tell her.

"It's an emergency," Mom says. Then Dr. Rickman must answer, because she says, "Rebecca?" There's a pause. "It's Alice." Another pause. "Frostbite, I think...White and puffy...I don't know...hold on."

She puts the phone down and says, "Sorry, honey, but this may hurt." She reaches under the blankets covering my feet and touches one of them. They're already on fire. Her finger feels like a hot poker pressing against my foot and I call out in pain.

Mom says into her phone, "Puffy, but soft." She waits, and then a small smile creeps across her lips. She nods and says, "Oh, thank God."

"What is it?" Dad says.

"She thinks second-degree frostbite."

"Is that good?"

"Third degree means they may have to amputate."

"Holy shit!" My voice sounds high pitched and reedy, not like mine at all.

"She says second-degree is better, but it's not good. She says we're not out of the woods yet."

Mom turns her attention back to the phone and nods a lot as she talks. She ends the conversation with "Okay, see you soon."

"What's happening?" Dad asks.

"She's coming over."

"Shouldn't we be taking her to the hospital?"

"And tell them what? In case you haven't noticed, the weather hasn't exactly been cold enough to do this to use the sleepwalking story again."

Mom hands me a box of Kleenex, leans in, and kisses me on my forehead. "Can I get you anything?" she asks. I shake my head. What I want—to get this damn gene, or chromosome, or telomere, or whatever it is out of my body—she can't give me.

"When the hell were you, Al?" she asks, and I start to cry. By the time Dr. Rickman arrives, I've told her everything.

28

Alice is 14 and 14

My frostbite was nasty, but not fatal. Since most of my adventures in time seem to be triggered by extreme stress, Dr. Rickman felt the best course of action was to keep me sedated until my feet healed. I spent most of the month after that particular jaunt in bed, sleeping. Her theory assumed that if nothing stressful happened during the day, I'd be guaranteed sweet dreams all night long, and I'd stay put overnight. Turns out she was right.

Dad used my wheelie desk chair as a kind of wheelchair to get me from my bed to the bathroom. He carried me downstairs every morning so I wouldn't have to stay in my room all day, and then back upstairs at night, joking all the while that he was the Hulk, or Superman, or something like that, but the smile he flashed when he joked never reached his eyes. I knew the brave face was a show, and that he was really crying on the inside, and I hated that.

I told Pete and Tina that I had measles so they couldn't come over, but we called each other and texted. We couldn't Skype or Face-Time because I really didn't have measles, and I was worried one of them would figure that out if they saw me with clear skin.

When my month of confinement was over, I went back to school. My feet were scarred on the soles when the blisters popped, but if you didn't know to look for them, you probably wouldn't notice. I spent a lot of days withdrawn from class with the Students-At-Risk teacher we all called "The STAR Teacher", and a lot of evenings with tutors to get caught up.

Winter arrived, bringing with it a sense of foreboding. Pete looked just like he does now on that night. In spite of this, when it finally happens I'm caught unawares. I call Pete, and it rings a long time before he answers. He says nothing after the click, so I say, "Hello?" a few times. I hear ambient noise, muffled talking, like when someone pocket dials you.

Pete stutters when he answers. "Who..." he says. He clears his throat and tries again. "Who is this?"

"It's me, Pete," I say, not clueing in yet. "It's Alice."

Pete says, "Look, I don't know who you are or how you got this phone, but you're not Alice. I'm sitting right across from Alice so you can't possibly be her."

I can't tell whether I read panic or anger in his voice, but as I'm trying to figure it out, I hear my voice say, "Pete," coming through the phone, and my heart starts to beat faster, and my stomach feels like it might fall right out of my body, and I realize tonight's the night.

"Pete?" I say, feeling the panic mount. "Oh, my God! Pete? Who are you with? Where are you?" I know where he is—he's at the Timmy's near our school. I know who he's with—he's with a past version of me, the one who might never have to go through the agony of frostbitten feet if she just stays put. And, okay, so the police were there, and they might have taken us in on suspicion of being runaways, but when I look at the alternative, better being in the back of a warm squad car than running on frozen concrete in stocking feet.

I know everything that happened that night, but I'm still not convinced the past is immutable, I mean, every single movie and TV show you see is all about how people try to change the future by changing the past, and succeeding. So if Pete decided not to go to Timmy's that night, I wouldn't know where they were. And if I didn't know where they were, I wouldn't be able to pull a Bill and Ted—you know, remembering to go back and put a crucial item in a place where it would be safe, so you could find it when you needed it, and be successful in whatever mission you were on? Anyway, if I could meet them at the Timmy's...

Mabel whispers something that I can't make out because I'm too busy trying to confirm where, exactly, they are, but what I know is, "Tell her you'll call her back," because I remember saying it.

Stupid Mabel. Too afraid Pete will think you're crazy, and it's much better to sacrifice your feet than your secret.

Stupid Mabel. Too dumb to even consider frostbite was a possibility.

I hear Pete say, "She wants to know where we are," and then Mabel says, "Don't tell her."

Stupid bitch.

She tells Pete, "Just...tell her you'll call her back, Pete," and then Pete comes back on the line, tells me he'll call me back, and disconnects.

I jump out of my bed and race down the stairs calling Mom. She comes out of the kitchen, wiping her hands on a dishcloth. "Where's the fire?" she says.

"The Tim's by my school," I tell her. Frostbite certainly feels like fire when you're in the throes of it.

"Seriously?"

"It's Frostbite Night, Mom." The blood drains from my mother's face until it looks as pale and white as my feet did when I turned the light on and started screaming at the sight of them.

"Boots," Mom commands. "You can wear shoes." She drops the dishcloth and rushes to get her coat. "Pants, too." I had minor first-degree patches of frostbite on my legs, but nothing compared to my feet.

"I don't think it matters much, seeing as we'll get her into the car." I'm too driven by the thought of saving Mabel, the fact I'm actually going to pick myself up and get back a month of my life doesn't occur to me.

Mom grabs her purse and slips into her boots. We take off without telling Dad where we're going, without setting the alarm, without even locking the deadbolt on the front door, and drive to Timmy's as quickly as Mom can. I don't draw attention to the fact she drives over the speed limit most of the way.

When we get there, Pete and Mabel are gone. "Let's go in," Mom says. She puts the car into park and turns the key in the ignition to cut the engine.

I shake my head. "It's too late."

Mom turns to face me and brings a hand up to caress my cheek. "It's never too late, Al. Maybe they're still in there somewhere." Mom unbuckles her belt, but I grab her hand before it can reach the door latch.

"You don't understand," I tell her, tears collecting. "We sat right there. In the corner. In front of the window. If we're not there, it means we've already left for the school."

"So let's go to the school, then," Mom says.

"Don't you get it?" I let go of her hand and fling my back into the seat. "If we're at the school then it's too late. I already have frostbite. We failed our mission."

"What?" Mom says. "What are you talking about, Al? What mission?"

"To save my feet," I say through the sobs.

"Was that what all this was about?" I look at her out of the corner of my eyes and nod. What the hell else would it be about? I want to scream, but I'd never ever think of talking to Mom like that, not in a million years, not after everything else I've put her through.

"Alice," she says, "What's done is done—"

"That's just it, Mom. It's not done. Somewhere out there I'm back at the Timmy's, sitting in that window, having hot chocolate and doughnuts with Pete when he gets the phone call and hangs up on me. And then the police come, and we run, and any way you tell it, I spend an entire month of my life drugged out of my mind in isolation."

"And that's in *your* past. It may be in one of the Mabels' futures out there, but it's in Alice Carroll's past. You have to accept that you can't change the past."

"When we left the house it was still in our future."

"No, dear. It was Mabel's future. And as strange as it seems, you're not her."

I can't get my mind around that: Mabel is Mabel and I'm me. Mom's right: I have to realize that whatever happened in the past is Mabel's business. The same goes for the future. Whenever I leap through the calendar like I do, I'm just visiting.

Nevertheless, it's a lot to take in. I can't change Frostbite Night, which means I can't get Frostbite Month back. And sometime in the not so distant future, Pete leaves me for Tina. Sometime in the future, I give Pete my list, which means sometime in the future I share my defect with him.

Just then my cell phone rings.

It's Pete.

Maybe tonight's *that* night, too.

29

Alice is 14

Pete and I find a quiet corner in the library at lunch the next day. We hide in the stacks, Pete lying on the floor, his head propped up on his backpack, my head propped up on his belly. He holds my hand, tracing the lines on my palm with his index finger. "So, how does it work?" he asks.

"How does *what* work?"

"This whole...time travel thing." He whispers the words "time travel".

"What do you mean, how does it work?"

"I mean, how do you do it?"

"I don't know. I just do."

"There's no precursor to it happening? No precipitating event?"

I start to answer but then I sit up and say, "I don't want to talk about it. Not here, not now anyway."

"Okay, Al. I didn't mean to...look, whenever you're ready, okay?"

I nod and lie back down. This time I take *his* hand and trace the lines on his palm with *my* finger. After a minute of silence, I say, "It's not like I have any control."

"Over what?"

I turn my head toward him and mouth, more than whisper, "You know."

Pete gives an exaggerated nod.

"Sometimes when I'm stressed—"

"Like before a test or something?"

"No, dork, I mean like last night when Mabel revisited the grade three classroom—"

"Wait—who's Mabel?"

"It's what me and my family call the me that's out of time."

"Why Mabel?"

I shrug. "It's my middle name."

"Oh."

"It also happens every time I dream about that horror show."

Softly, tentatively, Pete says, "You still dream about it?"

I nod. "Nightmares, actually. Don't you? Have nightmares about it?"

"Not for a while now." So it was official. I was the only freak show that couldn't get over the most horrendous thing that ever happened to me.

After a moment of silence, Pete says, "Al? If you could go back to that day and change anything, would you?"

I sit up so I can look at him while we talk. "I can't change anything, Pete."

"How do you know?"

"Look at what happened last night. I tried to change it by calling you, and the same thing happened that happened months ago."

"But that was *before* I knew."

I think about that for a moment. What if either one of us had known that by taking my phone call, by waiting for Mom and I to come, by not running, I could have been saved a whole bunch of agony? Would it have made a difference? "Something else probably would have happened to derail my rescue mission."

"But what if it didn't?"

"The Macbeth Conundrum," I say. The Macbeth Conundrum was what our English teacher dubbed the fate vs. free will argument in the play. Given his prophecies, Macbeth has the choice to sit back and wait for his fate to play out. Instead, he takes matters into his own hands and goes on a killing spree to secure Scotland's crown. Had Macbeth not killed the king, had he not continued to kill to keep the throne, would he have eventually become king anyway? We staged a debate that lasted days, and in the end we were still a class divided. Half the class argued that if it were his fate to become king, then we can never know if he would have become king without acting on his own, because he didn't wait long enough to find out. The fate people argued that the reason things turned out so badly for Macbeth was *because* he took matters into his own hands and chose his own path. The other half of the class argued that the witches were playing with Macbeth when they made up the prophecies and he only became king *because* he took matters into his own hands. He chose to take the crown by spilling blood, so it was only fit Macbeth's blood was spilled at the end of the play, divine retribution and all.

"My point exactly," Pete says.

"So you're saying it's my fate to float through time because I deserve to be punished like Macbeth?"

"I'm saying you have a choice to accept floating aimlessly through time or do something about it."

"But either way it ends badly."

Pete shakes his head. "Shakespeare had a formula to follow, Al. If he wrote a tragedy, his structure was bound by his own formula for a Shakespearean tragedy."

"Impressive," I say.

"I listen," Pete says, sort of comically. "My point is: how do you know you can't change anything if you don't try?"

I want to point out again that I did try. That calling him last night was me trying to save my poor feet, but I don't want to harp on his culpability in the whole Frostbite Incident.

"So, if you could go back and save someone, who would you save: the teacher or a kid? And if you choose kid, which one?" I ask.

"Tough call," Pete says.

"You brought it up."

I look at him and he looks like he's thinking, like he's *really* thinking. Pete chews on his upper lip and focuses on a point in the distance, like he's agonizing over which letter to bubble on the Scantron on a test or something. "The teacher's already proven she's devoted her life to doing good, shaping young minds and all that, but the kid's like a lump of clay. He—"

"Or she."

"Or she—could turn out to be anything—"

"A mass murderer, or discoverer of the cure for cancer, or something."

"Exactly," Pete says.

"Tough call," I repeat.

"Exactly." The five-minute warning sound chimes. Pete stands up and offers a hand to help me up. "We should look into this sometime," he tells me and hands me my backpack.

"Yeah," I say, petrified at the thought.

"Meet at my locker after school and we'll recon the grade three class."

"What? Today?"

The librarian uses a bullhorn to usher us to class. "Class starts in less than five minutes, people. You must leave the library and go to class." She repeats this over and over, like she's a recording.

"*Carpe diem*, right?"

I take a deep breath and follow Pete out of the library. "Seize the day," I whisper to myself, not sure I really want to.

30

Alice is 14

We meet after school and walk to Chris Hadfield P.S. Pete waltzes straight in through the front door as if he still belongs there, but I grab his hand and pull him from the doorway. "Are you sure this is okay?" I ask. Cheers come from deep within the school, as if there's some sort of sporting event happening in the gym. Three senior students sit at a collapsible table, six or so feet into the foyer, selling bags of potato chips, pizza slices, and pop.

"I'm sure." He takes both of my hands in his and presses his cool forehead against mine. "Look, Alice, we don't have to do this if you don't want to."

I *want* to learn how to control my milling about through time. I think about how great it would be to suppress the power of that gene, to stick my tongue out at it every time it wields its ugly head and threatens to ruin my life and tell it to GTFO, that I won't yield, that my body and what it does is no one's decision but my own. What I don't want is to get flustered at the sight, drift off somewhere or some*when,* and wind up with frostbite, or beaten, raped, or worse. "I want to," I whisper.

"You sure?" Pete asks.

I nod my head and his bobs along with it.

He lets go of one hand and leads me into the school, past the Refreshment Kids, and down the corridor to the third-grade classroom. We step through the open door and over the threshold and hear, "Can I help you?" A teacher sits at the desk in the classroom. I look toward my right, the cloakroom, and swallow hard.

Pete squeezes my hand and says. "I'm sorry to bother you, ma'am," though the woman hardly seems old enough to be called ma'am. She has short, black hair cut in a bob, and peers at us over thick, black frames. Her lips are deep, dull red, the colour of an unpolished apple. "We, my friend and I, were here, in this class, the day of..." he swallows hard, "five years ago on *That* Day." Voldemort Day; the day that shall not be named. "Our shrink thought it might help us, might be a good idea, if we looked around a bit."

The teacher smiles. "You have therapy together?"

"We see the same psychiatrist, Miss," I intervene. "She told us—"

"Separately—"

"That we should come back here, to visit the scene of the crime, so to speak."

"Please, Miss," Pete says, taking the ball, "it might really help us in our therapy—"

"Individually—"

"In our individual therapy."

The teacher takes her glasses off and rests them on the desk on top of the papers she's been grading. "You have fifteen minutes," she tells us. She stands and smoothes her skirt down. The skirt is a beautiful shade of yellow with a tulip petal hem. Her blouse is short sleeved, gauzy, and royal blue. She walks out of the classroom, exuding this regal air, and I know I'm going to pester Mom to buy me the exact same outfit, first chance I get.

Pete wanders to the centre of the classroom. He seems to be staring at his feet when he stops. I wander over to stand beside him and look down. There's a patch of about eight tiles lighter than the surrounding tiles. I squat down so I can touch them. "This is where Miss

Dinah died," I say, confident in my assertion, though I have no way of knowing for sure. When hell broke loose, I was cowering in the cloakroom.

Pete nods his head silently.

"Where were you, Pete? When it happened?"

"We heard shots down the hall. Miss Dinah grabbed my wrist and pulled me close to her. She sat there, cuddling me behind her desk until the doorknob was shot, then she stuffed me under the desk." He looked toward the teacher's desk. It was a huge, grey, metal monstrosity, enclosed on three sides so you couldn't see the teacher's legs when she sat. "I wonder if it's the same one," he says, and ventures toward it.

"So, you were safe?"

"As safe as you can be behind a thin plate of metal." He bends down in front of the desk and gives the metal sheet a rap. "I wonder if the gunman would have...if he'd have shot...if it would've been enough."

"I guess the best part was that you were hidden, so he wouldn't have known *to* shoot."

Pete caresses the front of the desk. "I guess," he says.

I stand up and examine the rest of the floor. There's another, smaller patch, closer to the window at the back of the classroom. "What do you suppose happened here?"

"Michael Barrie, I think."

"Did he live?"

Pete looks at me gravely and shakes his head slowly. How awful. That could have been Pete. It could have been me. It could have been any one of the twenty or so children in the room that day.

I walk over to Pete, still kneeling in front of the teacher's desk, and put a hand on his shoulder. He stands, turns to face me, and engulfs me in this bear hug that nearly takes my breath away. I return the favour, and we stand there for a moment, feeling each other's bodies shake and heave. When we separate, each of us has a wet patch on a shoulder from the other's tears.

"I was here," I tell him.

The cloakroom is separated from the rest of the class by a cinderblock wall that runs the length of most of the classroom. There's an entrance at either end of the room, one near the door, and one near the windows at the back, probably designed to allow for maximum natural light on both sides of the wall. I enter the room through the back passageway, the one by the windows. The space is narrower than I remember. There are a series of wooden cubbies along each wall, each separated into an upper compartment—consisting of a shelf; a middle one—containing a single, metal coat hook; and a lower one—opening onto the tiled floor for shoes or boots. A narrow bench runs almost the length of the room, really nothing more than a wooden plank suspended on a series of metal bars secured to the floor. The teacher's cubby, the only one with a door on it, is in the corner nearest the hallway entrance.

"Where?" Pete asks.

"I tried to climb under the bench, here," I say. I caress the wooden seat with the palm of my hand. Sure enough, the tile in front of the bench has also been replaced.

Pete must notice this, too, because he asks, "Were you shot?"

"Not me."

"Then who?"

I shake my head. "I don't know. This...woman. She came out of nowhere. Used her body to shield mine. I think she must've..." The thought is enough to get me going. If it weren't for Miss Dinah sacrificing her life for Pete and the other kids...if it weren't for my mystery woman shielding me...

I swallow hard and say, "Pete?"

"Yeah, Alice?"

I try to speak, but can't catch my breath enough to form the words. All I can do is shake my head. I catch a glimpse of myself, that freaky, distorted mask of my face in the chrome plated legs that I saw on That Day.

I blink, and Pete's gone.

31

Alice is 14 and 3

Whenever I am, the school is emptier than when I left, and Pete's nowhere to be found.

Now that I know where I am—the grade three cloakroom—I can move on to the next order of business—figuring out *when* I am.

The classroom side of the cinderblock divider looks familiar. Eerily so. From where I stand, I can see a small placard on the teacher's desk. It reads "Miss Dinah". My chest feels like it did that time I went on the Drop Zone Tower at Canada's Wonderland, like I've fallen about twenty stories and left my heart and stomach behind.

She's still alive.

Pete and I came here trying to navigate my trips back in time and I wound up *here.* In the classroom, before the Big Bad that changed my life. Changed *everyone's* life. If Miss Dinah's still alive, maybe my mission is to warn her so she can warn them and save everyone's life, including her own.

There's a calendar on the flip-board easel. It's my third year of life, my birthday month. Pete's not here because he's three, too. Both of us barely out of diapers and yet to meet. All we know about school is that it's this place where we're supposed to have fun and meet other kids and that it will prove we're Big Kids and not Babies, something for which all toddlers strive. School is also this place of extreme anxiety because it means we'll have to survive for hours without the comfort afforded by our fathers' hands in ours, or our ears against our mothers' bosoms.

My heart drops further and my body gives an involuntary shudder. Even if Pete had this date on his list, he couldn't help. My parents wouldn't be coming any time soon either, because they don't find out about my condition until I'm four. Even then, they write it off as some kind of group hallucination until I give them the head's up that it actually happened when I'm twelve.

It's dark out. That means Miss Dinah's gone home for the evening. I race behind her desk and try the drawers. If her address is somewhere, her phone number...but I find nothing.

I can't save her. I can't save anyone. Hell, I couldn't even save myself from frostbite. What's the point of having this ability if I can't do anything with it?

Screw ability. This is more like a curse. I'm doomed. Doomed to re-live the worst day of my life. Doomed to miss opportunities to change it. Doomed to have my defect put my life in danger, time and time again. Doomed to have to rely on Pete to get me out of it.

Someone tries the door handle, probably the caretaker doing his rounds. Thankfully, it's locked, and I go undiscovered. I wait in the room another fifteen minutes or so, long enough for the caretaker to clear the corridor so I can escape. I put a piece of tape over the doorplate so it won't lock behind me, just in case I need to duck back in for cover later.

It's nice outside, early autumn. In Toronto, that could mean anything from flash snowstorm to skyrocketing UV levels. While it's not cold enough for snow, and it's not hot enough to warrant shorts, it's still too hot for the sweater and sweatpants I'm wearing. I'd stick out like a sore thumb if it were still daylight and there were people enough on the street to notice.

I decide to check out the mall.

After Frostbite Night, my mom went to a bunch of local spots, Tim Hortons, mostly, and left my picture and a gift card with the instructions that if I were to show up, they were to feed me and take the money off the card so I wouldn't starve in case I were stranded. What she didn't count on was that I might be stranded in a time before that night. A time before either she or Pete knew I was there. A time that wasn't on my list.

It wasn't the most hygienic of plans, but I aimed to go to the food court and graze on what people had left behind on their trays. Gross, I know, especially considering the array of diseases people carry with them in the twenty-first century, but time travel takes a lot out of me, and my stomach is growling like a son-of-a-bitch, and I have no way of knowing how long I'll be stuck in this time, no way of knowing how long it'll be until my next meal, so any port in a storm, as they say.

The mall is dead, and when I find a clock I know why—it's eight-thirty already, and near closing time.

The food court is dead as well. People were being nice to the wait-staff as few tables have trays on them, and the ones that do have nothing more than empty paper or cardboard containers.

A security guard passes by me and then circles back around to check me out. I guess a kid, looking more pre-teen than teen, wearing unseasonal clothes, and poking around in other people's garbage seems a bit hinky to him. I sit down at the nearest table with a tray on it and pretend-chew my pretend last bite of food. I pretend swallow, stand up, and bus my tray, taking it to the garbage, dumping its contents, and stacking it on top of the receptacle. I smile at the guard, nod, and leave the area.

My stomach is so empty it hurts. I have to figure something out before I die. And while I'm not above outright stealing, I'm not stupid enough to do it in front of a mall cop.

I sense more than see the security guy walking a few paces behind me. I know I have to do something or blow my cover. In this time, chances are my parents would deny knowing me, so if he called home, he'd have no option but to believe I was a runaway and call the real cops, who would take me to a shelter or something for the night. When I eventually disappear, they might let it go—bigger fish to fry and all that—or they might pursue it, and I'd be on the real lam every time I got unstuck in time, not just avoiding the police to keep the peace, but avoiding them as a fugitive.

It's at that very moment I see him. I've seen him before, over the years of coming to the mall as frequently as we do. In spite of that fact, his appearance still fascinates me. We'd nicknamed him Barry Ballerina in my house when I was younger, because I thought he needed a name. Barry is tall, over six feet, and heavy—Dad once imagined him to be at least two-fifty, if not more. But what makes him so interesting to mall patrons (and what led me to dub him with the name I gave him) is neither his height nor his weight; it's the way he dresses. Barry wears black ballet slippers on his feet, white tights on his legs, a rainbow-coloured, tulle tutu, a tweed jacket, vest, white dress shirt, and a Lincoln-style top hat with a huge pink bow around it. A puffy cottontail pokes out from the slit at the back of his jacket. He lines his eyes with thick, black eyeliner, wears bright, sparkly blue shadow on his eyelids to a point just beneath his perfectly shaped eyebrows, a spot of hot pink blush on the apple of each cheek, and bright red lipstick. He does nothing in the mall, to my knowledge, other than walk, patronize the odd store, or sometimes have a coffee at one of the shops.

Just when I think he's coming toward me, he veers off to my right and into one of those shops. In an effort to get the security guard off my ass, I duck in the other entrance and stand next to Barry at the register. Barry orders coffee and a muffin. There's a brief moment of awkwardness that passes between myself and the barista when he asks me for my order. I nod in Barry's direction in an effort to say, "I'm with him," without Barry noticing.

Barry takes his coffee from the man, sits down, and I slide into the chair opposite him.

"Well, hello," he says to me in a deep voice, a paradox to his appearance. "What can I do you for tonight, love?"

"I need to ditch the security guard," I tell him, thinking honesty's the best policy.

Barry looks at the guard blocking the entrance to the shop. He turns to me, leans forward and whispers, "What did you do?"

"Nothing," I say, not a little bit defensive. "I just...I'm hungry, and I was...looking for something to eat, and he...thought it suspicious." I hope I don't sound as pathetic to him as I do to myself.

Barry motions for the security guard to come to our table. There's a moment in which I wish looks could kill, and send out the killing-look vibe to Barry with the sick notion that he's going to turn me in. Instead, he says to the guard, "It's okay. She's with me." The guard crosses his arms over his chest as if trying to decide if I really am okay, if this guy, dressed the way he is, is in any position to vouch for me. "My niece. Visiting from out of town."

"Keep an eye on her, okay?" the guard says, and he leaves the shop.

"You're not a runaway or anything, are you, kid?" Barry asks when the guy's out of earshot.

I shake my head. "Things are just a little weird at home. I left so things could cool down a bit, but I forgot my purse when I did."

"Parents fight a lot, do they?" he asked.

They didn't. Hardly ever, in fact, but I wasn't going to tell him that. I nod.

"Can I interest you in half a muffin?"

"Yes, please," I say.

"Before we break bread, I think introductions are in order."

He looks at me waiting for me to make the first move, so I say, "Mabel."

"An oldie but a goodie. Bet you're always the only Mabel in your classes, aren't you?"

"Yes, sir," I say, feebly.

"No last name?" he asks.

I shake my head. "Just Mabel."

He shrugs and says, "Pleased to meet you, Mabel. Name's William Tibbar, but folks call me Bill." His voice cracks a bit in the middle of saying this, but he just clears his throat and pays it no mind. He pronounces his name "Tih-bah". It reminds me of that time on *Saturday Night Live* when they were being the Kennedys and they kept on saying Bah-hah-bah, and the audience and Dad laughed their asses off every time, so I asked him what was so funny and he said, "He's saying Bar Harbor." I sought to find the humour in that and when I couldn't, I frowned and said, "Yeah...I don't get it," and Dad said, "Bar Harbor's a place in New England." I thought again. "Still don't get it," I said. "It's the accent," Dad said. I looked at him trying to figure it out. "It's funny," he said. "But why?" I asked. Dad got frustrated, shook his head, and said, "Just watch TV."

I think about Bill's last name and the way he said it and I ask him, "Are you from New England?"

He laughs at that, tears the muffin in half and says, "Why would you ask me that, silly goose?"

I shrug one shoulder and say, "No reason."

Bill places half of his muffin on a napkin and slides it across the table to me. "It's bran. Blueberry bran. It's good for the digestion." He pats his ample stomach.

I thank him for the food, tear a piece off, and shove it into my mouth, which begins to produce enough saliva to drown a small animal.

"So what's your story, Mabel?"

I shake my head and say through the muffin, "No story."

"You're what, twelve?"

"Fourteen."

"Excuse me. Fourteen, in the mall near closing time, alone, and dressed hideously." I know what you're thinking, but the man saved me from the mall cop, and he was giving me food, and I have enough sense not to alienate him by stating the obvious. "You have to have a story," he says.

"I told you mine already. You tell me yours."

"I don't have a story," he says. He takes a sip of his coffee. "What makes you think I have a story?" He looks at me expectantly as if daring me to say something, but, like before, food wins out over smart-assery every time.

"Nothing," I say. I finish the last bit of my muffin-half, nod to his sitting prettily, still untouched on the torn-open serving bag, and ask, "You going to eat that?"

32

Alice is 14 and 3

Bill withdraws a pocket watch from one of his vest pockets, checks it, and says, "Oh, dear. I have to go. I'm late." He puts the watch away and says to me, "Thank you for the lovely company, my dear."

"Thanks for the muffin," I say. "I don't know how, but I'll figure out a way to pay you back somehow."

"Don't you worry your pretty little head about it, my dear," he says. "Can I walk you home?"

I'd like nothing better, but I can't go home, not at this time, so I shake my head.

"At least let me walk you out so as not to arouse the suspicion of security?"

I imagine Tina giggling at Bill's use of the word "arouse" and stifle a grin.

"Deal." We leave the mall together, parting ways with a hug and a wave in front of the main entrance door. I watch him walk off, oblivious to what anyone else thinks, happy just to be Bill Tibbar (Tih-bah) being himself. At least he has a place to go. Unlike me. I can't go to Pete—he's only three. I can't go home—Mom and Dad don't find out about my death-defying feats for seven years yet. I can't go back into the mall—the security guards will be on the lookout for the homeless seeking overnight shelter. The only chance I have is to go back to the school and lay low until I don't need to anymore.

It's Cub night at the school. Parents—mostly dads—lead young boys dressed in beige, knit, long sleeved shirts, black short pants, burnt orange ties, and beige baseball caps. Getting into the school is no problem—just a girl there to pick up her kid brother from Cub Scouts.

The tape is still on the doorplate of the door to the third-grade classroom. The door pushes open and I go inside. I'm drawn to the cloakroom, the spot on which I cowered, hunkering low to the ground, my hands over my head, thinking I was about to die until I wasn't there anymore. Because the tiles have yet to be replaced, I have only the GPS of my memory to lead me to the exact spot. I stand there and look around.

What am I doing here?

Attempting to take charge of my life. To get a handle on my defect.

And now that I'm here? Now, what?

I have to save Miss Dinah. I have to save Miss Dinah and everyone else that was killed, hurt, or emotionally scarred that day, but how could I possibly do that?

I could wait here until morning, but there's no guarantee I'd make it through the night. Even if I do make it through the night, there's no guarantee I won't be found and evicted, and then what? I have no ID, no way to prove I am who I say I am. Would my three-year-old mom be as understanding as my four-year-old mom? If they were called to come for me, would they? Or would they insist the police (or the principal or the custodian or whoever was calling) had the wrong number? Would they insist their Alice Carroll was in her junior bed, snuggled under her princess comforter and sheets, and fast asleep?

My only recourse is to leave a note and hope it's enough to save her.

On Miss Dinah's desk, I find a marker—a green one, the same colour she'll use to assess my work seven years from now—and a blank piece of paper and write, *Dear Miss Dinah,*

Now, what?

Dear Miss Dinah, on this date you will die.

Sounds too much like a threat.

Dear Miss Dinah, on this date a gunman will enter your classroom.

Not much better.

Dear Miss Dinah, you don't know me, but...

Great. If you're writing one of those chain posts on Facebook, you know, if you don't share this post and tag ten people on your friends list, bad luck will come to you. Definitely not the tone I'm going for.

A swarm of bees buzzes inside my ear canal and the air in the room starts to thicken. Not a good sign. It means I'll be gone before long.

Dear Miss Dinah, don't come in to work on this date.

That might save her, but what about the others? What can I say that will get them to close the school, or at the very least, have some sort of police presence around?

I blink hard and try to will the world to stop spinning.

I feel like I'm moving underwater.

I crumple the paper I've just written on, throw it to the floor, and begin to write once more, but it's too late. My last vision of the room is of Miss Dinah's desk, crumpled papers all around, and one uncrumpled sheet on the desktop. On it, written in green ink, is Miss Dinah's name and a date.

33

Alice is 14

I wind up where I left off, back in the cloakroom of the third-grade classroom. It takes about a second before I start to heave. Before I know it, Bill's muffin is on the floor, half-digested and in a pool of stomach acid. Someone goes, "Psst," and I turn around to see Pete peeking in through the open window.

I hear myself say, "Oh, God," and my stomach heaves again. "I'm sick," I tell him.

"I can see that."

"Dorkus." I hawk a small lugie to clear the grossness from my mouth.

"No directioner."

I suck air in as if I've just touched a hot stove burner.

"Relax, dweeb," he says, "I take it back," but I'm not letting him off the hook that easily. Some things just cannot be taken back, such as messing with the sacristy of my British boys.

"What do you want, Pete?"

"I waited, hoping you'd come back before it was too late and my parents called looking for me."

"I guess today's your lucky day, then."

"I guess." He looks at me through the open window, appearing nothing more than a silhouette, backlit by the streetlamps and moonlight the way he is. I glare at him over my shoulder, make a face at him with eyebrows raised and wide eyes. "What are you waiting for, Al?" he asks. "Let's go."

I'm still a little pissed at the One Direction low-blow he pulled earlier, so I don't answer him right away.

"I'll meet you at the side doors." He points to the stairwell beside the class, the one I used to sneak out earlier.

"Wait," I whisper, loud enough so he'll hear. "I have to clean this." I point with my hand to the sick-up puddle on the floor.

"Caretakers'll get it," Pete says.

I nod, and though I feel guilty about the mess I've imposed on the poor, unsuspecting caretakers, I leave the third-grade class, careful to check the hallway before I do, and close the door quietly behind me.

We walk halfway home in silence, cutting through the neighbourhood park. Pete grabs my hand near the swing set, pulls me off the path, and into the gravel patch under them. He sits on the closest swing. When he lets go of my hand, I sit in the swing beside him, but facing the other way. We swing a bit without talking. Before long, Pete starts poking me in the side when we cross paths.

"Quit it," I tell him, but he doesn't. Instead, he changes the pokes to quick tickles. "Stop it, Pete," I say loudly.

"Sorry," he says.

Soon the arcs our swings draw in the sky narrow until we're not doing much more than rocking back and forth, our feet never leaving the ground, our eyes fixed on our dusty sneakers getting dustier by the minute. Pete says, "What I said before? I didn't mean it. It's just that...we do this thing, you know? This insult thing? And it's kind of cute, because you know that I don't mean it, and it's our thing. I guess I took it too far.

"I *am* a dweeb. I don't know where to draw the line sometimes."

I look up at him through the corner of my eye and say, "You're not a dweeb, Pete." We start to sway left to right until our swings collide. Sometime after the first hip bump, my eyes start to burn. Before long, they brim with tears. I blink and they stream down my cheeks. I sniffle, and Pete turns to look at me. I look back at him, wipe the tears from my cheek, and laugh. "I don't even know why I'm crying," I tell him.

Pete takes hold of the swing chain and pulls me close. "What happened? When you were gone, I mean." And so I tell him the story, about landing in Miss Dinah's class with the original flooring, about taking off to the mall, having coffee with Bill, and about the note I tried to leave.

"Wow," Pete says, "heavy."

It takes a few moments for me to get my sobbing under control. When I do, I say, "Why are things so heavy in the future? Is there a problem with the Earth's gravitational pull?"

When I first told Pete about what I could do, he proclaimed we needed to brush up on our time travel lore. To that end, we watched all three *Back to the Future* movies, marathon style, on Netflix one afternoon, gorging ourselves on popcorn, potato chips, pop, and pizza all the while. Then, for good measure, we watched the first one again. I left Pete's house with a wicked case of indigestion, vowing never to ever so much as look at another piece of junk food again (a resolution I kept less than twenty-four hours when Mom proclaimed she was going on a frozen yogurt run the next afternoon). Pete later confessed to me he'd watched the first two in the series at least half a dozen times more over the next week or so. I didn't see any reason to myself—Marty uses Doc Brown's DeLorean time travel machine, he doesn't develop the ability to time travel after being caught in a flux capacitor explosion. No parallel between Marty McFly and Alice Carroll, if you ask me.

"Goof," Pete says.

After a few moments, I say, "I couldn't do it, Pete."

"Couldn't do what, Al?"

"I couldn't save her."

"Who?"

"Miss Dinah. I couldn't save her," I say, and then my sobbing begins anew. "I tried." Heavy sob. "I failed." Lighter one. "I couldn't do it."

"Rome wasn't built in a day, you know."

I exhale loudly. "Oh, Pete."

"Open foot; insert mouth," he says.

I take hold of his nearest shoulder and squeeze. "It's okay."

"What I mean is this is your first attempt at controlling your power—"

"You mean my *defect*."

"I mean your *super*power. You concentrated your efforts and you landed in the right place, but the wrong time."

"That's putting it mildly."

Pete smiles his winning smile at me, the one that balls up the apples of his cheeks and brightens his eyes. He makes a "come here" gesture by jerking his head. I stand and he pulls me close until his head rests on my breasts (new blossoms, Mom calls them). He plants his hands, palms open on my back, and squeezes me tightly. After a minute he lets go and slaps his thighs. It's a little awkward, but I step into the pocket formed by the swing chain and his butt with my right leg. He reaches around my body and rests his hands at the small of my back so I don't fall when I do the same with my left. When I sit, it's on his lap, facing him, our legs forming a four-legged spider. I rest my head on his shoulder as he rocks us in narrow arcs.

"Remember in *Man of Steel* when Clark Kent learned he had super hearing and x-ray vision, and he had to learn how to control it?" I remember it well. Pete and I saw it together on Netflix. I thought Henry Cavill was hot, but I didn't let on about that to Pete. He tolerates my British boys, and that's more than one boyfriend could be asked to handle. "Your ability to time travel is no different. One day you'll get the hang of it."

"What if I can't change anything, though? Or what if I can, but stuff starts disappearing, like in that picture in *Back to the Future*? Or what if I change everything, like when that guy steps on the butterfly in that story we read in English?"

Pete chuckles.

"What's so funny?"

"Nothing."

I push back from him and playfully slap his shoulder. "Are you laughing at me?"

"It's just...you're cute, comparing your real life to the fictional ones."

I have to chuckle about it, too. Pete's usually the one making fictional connections to real ones, not the other way around. "Goof," I say.

"Brainiac." He pulls me close again and smoothes the hair at the back of my neck. "You, Alice Carroll, are unique. There has never been anyone else in the world like you, and there may never be again. You're operating in uncharted territory here, and your first imperative is to learn to control your ability. We'll cross the other bridge when we come to it, okay?"

I nod into the crook formed by his shoulder and neck and wonder if he'll ever sit this way with Tina, hold her in his arms, rock her gently, and tell her everything will turn out okay.

34

Alice is 14

There's an incident in the spring of my grade nine year that scares the shit out of me and everybody else around me. I leave school feeling zonked as all get-out after fourth period Math class, visions of equations with two unknowns dancing in my head. Pete and I walk out of the school and onto the driveway to cross over to the sidewalk, and a car comes at us going the wrong way. We don't see it initially, because we are flirting and giggling, and making fun of a teacher who has a strange accent, halfway between German and British, and tends to look at the ceiling more than her students as she teaches. When she does, she flutters her eyelids as if they're blinds that have been pulled hard enough to fly up and spin on the dowel.

The car revs its engine and both Pete and I turn to look. We stand dead in its path. Rather than hit the brakes, the driver seems to speed up, closing the distance between the car and Pete and me, fast. There's a split second when I catch a glimpse of us dodging the car, midair, in the hood of the car as Pete pushes me out of the way.

When I land on the ground, Future Pete's there waiting for me.

"Christ, Al, you nearly materialized right on top of me that time," he says. This accompanied by the image at the end of *The Philadelphia Experiment*, the one where the camera shows sailors partially encased in the concrete of the dock after the climax, and a full-body shudder.

"Can we go?" I ask.

Pete escorts me to a car parked in the visitors' section of the school lot. He opens the passenger's door remotely, gets in behind the wheel, and starts the car. If he has his licence, he must be at least sixteen...wait, no, seventeen—you can't drive without a licensed driver until you get your G2 licence, which comes a year after earning your G1 at sixteen. If Pete's seventeen, I wonder if that night at his dad's, the one where I threw myself at him, has happened yet.

"Tim's okay?" he asks, and I can't help but grin.

Before that night. Definitely before.

"That's our place, isn't it?" I say. Lots of teens hang at Tim's because it's cheap, and you can eat either healthy, or junky, or both at the same time.

As luck would have it, the Tim's we go to, though not the one closest to school, is one that has that deal with my mom, and so coffee's on me this time. "When are we?" I ask Pete after we sit.

"I don't know if I can tell you that, Al. Per your instructions, remember?"

I don't, but that's because Pete's working from a list in my future that I haven't fully penned yet. "Okay, how old are *you*? Can you tell me *that*?"

"Don't get all snippy with me, okay? I'm playing by your rules, not mine."

"Okay," I say. "I'm sorry."

Pete looks at me for a minute and says, "The least you could do is say it like you mean it."

I smile at him and take a long sip of my Iced Cappuccino. Though I hold it in my mouth until it mostly melts, there's still a moment—a really long moment—when it feels as if my head might explode.

"Brain freeze?" Pete asks.

"Whoa, yeah."

He waits until the worst has passed and I finish wincing before saying, "Eighteen," and I must look at him like he's speaking Klingon because he repeats, "I'm eighteen. You?"

"Fourteen."

"I remember Alice Carroll at fourteen—"

"Almost fifteen," I counter.

"Headstrong, stubborn, loads of attitude, and I mean *loads*."

"What about me at eighteen?"

Pete shakes his head. "My lips are sealed."

I take another big sip of my Ice Capp, hoping that when this bout of brain freeze passes it'll take the question on the tip of my tongue with it, but there's no brain freeze, and the question has to be asked. "How's Tina?"

"Tina?"

"You remember Tina, don't you? Tina Bell? My best friend growing up?"

He forces a frown and shakes his head slowly. "I wouldn't know. I think she went away to University. Waterloo? Guelph, maybe?"

I think of The Other Future Pete, not much older than this Pete, receiving a call from a grown-up Tina, cell playing *My Girl*, like some sort of tribute to her, and the intimate conversation that followed, and think I might sick-up my drink. "Tina went to university?"

Pete nods. "Turns out she's like a prodigy when it comes to computer programming."

"Huh," I say.

Pete opens the box of Timbits I got and offers them to me. I select an old-fashioned glazed one, nod my thanks, and pick off a small piece. "Pete?" I say. "Do you remember that time we almost got ran over and you pushed me out of the way and I left?"

"Do I? I wound up flat on my face. Knocked out one of my front teeth." He smiles toothily and taps on one of his incisors. "Had to get an implant to replace it." He pops another doughnut hole into his mouth and chews a bit before continuing. "I don't think anyone realized you were walking with me. I guess they just thought I'd tripped and fallen."

"I'm sorry," I tell him.

"I know."

I take a bite out of my old-fashioned and ask through a full mouth, "Do I ever learn to control myself? I mean, my..." defect, I want to say, but manage to restrain myself. This is no time for wallowing. "...my ability?"

"Tick-a-lock, Al," he says. He turns an invisible key in front of his lips and mimes throwing the key away.

"I'm Mabel," I tell him, still feeling a bit sorry for myself.

After Tim's, Pete and I go back to school and wait until my time with him is done.

35

Alice is 14

Knock, knock, knock. "Alice."

Groan!

Knock, knock, knock. "Alice."

Mom. Doing her silly Sheldon Cooper thing. "Go away!" One more volley and she'll be done.

Knock, knock, knock. "Alice." I hear my bedroom door unlatch.

"Close my door."

She turns the light on instead. "Not till I know you'll get out of bed."

"I'm not." I wrap my comforter around me, cocoon-like.

"You have to go to school."

"No, I don't."

"Actually, you do, young lady. The law says so."

"I said, leave me alone." This time I bury my head under the pillow to drown out the sound of her voice. I feel something graze my shoulder and tumble onto the mattress in front of me. Allie the Alley Cat. Mom lobbed it at me before she closed the door.

I must doze a bit because the next knock on the door startles me back to the land of the living. This time, the rap is all business, devoid of Mom's playfulness. Must be Dad.

"I'm coming in," he says.

"I'm not dressed," I tell him. He tells me the same thing when I knock on his door and he and Mom want privacy. It doesn't work as well for me as it does for him.

"Bull-shtak," he says, borrowing the word from that show he watches, the one that has a video game...*Defender? Defiance?*

Dad opens the door. There's a brief moment of silence and then he rips the comforter from my body. I'm left in a fetal position in my shorty pajamas, shivering against the sudden change in room temp.

"You're going to school."

"No, I'm not."

"Yes, you are." He kneels beside the bed, hooks his hands under my armpits, and yanks me from the mattress. I play rag doll, hoping he'll let go, which he eventually does. I curl up into a ball on the floor. Dad nudges my ribs with the tip of his stocking toe.

"Alice," Dad says, pleading.

"John," Mom says, calling Dad by name. "Let's go."

"Today. You got today. But back to school tomorrow," Dad whispers in my ear. He closes the door behind him.

"Like hell," I say. I climb back into bed, huddle beneath the comforter, and hug Allie the Alley Cat. "I'm never going back there again."

Not ten minutes later, there's another knock on my door, three short raps, and then I hear the click of the latch. "Sweetie?" Mom says. But it's not just any Mom. This is Good Mom, here to appeal to my common sense, the Mom who claims to believe you can bag more flies with honey than with vinegar. "Alice, honey?" Her bare feet pad over to my bed and she sits on the edge. She digs my head out from under the blankets, brushes my hair from my forehead, and brings her cool lips to it. "You're cool as a cucumber," she says for about the millionth time in my lifetime.

"I'm not sick."

"Paralyzing fear is a kind of sickness," she says and just like that, we're replaying the scene from *The Big Bang Theory*, the one where Sheldon is locked out of his house and spending the night at Penny's, but he can't sleep. Sheldon says he's not sick, and Penny says, "Homesickness is a kind of sickness." Mom doesn't disappoint—she asks if I want her to sing "Soft Kitty" to me. Or maybe she does disappoint. I mean, here I am, scared to frozen that if I go to school I'll one day dematerialize in front of people in an imperceptible poof of air, and all she can do is play out a corny scene from a stupid television show. I know she means well, to ease the tension in the room, but come on!

I want to give her shit for that. Tell her she's being an insensitive bitch. But let's get real here: she's my mom. And just because I'm really pissed at her at this particular moment doesn't mean I want to burn any bridges that can't be mended. "Go away," I say, instead.

"Alice Mabel Carroll," she uses her stern, I-mean-business-this-time voice, "you get out of that bed, get washed, get dressed, and go to school."

"No," I say. And then for emphasis, I repeat, "Go away." My fingers find Allie the Alley Cat's hair and twist it between them.

The springs of my bed creak as Mom stands and pads back to the door. "I'll call the school and let them know," she says, resigned, and then adds hastily, "but just for today. Tomorrow you're going right back, young lady." She gently closes the door.

"Fat chance," I say when I figure she's out of earshot.

* * *

Around noon, I hear the front door open. Footsteps. Women's voices. At least one of them is Mom. I pull the comforter tighter around me and bring a flap up and over my head. I wish she'd leave me alone. I wish everyone would just leave me alone.

I wish I'd materialize in front of a moving vehicle, preferably a bus. Its brakes would squeal as the driver tried to stop, but it wouldn't come to a standstill until it's well into the next block. Someone will inevitably call 9-1-1 but I'll be mush long before then. I'll float above my body, watching as paramedics try to revive me in vain. That would show my mother. Force me outside, will you? Make me go to school? You might be surprised to find out that Mom doesn't always know best.

There's a light tap on my door and I hear it open. "Alice?" Mom says, tentatively.

I don't answer.

There's a shuffling at my door and then I feel the springs depress at the foot of my bed. "I understand you're not feeling so well today," someone says. It's a female voice, not my mom, but familiar, nevertheless. "Do you think you could come out and talk a bit?"

I roll over and peek out over the blankets to see Dr. Hatfield. She unwinds a fuzzy, mauve scarf from around her neck. "It's been a while," she says.

I haven't seen Dr. Hatfield in more than a year now. I decided that since my problem was more genetic than mental, and since Pete was helping me get control over my time skipping with his movie therapy, I didn't have to see Dr. Hatfield anymore. Obviously, Mom doesn't agree.

"My, you've grown," she says.

"I don't want to talk."

"I brought you something."

I turn a fraction more so I can see what she has. The winged, pink unicorn from her office. "What did you used to call her?" she asks. "Princess something or other?"

"Pinkie Pie," I say. "Princess Pinkie Pie."

"Right." She holds it out toward me. "I always thought it such a clever name." When I don't take it from her, she stands it on my hip.

"It's a *My Little Pony*," I say.

"Hmm?" she says distractedly. I catch her taking in my Wall of Devotion, eyeing the pictures of Taylor, Demi, Leondre, Jordi, and my other British boys.

"The name. It's after a *My Little Pony*."

"So, you didn't make it up?"

I guffaw. "No." I take hold of the tattered unicorn. Her hair is matted in places from years of kids' sticky fingering. Her colour's faded, too. Random sparkly threads hang from her horn, making it look hairy. Clutching Pinkie Pie, I push myself into a sitting position.

"Mom's worried, you know."

"I know," I say, combing Pinkie Pie's mane with my fingers.

"You can't not go to school, Alice."

"I can't *go* to school either."

"Why?"

"You heard about the latest incident?"

"I did."

"What if that happens again the next time I have stress?"

"Alice." Dr. Hatfield clutches my ankle through the comforter and squeezes.

"High school's very stressful, you know, all of the tough guys causing problems for the teacher—"

"But they don't cause problems for you, do they?"

"Doesn't matter. It's stressful to watch.

"The cafeteria's like the 'Hot Lunch' scene from *Fame* and I hate taking tests. I could get so worked up during a test that I just...wink out, and then I fail the test because when the teacher comes to collect it, all he finds is a blank test paper, and an empty seat where Alice used to be."

Dr. Hatfield chews at the inside of her cheek and begins to shake her head. Her hair is tied back in a ponytail and it sways with the movement. She sighs and says, "What's really bothering you, Alice?"

Hasn't she been listening? "I told you: I don't want people to see me as a freak."

"So, you're afraid people will find out about your ability—"

I snort. "More like defect."

"Defect? Is that really what you think?"

I don't answer her. I try to work out a knot in Pinkie Pie's mane instead.

"Alice," she puts a hand on my knee and leans in a bit closer. "You're perfect just the way you are."

"Easy for you to say. You don't flicker out of existence the second the going gets rough."

Dr. Hatfield sighs. "No, I guess I don't." She shimmies up the bed toward my head. "You know," she says, brightening, "they say God never gives us more than we can handle."

What's God got to do with it? What's God got to do with anything, least of all this psychology bullshit? "If there were a God, I can't for the life of me figure out why he chose to saddle *me* with this...this—"

"Defect."

The fact she agrees with me shocks me for a moment. Dr. Hatfield looks at me, worried, like she's not sure if she's said the right thing, or if I'll choose that precise moment to pull the knife from under my pillow and end it all, or turn it on her before I end it all. Thin lines draw on her forehead and between her nose and lips. And then I laugh and she joins in.

By the time we're done, both of us have tears in our eyes. Hers from laughing, mine from frustration. She play-slaps me on my leg and says, "You're a strong girl. I know you'll get through this." She squeezes my thigh. "Somehow," she says, forcing a grin.

36

Alice is 15

After much convincing, Dr. Hatfield's visit notwithstanding, Mom agrees—reluctantly so—that I'd be better off homeschooled. Actually, I more dig my feet in and refuse to go back than convince. My argument begins with a treatise on how I narrowly escaped complete and utter mortification when I disappeared due to stress at the thought of being flattened by the SUV, and that Pete wouldn't always be around to use his body as a human shield to mask my defect. From there, I segue into a rant on the many stresses modern students meet, and how school today isn't like school was in the stone ages, when Mom and Dad were kids (I think that argument is more in favour of pissing Mom off than swaying her to my POV, but you can't unsay something once it's been said).

My "School Is Stressful" line of reasoning begins with the fact that I'm likely to meet stress each and every day in the impossible tasks my teachers assign—especially in Math—and it's possible my time-bubble will burst at the least provocation, seeing as I haven't yet learned to control it. My next claim is in defense of Pete, that it isn't fair to ask him to run interference and cover for my disappearance whenever my PTSD feels it necessary to rear its ugly head. Case in point, the SUV incident. My last argument is similar to the first—what if I were writing a test and got stressed and vanished?

Mom counters this by arguing that my IEP, the Individual Education Plan outlining accommodations for my education in light of the mental delicacy I suffer as a result of The Incident, allows me to write in a separate room with teacher support, and extra time if needed.

I respond that if something happens, it will open a whole other can of worms, even if I disappear when isolated. *Especially* if I disappear when isolated. Queue the complete and utter mortification proof. Granted it'll only be amongst the teachers, but the result is complete and utter mortification, nevertheless.

In the end, Mom agrees to homeschooling via virtual school, which means I'd take my courses at home and online. While the issue of dematerialization due to stress is not alleviated owed to the in-school, face-to-face final exams, I'm still satisfied with the compromise.

I sign up for English, Math, Careers and Civics, and History, and do just enough to keep the teachers happy and Mom and Dad off my back. My ulterior motive in this plan is to have time to myself to study my problem (Dr. Rickman is still on the case with geneticists, in search of some designer drug with minimal side effects, but the wheels of progress in the field of genetics are so slow, they seem to have ground to a halt where I'm concerned).

Mostly what I do is look stuff up online. Searching up *Time Travel and Genetics* gets me over four million hits, and I'm determined to check out each and every one. After a few days, though, it becomes clear that the general consensus in cyberspace is that I am a one of a kind anomaly, if not an impossibility. Most people agree that, even if one *could* develop my "superpower", the reason for it wouldn't—couldn't—be found in one's genes. The TVtropes website writes me off as a convention writers use. The site says, and I quote, "genes are only responsible for protein synthesis" and that, at best, my genes could only be producing "Phlebotinum [which] acts on quantum forces not yet discovered", whatever that means.

Over to dictionary.com to figure it out. No entry for phlebotinum. The closest entry is phlebotomy which is the study of veins. So my genes may be coded to create a network of small veins that have some sort of quantum effect on my blood?

Whatever.

I print out the TVtropes gobbledegook anyway and stick it in a purple folder I find stashed in a drawer in Mom's desk.

Pete comes by nearly every day after school for a study date. Most of the time we really do study. Sometimes Tina tags along, but those sessions are *tres* uncomfortable. Totally my fault, given what I know about their futures, but uncomfortable, nevertheless.

On weekends, sci-fi geek Pete brings me movies to watch. My favourites are *The Time Traveler's Wife*, in which a man has a genetic abnormality called "chrono-displacement" that allows him to travel through time; *The Butterfly Effect*, in which a man's consciousness is able to travel back in time to inhabit his younger body; and *Jumpers*, in which a boy learns he can teleport, though not through time. We watch all five seasons of *Heroes* (including *Heroes Reborn*)—in which original character, Hiro, and new character, Nathan, can control time and space—over a single weekend; and all of *Journeyman*—in which a man learns he can jump randomly through time—in a single day, but none of it helps me understand why this is happening to me.

More importantly, none of it suggests how I might control it or stop it entirely.

Dr. Rickman and her team are at a loss. She contacts Mom one day to ask permission to publish an article about me in a scientific journal with the hope of seeking out other doctors worldwide, in case I'm not just one in 7.108 billion. We agree when Dr. Rickman swears she'll refer to me only as Patient X, rather than Alice Carroll, Genetic Freak.

Mom tells me to stop being melodramatic.

One day, Mom knocks quietly on my door when I'm "studying"—no triple-knock Sheldon bullshit this time—which means something's wrong. I click Chrome's PanicButton icon, a handy app that minimizes all my tabs so Mom can't see what I'm really working on. Mom has a folded newspaper under her arm. Both Mom and Dad are techno-mavens, so this is the first time I've ever seen her with an actual flesh-and-blood newspaper in, like, ever.

Mom sits slowly on the bed, smoothes the comforter beside her, and pats the spot.

"Now's not the time for a heart-to-heart, Mom. Studying," I tell her without turning around. I pretend to be interested in an article detailing the difference between the Liberal, Progressive Conservative, and New Democrat parties under the guise of studying for Civics.

"That's not what this is."

"I'm on a deadline."

"Alice!" she says. I swivel my desk chair to look at her. Her face is all business, all frowny and knitted eyebrows. "Please don't fight me on this." I can tell she's seriously perturbed, so I drag myself over with exaggerated effort and drop my butt heavily on the bed.

"What?" I say, meaning every drop of attitude I hope she reads into it.

Mom hands me the paper, today's issue of the *Toronto Star*. I unfold it to find a picture of a man in handcuffs being lead away by two policemen. "So?" I say.

Unless this guy's a geneticist and my last, best hope, I couldn't care less.

"That's him. Charles Dodgson. The guy responsible for your...your thing."

"My *thing*?" I say, sort of mockingly.

"Your PTSD."

I look at the guy in the paper, head down, bangs from his Justin Beiber-do blindfolding the cut of his brow, and the shape and colour of his eyes. For years I've heard the tap-tap click of his heels, the swish of his pants legs, the wheeze of his breath, and saw that face in my dreams—or so I thought. I'd recognize that face anywhere, I used to tell myself, but now I'm not so sure. "*That's him?*"

Mom nods.

"The gunman?"

She nods again.

"How do they know?"

"He confessed."

"About me?" Of course not. I'm probably one of his many nameless, faceless victims, as surely as up until a single moment ago, he was one of those nameless, sort of faceless perpetrators I read about and watch on the news. "About the shooting?"

"About another shooting. One he was planning."

"Why? I mean, after all these years?"

Mom shrugs. "I just wanted you to know," she says. She leaves the paper behind and shuts the door when she leaves my room.

I Am Alice

37

Alice is 15

I clip the article Mom gives me and put it in the purple folder with the other stuff I've been collecting on my glitch, but I get an idea after watching one of those *CSI*-type shows on TV. I need a board, but it has to be a secret one. One that's hidden, like Tommy Lee Jones's weapons room in *Men in Black*. Then it dawns on me: my closet. If I push the clothes out of the way, the back wall of my closet would make a super-incognito case wall.

I begin by pasting the picture of the perp (I learned that on one of those *CSI*-type shows, too) in the rough centre of the wall using green masking tape so I won't remove paint and Dad won't have a cow when I take it down. I arrange the other clippings, mind map style, connecting the clusters of paper with yarn I teef from Mom's knitting bag. When I'm done, I pull my clothes to the centre of the closet so it covers my work, drape-like.

Citypulse News reports Charles Dodgson, 28, was arraigned in a downtown courtroom after police learned of his plan to plant a homemade bomb near the Registrar's Office at a local college. Says the reporter, "Dodgson is no stranger to trouble. He was arrested six years ago after calling in a bomb threat to a local high school.

"Dodgson is also under investigation for a shooting taking place at his elementary school when he was 18.

"A source close to Dodgson told a CP24 reporter that Dodgson was disappointed in a school system which he believed had failed him as a youth." Here the video of the reporter's talking head is replaced by a picture of Dodgson, looking every bit like a mug shot. "Repeatedly suspended from school, Dodgson was eventually expelled when he was arrested for dealing drugs on campus.

"Dodgson's vendetta with the college began after his applications to attend the college were rejected on several occasions."

I find the copy for the news report online, print it out, and add it to my case wall.

38

Alice is 15

Pete comes over for our regular study date. English. It's not his strong suit. He's much better at Math. As fate would have it, Math's not *my* strong suit. We count that among the reasons why we're perfect for each other.

Pete's got *Hamlet* stuff to do. "Why doesn't Hamlet kill Claudius when he has the chance?" he asks. "I mean, isn't it best to get him when his guard's down?"

"He's confessing."

"So? He may not get another chance."

"If he kills him after he's confessed, Claudius will go to heaven. Hamlet wants him to suffer in the afterlife as much as his father's suffering."

"How does he know his father's suffering?"

I roll my eyes. "What do you do when your teacher's teaching, Pete?" I sigh. "The fact that he sees his father's ghost means his soul isn't at rest. In other words, he's suffering."

Pete nods an exaggerated nod and pretends to read the scene again. A few minutes later he says, "'Help, angels! Make assay! Bow, stubborn knees; and, heart with strings of steel, be soft as sinews of the newborn babe! All may be well.'"

"That's not random," I say.

"Shut up, Al. I'm trying to say something."

I close my laptop and place it on the floor beside me. Pete looks grave. His eyebrows knit together and his lips are pressed into a thin line. "I'm all ears," I tell him.

"I have a confession to make."

"Uh-oh."

"I'm serious, Al." I can see that. He looks about to shit his pants.

Then it hits me. He has a confession to make, a *serious* confession. This is it—he's going to come clean about Tina.

It can't be that, not Tina. Future Pete said Tina's away at university. But if not that, then what?

Pete continues to look at me with that gargoyle face he's making, and I'm convinced that he's decided having a girlfriend that could pop up at literally anytime is too much for him. Tina or no Tina, he's going to break up with me. My eyes start to burn. I reach out, pull Pinkie Pie from under my bed, and squeeze.

"I hate school," he says. "It's not the same without you."

The dryness in my throat and constriction around my heart begins to let up a bit.

"I can't wait for the dismissal bell so I can come over and be with you."

"You're a colossal ass-hat, you know?" I throw Pinkie Pie at him. She plants her butt in his face.

"*I'm* a colossal ass-hat?" he says with a smile. "Me?" He throws Pinkie Pie back at me, hard.

"Goof."

"I confess my feelings to you and you call me a name and *I'm* the ass-hat?"

"If the hat fits..." I say, throwing Pinkie Pie back at him.

He catches her, tosses her aside, lunges at me, and I fall backward. Pete's in a half-plank stance over me, knees between my legs, his weight supported by his forearms.

He looks at me with those smoldering chocolate pools and then plants one on me.

Dry, relaxed lips, just the right amount of pressure, no tongue.

He breaks the lip-lock and I get a case of conscience.

If Pete can share his secret with me, then I can share mine with him.

My case wall obsession.

If anyone would understand my need for such a thing, it would be Pete.

He leans in for another kiss, and I let him, responding in kind, my hands reaching up, fingers entwined as best as they can in his short hair. This time he finishes by touching his tongue to my lower lip before pulling away, and I shiver.

Forget the confession; I want another kiss.

His face hovers above mine. He smiles, and then rolls over and lies beside me.

I lie still for a moment debating my options: go in for another kiss, or show him my case wall?

Pete's pretty. He's fun. We have a lot in common. His feelings for me are out in the open, floating above our heads like a thought-bubble filled with rainbows and unicorns, while my case wall remains secreted away in my closet, a monster hiding, snarling, waiting for the best moment to pounce. The best remedy for a child fearing the monster in her closet is to open the closet door to reveal there's nothing there but childish fancy.

What's the best way to remove a bandage?

"Pete?" I say.

"Yeah?"

"I have a confession, too."

"Yeah?"

"Yeah." I get up and go to my closet, open the door and part the clothes on their hangers in the middle, sliding them off to the sides.

"You got a batcave entrance in there, Al?" Pete asks as he stands. I don't answer him.

When he's standing behind me so he can see what I've done, he says, "Whoa," in a sort of whispery voice. He steps around me and stands practically inside the shallow closet. "Sick," he says in the same whisper.

"I am, aren't I?"

"Not you, Al, this wall. In a good way"

"Oh."

"Walk me through it."

"Yeah?" I don't know why, but my eyes are burning. I blink, and a tear streams down my cheek.

"Yeah," Pete says.

I explain everything: all of the images, all of the yarned connections, all of the notes.

In the rough centre of the mind map is a picture of me as a child in grade three.

Above my picture are three photos: Miss Dinah, Michael Barrie, and Mr. Lewis—the three killed in the shooting.

Below my picture is the news article Mom gave me, the image of Charles Dodgson, detailed in black and white pixels on newsprint. Under that, a class photo, Dodgson's face circled.

"Where'd you get that from?" Pete asks.

"The elementary school posts graduating class photos online."

"So this guy, Dodgson—"

"He did it."

"How'd you know?"

"Confessed." The stress of sharing is taking its toll. There's a faint hum in my right ear. I sit in my chair and practice breathing long breaths in through the nose and out through my mouth.

Pete's finger traces a line drawn in puke green yarn (the colour of one of my mother's failed attempts at knitting an infinity scarf) from my picture to a rather poor drawing of Bill. Pete looks at me and I explain.

From each of the three victims' photos is another line of chartreuse yarn, ending at an obituary. Another length of yarn trails from my picture to an article covering VD—Voldemort Day.

"This is...weird, Al."

The hum intensifies to an all out drone. "I knew you wouldn't understand."

"Hey," he says, turning to face me. "Chillax. I said it was weird, not that I didn't understand." He kneels in front of my chair. By this time I'm all out bawling. He rests his head on my lap and hugs my legs under my knees and the drone quiets to a purr.

"I get it," he says. "If my body reacted the same way yours did, I don't know how I'd handle it. Hell, I don't know *if* I could handle it." He looks up at me with these watery doe-eyes. "If this is what keeps you grounded, then I'm all for it."

He lets go of me and stands back in the closet archway. "Do your parents know?"

"God, no!"

Pete's head bobs in a nod.

"And I want to keep it that way, so no double agent shit on your part, okay?"

Pete turns to face me, hand on his heart. "I would *never* betray your confidence, Al."

He looks at me once more, doe-eyes aglow and I know I can trust him.

39

Alice is 15

Pete texts: *Flash party 4 Tinas bday @ house tonight*
Which house? I text back.
Hers
Thats nice
Get U @ 8
It's Tina's fifteenth. One year away from sweet sixteen. *Not going*
U R!
I love Tina, in spite of what the future holds for her and Pete, but I am not going to a party at her place, or anywhere else.
NO!
My phone starts to buzz, two short ones followed by a long one. Pete's picture, the one we took at the mall of him wearing funky glasses with a lime green moustache hanging from them, displays on the screen, the words "Peter Flay" above the slider.
I decline the call with a message: *Not available.*
Answer the phone Al! he texts.

Not available, I type as my parents' landline begins to ring. A moment later, Dad calls up to me to get the phone.

I pretend I don't hear him. Just when I think it works, that maybe he'll figure I'm asleep, or I've ducked out the back window and down the trellis, or something, I hear the tread of his foot on the stairs, and then he knocks as he calls my name. "What?" I say, icy as I can.

"Pete's on the phone."

"Not available," I say, sing-songy.

"I'm coming in." The doorknob rattles with the weight of his hand, but I throw myself against the door, and slide my butt to the floor to act as a doorstop. The door bucks from Dad's weight but remains shut.

"Leave me alone," I tell him. He walks away muttering conciliations to Pete.

Pete texts, *Not cool,* a few minutes later.

The doorbell rings just after eight. I hear Dad at the door talking with a male and a female voice. Just when I'm ready to write the voices off as the latest round of Latter Day Saints, Jehovah's Witnesses, or Lubavitchers (we get them all in this area) come looking for donations, Mom calls, "Tell them to come in," from the kitchen.

Before long there are too many rings to count, and I hear footsteps on the stairs, and then in the hall outside my room, and then the door flings open, and Pete and Tina barge in. "Flash party at *your* house!" Pete says.

"You wouldn't come to the party so the party came to you," Tina says.

I'm in bed when they come for me, snuggled under the comforter, wearing a rainbow striped onesie, with a goofy monster face on the hood, and mismatched fuzzy socks. "Go away," I tell them.

A moment later I hear Pete calling, "We're going to need help," and a herd of elephants tramps up the stairs.

Before I know it, someone's got me around each of my ankles, Pete's at my head, arms hooked under my armpits, and they're lifting me from my bed and carrying me down the stairs. At the top of the stairway, I hear the base of Macklemore and Lewis's "Thrift Shop" and Mom's voice over it saying, "Watch the stairs," and then, "They're going to drop her, John," to my dad, and then I'm being hooked around the banister and toward the basement staircase.

"Be careful," Mom says, and then I'm near-body-surfing down the stairs and into the basement.

The boys dump me in this big, blue easy-slash-rocking chair that threatens to topple over when I land. No sooner am I free from their grip than I stand and scope out my exit strategy. Before I can take even a single step, Pete's standing in front of me handing me a plastic cup of cola. Remembering his earlier text, I say, "*This* is not cool, Pete."

"What? Throwing a birthday party for your best friend?"

"I'm not dressed."

"Who cares." He throws an arm around my shoulders and swivels my chair around so I can take in the room at a glance. "Everyone's having a great time. Your mom's ordered pizza, there's munchies, Tina's mom threw in the cake.

"You've been holed up in your room for so long." He twists me so I'm facing him, grabs both my shoulders and gently shakes me. "You need to relax, Al."

Tina flits by us. "OMG, Al! *Great* party!" she shouts into my ear as she passes.

Pete pulls me to the sofa and down onto his lap. He hugs me tightly. I want to cry, I've missed him so much, but my body won't relax into his, no matter how I try. One thought plays over and over in my brain, demanding to be heeded, refusing to shut up: Did you remember to close your closet door?

40

Alice is 15

"Royals" by Lorde is on the stereo, and Pete drags me up to dance. The party's still in full swing. We've gone through at least a dozen bags of chips, the same number of pizzas, and at least two cases of pop.

"Let me be your rumour," Pete sings in my ear. His breath, hot and moist, sends a shiver down my spine. No mean feat, considering my attire.

"You cold?" he asks, and he holds me tighter, as if he could transfer his body heat to mine.

When I don't answer, he stops our slow and clockwise twirl and cranes his neck so he can look me in the eye. "You okay, Al?"

I consider this question for a moment: *Am* I okay?

I'm in the arms of a boy who still sets my body a-tingle, even after all these years: okay.

I'm standing in the middle of my basement rec-room, surrounded by pretty much everyone in the tenth grade, frightened to death I might lose my shit and vaporize at any given moment: not okay.

I'm standing in the middle of my basement rec-room, surrounded by pretty much everyone in the tenth grade, a fairly large human shield to mask the fact that if I lose my shit and vaporize at any given moment, no one will probably notice: okay.

Reluctantly, I nod. "I'm fine."

Pete smiles a crooked smile, the right side of his mouth reaching a touch higher than the left. As if trying to reach the high side, his right eye squints into a near wink at the same time. My heart warms at the look of him, my face flushes, and I feel as if I'll either swoon or dematerialize when he takes my face into his hands and kisses me, hard, on the lips. My lips respond as if they have a mind of their own, and move in time to Pete's. His tongue glances my front teeth sending goose pimples to my flesh.

It's my first real kiss—my first real *tongue* kiss. It's sort of wet, and gross, and kind of nice, but it ends all too quickly when the door to the crawl space under the stairs flings open, and Tina rushes out. Dashiel follows her out, calling, "C'mon Tina, don't be like that." I want him to follow her up the stairs and make it better, but he stops short, turning at the foot of the stairs to address the crowd.

"Let me be your loser. You can call me James Dean, and baby, I'll screw..." he croons in time to the music as he walks over to the nearest female wallflower and pulls her from her safety to dance.

"Pete?" I say.

"Yeah, yeah," Pete answers, "go to her." He frowns at Dash. "Bastard," he says.

Dashiel—Dash—is a known philanderer, a different girl every week. Tina thought he was fun, and said she'd like to get with him one day. Well...happy birthday! "Who invited him anyway?"

Pete kisses me on the forehead and nudges me toward the stairs.

***

The last thing I want to do is commiserate when I have my own problems to deal with. But it *is* my party and—role of future boyfriend stealer aside—Tina *is* still my best friend.

I find her outside, sitting on the roadside curb in front of my house. If I listen hard enough, I can follow Lorde's bass as "Royals" ends. "Hey," I say, occupying the space next to her on the cold concrete.

Tina's sniffle turns into a snort. "Sorry," she says.

"NP", I tell her, text-speak for "no problem". The music bass changes. I think someone's put on "Gangnam Style". I wish I were inside watching Pete dance. He does an imitation of Psy that's just roll on the floor laughing (or ROTFL). I can only imagine all of the boys lined up can-can style, bucking their legs and flicking crossed wrists *à la* Psy in the video. What's one degree more than ROTFL?

I collect myself and say, "What happened?"

Tina sniffles as she speaks, her voice catching on the occasional hiccup. "I'm worthless," she says. She sighs, her breath pungent and bitter—has she been drinking?

"You're not," I tell her.

"Ach." She leans forward resting her head on her palm. "I can't believe I was so stupid."

"You're not stupid," I tell her. "You're smart. *And* you're pretty." It's a dumb inside joke, one we usually write in response to a lame post online.

"Not funny," she says.

We sit side-by-side on the curb, my arm over her shoulder for a moment or two. "Look, are you going to tell me what happened or not?" Not exactly pathos at its best, but I have a whole houseful of people I've left in Pete's care, which isn't fair to him.

"Dash's an ass."

"Tell me something I don't know."

Tina's shoulders hitch. She begins to sob something fierce. She stops long enough to gulp some air and snort. "I'm still a virgin," she blurts, in the tone you might expect someone to blurt she has cancer.

"What?" I say, but not because I didn't hear her. I just can't believe that Tina Bell—*my* Tina Bell—could still be—

"I said I'm a virgin, okay?"

"A virgin?"

She nods her head.

"As in never—"

"Ever!"

I can't help but laugh at her admission.

"Why are you laughing?" she asks.

"It's just that...I imagined the worst, that Dash...and all that happened was...what?"

"He turned me down!"

"Dash did?"

She nods and begins a fresh volley of sobs.

"But Dash's a—"

"Man-slut? I know." She stretches out the O in "know" to a wail.

"He bruised your ego?"

"He'll ruin my reputation."

"I don't understand."

"Ever since Rowland Knight in sixth grade, people have thought I was...you know—"

"A lady-slut?"

"Gee, thanks!" She feins being miffed, but sort of half-smiles when she does.

"So you didn't do anything with Rowland?"

She shakes her head.

"But you told everyone you did."

"*Rowland* told everyone I did. It made me popular. Boys wanted to date me and girls wanted to hang with me, so I went along."

Something in her story doesn't add up. "So why decide to make your first time with a sleazeball like Dash?"

"I don't know. I went under the stairs to fool around, and I knew he wanted to...you know. I could even *feel* he wanted to, and I told him I wanted to be with him, and he turned me down." She sighs and then says, "Al?"

I answer, "Yeah?"

"I think I'm drunk." As if to confirm this confession, Tina gags and spews a mixture of clear liquid and something bright orange like Cheezies between her legs.

"Where the hell'd you get the booze from?" My parents don't usually drink, but I think there are bottles of some sort of fruit flavoured concoction in the fridge upstairs. Please don't be my parents' stash, I pray, awaiting her answer.

Tina reaches for her purse, still slung over her shoulder. She opens it, and it's jam-packed with miniature bottles of alcohol. "My dad collects them," she offers.

"Won't you be in trouble when he notices them missing?"

Tina shrugs. "I only took duplicates." It seems to me that, if it were a true collection, he'd be aware of the exact number of duplicates he had of each and every bottle, but given her state, Tina probably wouldn't see the logic in it if I told her so.

I become aware of the change in music bass once more and Tina says, "Oh!"

"What?"

"I love this song." And just like that, her tone takes a total one-eighty. She gets to her feet, doffs her purse on the grass at the side of the road, kicks off her heels, and says, "Come dance with me," like it's a request, but before I can respond she grabs my wrist, pulls me up, links arms and drags me to the middle of the front lawn where at last I recognize the music—The Temptations: "My Girl".

She sings, loud and out of tune, sweeping her arms above her head, pointing to the sky for the words "sunshine" and "cloudy", stretching both of the words out.

"We should go inside," I tell her, worried that someone might call the police, for (a) the music, and (b) her caterwauling, not to mention getting my parents into trouble for (c) underage drinking.

She pantomimes being cold, giving a mock shiver and wrapping her arms around her body for warmth in time to the lyrics.

Pete comes out of the house, eyes wide, and shaking his head. I try to go to him, but Tina pulls me back.

She points to her eye, holds her palms up to the sky in an I-don't-know gesture, points to me, and points to her mouth.

She's drunk, I mouth to Pete.

She makes the I-don't-know gesture again, points to herself with her thumbs, the other fingers on her hands curled into fists, sings the title in the lyrics and follows with a whoohoohoo-oo.

"Don't just stand there, sing with me, Al. C'mon Pete."

Before I know it, the next verse is over, and we're all standing side-by-side on the lawn, singing "My Girl", and it hits me: this is why Pete has "My Girl" as Tina's ringtone. He uploaded it as a constant dig to the night she got drunk and made a fool out of herself standing on the grass, singing the song.

I sidestep until I'm next to Pete in the chorus line, standing between my best friend who doesn't steal my boyfriend, my best friend in the world who—if you disregard a huge white lie about her virginity—would never, ever lie to me, let alone take Pete away from me, and Pete, the best boyfriend in the world, ever.

We sing one more raucous rendition of the chorus before Dad comes to shoo us back inside.

41

Alice is 15

By the time the party's over, after all the cake and ice cream and coffee we force down Tina's throat, she's sober enough to fool her dad when he comes for her and Pete. I say goodbye to my BFF and my BBFF, lock the door, set the alarm, and make my way upstairs.

It was all a misunderstanding.

Tina's cool.

Pete rocks.

All is okay with the world.

Then I push my bedroom door open, see Mom sitting on my bed, and realize I was wrong. There's a pile of wadded up Kleenex on the bed beside her and another wad in her hand. Her eyes are swollen, her lips are pursed, and I can tell she's been crying. That's when I notice the mound of clothes on the floor in front of my open closet door, and realize Mom went snooping and found my case wall.

"What gives, Mom?"

"Funny," she says. She sniffles. "I was just about to ask you the same thing."

"You have no right—"

"Cut the crap, Al. This is *my* house. I pay the mortgage on it. I can do whatever the hell I please."

"Including invade my privacy up the wazoo?"

"Especially that."

"You suck, you know that?"

"Don't you talk to your mother that way, Alice," Dad chimes in from the doorway. "You've got some explaining to do." I think of Ricky Ricardo in those cheesy old *I Love Lucy* re-runs dad forces me to watch saying, "Lu-cy! You have some 'splainin' to do," and in spite of the gravity of the situation, stifle a giggle.

"I have to do no such thing!"

Mom stands up and says, "Lower your voice, young lady."

"Lower yours first," I yell back. I hate it when she does things like this, when she's wrong and tries to make it seem like it's me. As if to prove the point, she says, "I have every reason to raise my voice. You're the one in the wrong here, Alice, not me."

"You're pissing me off," I say.

"You have no reason to be pissed off. I thought we'd put this situation to rest. I thought giving you the Dodgson article would have put an end to this nonsense, but obviously I was wrong."

"Obviously you were."

"You're grounded, young lady," Dad tells me. "You're to take that garbage off your wall and leave this alone, do you hear me?"

He has no right.

I hear the buzzing in my ears like I've just stuck my head inside a beehive.

They have no right.

The room starts to swim.

This is *my* life.

The air grows soupy.

There is a split second in which I catch a glimpse of the three of us reflected in the dark backdrop of my bedroom window.

And then I blink.

42

Alice is 15 and 4

When I open my eyes I'm back in that fatal cloakroom. A little girl stands in the archway dividing the classroom from the cloakroom. She points at me, her mouth a big wide O, banshee scream pouring from it like someone's tarring her within an inch of her life.

Miss Dinah swings around the corner, lays eyes on me, and says, "Oh, dear."

Miss Dinah is beautiful. She's wearing a coral pink sweater, black pencil skirt, and black pumps. Her hair hangs loosely about her face. She has dark pink coral lipstick and small white pearl earrings. She bends down beside the screaming girl, twirls her around, and pulls her into her chest. "Oh, for heaven's sake," Miss Dinah tells me, "can't you find your jollies some other way?" in that matter-of-fact way she had about her, whenever you said something nonsensical. Like, if you told her, "I don't have my homework because the dog ate it, Miss." She'd point her finger at you, and straight as you please, say something like, "Well that's what you get for letting the dog do your homework."

Miss Dinah whispers something in the girl's ear.

"But, Miss Dinah," I say to her. I want to rush to her side and hug her. I want to tell her everything, that she can't be at school on Voldemort Day, that she has to switch classrooms on that day, or better yet, clear the school. But before I can she says, "Don't you dare move from that spot, young lady. I'm not done with you, yet," and I know she wouldn't believe me, even if I tried.

Miss Dinah leads the girl off into the classroom. I stand where I am, rooted to the spot, feeling more and more like an anomaly with each second that passes. Kindergarteners poke their heads around the divider every once in a while to catch a glimpse of me. One little blonde boy peeks in and lingers longer than the others. "I've never seen a ghost before," he says.

"Boo!" I say. He squeals and retreats back into the classroom. The other children echo the noise he makes with giggles and further squeals.

When Miss Dinah returns it's with a man whom I can only surmise is the principal. She whispers a few words to him. He looks at me, eyes drilling into mine. He says nothing, but points at me with his forefinger, turns his hand over, and bends and unbends the same finger in a come here gesture.

"Name?" The principal says to me. It's the first thing he's said to me in...ever.

The date on the desk calendar would put me smack dab into my fourth year of life. Based on the fact there may or may not be another Alice Carroll in attendance at the school, and my parents may or may not be aware of my condition yet, I realize I can't tell him. I shrug my shoulders instead.

"Stalking pre-schoolers is a serious offense, young lady. Your parents must be called."

I start to tell him that I wasn't stalking them but stop after the first few words. Even if I could get the words out, he wouldn't believe me anyway. I shrug again.

He sighs grandly. "I'm afraid you leave me no choice but to notify the police."

I feel my eyes grow large.

"Unless, of course, you've suddenly remembered your name?"

I didn't know Miss Dinah ever taught kindergarten. Maybe that's because I wasn't in her class. Even so, I spent my entire primary career at that school. You'd think I'd remember Miss Dinah as one of the kindergarten teachers. Maybe I've entered an alternate timeline this time. Maybe the atrocities of that Dodgson guy never happen in this timeline and I have nothing to worry about.

Dodgson.

Charles Dodgson.

The article Mom gave me said he was 18 when he went postal on the grade three class. If this is my kindergarten year, that means Dodgson won't strike for another four years yet. That also means he'd already have graduated grade school. Assuming, of course, this isn't an alternate timeline, because if you believed what you see in the movies, shit like that happened as well. You know, you might go back in time and kill Hitler before he orchestrates the Holocaust, or kill his mother before he's born, and you could return to the exact same timeline and nothing different would have happened because you killed them in a different timeline. All the same, if Dodgson were 14, he might be in grade nine at the high school, which wasn't more than a block away.

If I could just slip the principal's office and make it to the front hallway...

The principal sends me into the main office and tells me to sit by the secretary and wait.

Eventually, the lunch bell rings. A group of girls wanders into the office, blocking me from the secretary's view. When I'm sure no one's looking, I stand up and walk toward the office door, but just as I'm about to grab the handle, the door opens, and a uniformed policeman enters, forcing me back into the office. The principal must've given them a description of what I look like because he says, "Back to your seat, young lady." I'm mortified at having been caught trying to escape and have no choice but to comply.

43

Alice is 15 and 4

The policeman puts me in the back seat of a squad car. A sea of faces peeks out of the classroom window at the front of the school, watching, wondering about me, assuming the worst.

At the station, he leads me into a large office room, desks positioned head to head in neat rows, just like on television and seats me in a collapsible chair beside one of the desks. He sits behind the desk and logs into his computer.

"Name?" he asks.

I press my lips together, shrink into the chair and shake my head.

"Look, kid, do you see this badge?" He points to the badge pinned to his chest. "That means I'm a cop. You were caught trespassing at the elementary school. Depending on how this goes, that could put you in the same category as a pedophile. Your one saving grace is that you're still a minor, but it's only a saving grace if you cooperate." He gives me the kill-eye, looking me up and down before continuing. "You're in a whole heap of trouble here, so why don't you just cut the crap and give me your name." His voice rises in volume with the last statement. He's trying to be intimidating, and it's working.

I want to cooperate. I was raised to think the police were the good guys. If I were ever lost or in trouble, they would be my first line of defence in getting the help I needed. But now that I find myself in this topsy-turvy bizarro world where *I* am the bad guy, I'm not so sure. Even if I wanted to tell him my name—and I so desperately want to so he can call my parents, and they can come and get me, and this nightmare will be over—I don't. Something inside tells me that if I give in, I'll find the nightmare has only just begun.

"Look, are you going to tell me your name or not?"

I bite my lower lip and shake my head some more.

"Hey, Griffin," the officer calls. He's acknowledged by a female officer.

"Maybe you can get somewhere with her." He stands, holds his chair steady so the woman can sit, says, "Tag! You're it," and walks away.

The female officer, Griffin, is young, maybe Miss Dinah's age. She has no make-up on; her skin is naturally flawless. Her auburn hair is tied back in a bun at the nape of her neck. "Skipping off at your own school to trespass at the elementary school," she says.

I look at my hands clasped tightly together in my lap.

"This your first offence, sweetie?"

I nod.

"Why scare the kids like that?"

My first impulse is to defend myself, to tell her that I didn't mean to scare the kids, that I'm just as traumatised as that little girl in pig-tails, that I almost opened my mouth and screamed right along with her when I realized my predicament.

I thought of the series Pete showed me, *Minority Report*, the one based on the movie, where kids who can see the future—called Precogs—see a crime being committed, and the police arrest the offender before he actually offends. Do they have the right to exact punishment on a person who has yet to commit a crime, before he actually commits it? If I tell Officer Griffin I'm on a mission from the future to prevent a school shooting, she'll probably lock me up and throw away the key.

Not that it would matter; eventually I'd go *poof* and find myself back in my own time, anyway.

"I said," she repeats, "why scare innocent little kids like that?"

I shrug.

Griffin sighs. "I don't know what's gotten into you kids these days.

"You're allowed one phone call, at any rate. Maybe you can call someone who can talk some sense into you." She slides the desk phone over to me, hands me the receiver, dials nine, and leaves me alone at the desk.

There's only one person I can think of to call.

The police officers try everything to make me talk, plying me with cans of pop, stale sandwiches, and candy bars. I accept a ginger ale—it's the only thing I dare eat, lest I sick it up on the other end of my journey.

About forty or so minutes later, the first officer comes back and says, "Kiddo." He nods toward the front desk where a large man wearing a dark suit and fedora is showing ID.

Griffin escorts the man to where I'm sitting and pulls up another folding chair. "Says he's your Uncle Bill." She leaves us alone.

"So, Mabel? We meet again, huh?" the man says. If it weren't for the voice, I'd never recognize him. Barry Ballerina a.k.a. William Tibbar, a.k.a. Bill a.k.a. Uncle Bill.

Bill's got what my mom calls a five o'clock shadow on his cheeks and chin. His eyes look like thin slits in his round face without the blue eye make-up. He takes his hat off, and he's mostly bald, dark hair flecked with gray, in a fringe that runs over one ear, behind his head, and back up on the other side.

"What've you gotten yourself into this time, silly goose?" he says, and I start to bawl. I can't help myself (and believe me, I try). My eyes start to burn. Then they water. Then, before I know it, the waterworks are on full throttle. No matter what I do, I can't stop.

"It's okay, my dear," he says. He takes my hand. "I'll rescue you from this situation on the condition you share your story with me.

"Deal?" He plasters a thin smile on his lips. I look up at him, and he nods. "Do we have a deal?"

I nod profusely.

Bill calls Officer Griffin over to us. "My sister and brother-in-law are out of town, and my niece is staying with me. Is she being charged, might I ask?"

"Since this is a first offence, we're willing to let her go on her own recognisance, provided you have a talk with your sister about her behaviour."

"Yes, yes, of course," Bill says standing. He takes his hat in one hand and holds the other out to me.

"Tampering with children is not something you want to be charged with, little girl. Being forever branded a sex offender is not a prudent choice."

"Yes, Officer," Bill says, dismissively. "Thank you, Officer." He pulls me out of the station.

When we're through the front door he looks at me and asks, "Whatever did you do?" with a smile.

44

Alice is 15 and 4

I tell Bill everything in the car. When I'm done, he says, "*Alice Through the Looking Glass.*"

"Huh?"

"Have you never read it?"

I shake my head.

"What *do* they teach you in those schools of yours these days?" He looks at me and I shrug. Bill's attention returns to the road ahead. He says, "Alice went through a mirror in her parlour and wound up in a topsy-turvy world where nothing made any sense, and nothing was as it seemed. That's you."

"Does that mean you believe me?"

"And what if I don't?" He glances at me again. I shrug once more.

"Does it really matter?" he asks. He drives another block or so before saying, "If you believe it, it's good enough for me."

I smile, though I don't think he sees it. "Thank you," I tell him.

"You have a plan?"

I shake my head.

"You have to have a plan, my dear." He turns into my high school lot, finds a spot, and parks his car.

I tell him, "Thank-you," and reach for the latch, but he grabs my shoulder. I turn toward him thinking he's going to wish me luck or something. Instead, he says, "You need a plan. Let's hatch one now."

Hatching a plan sounds much more nefarious than I feel. I have no clue what I want to do. Go into the school? Find Dodgson? Then what? Kill him? I *could* get away with it. Chances are the stress of killing another human being would send me back to my own time. By the time I'm old enough to be recognized as the killer, the police might have forgotten about it. Even if they arrest me and it goes to trial, they'd be made laughing stalks trying to explain how someone who was four years old and napping in her kindergarten class at the time of the murder could possibly be held responsible.

I shrug at Bill.

"You really should take care of that twitch, my dear."

"Huh?"

"Your shoulders. They keep twitching."

I shrug again.

"There they go again." He reaches into the pocket of his jacket and offers me a sugar-coated jelly candy. I shake my head. This time *he* shrugs, rips open the wrapper, and pops it into his mouth. He chews a few times, and says, "Which class is he in?"

"I don't know."

"How do you plan to find him, then?"

"I don't know."

He uses his tongue to work the candy from his molars. "Let's say it's lunch. You go into the cafeteria and recognize him from his newspaper picture. What do you say to him?"

"I don't know...don't do it?"

"Don't do what?"

"I don't know...don't kill my teacher? Don't shoot up my grade three class?"

"Say he hasn't formed his grudge yet and he has no idea what you're talking about. He just looks at you dumbfounded. Then what?"

I imagine sitting on the witness stand and Bill is the lawyer questioning me. Though I've never read *Through the Looking Glass*, I have seen *Alice in Wonderland* movies. Lots of them. I imagine the Red Queen entering the courtroom shouting for the executioner, followed by an exclamation of "Off with her head!" and start to cry.

"Mabel?" Bill says. He reaches over and squeezes my shoulder. "That's no way to carry on, duckie."

The buzzing begins in my ears and I know I'm not long for this timeline.

Bill reaches over, pats my shoulder, and says, "There, there," and I imagine Sheldon reaching over, patting one of the other characters' shoulders awkwardly, forcing a grin looking every bit like the Joker but for the crazy skin colouring.

"I'm going to go soon, Bill," I tell him.

"What? Why?"

"I just am. I can feel it." My head begins to swirl like I've just come off an aggressive Tilt-A-Whirl ride. "Carry on with my mission." I hear a pop and I'm back in my room. My mother is asleep in my bed. I retreat to the bathroom as quietly as I can to get cleaned up; Mom doesn't so much as stir.

45

Alice is 15

The shadows in the room disappear in the light of day. So, apparently, has my case wall. I rush downstairs and peek in the kitchen garbage can, reaching in with my bare hands to tumble shit from last night's party around, but come up empty. I open the front door, aiming to check the recycling bins outside, but forget to turn off the alarm in my haste. It goes off with an array of deafening whoops.

"Christ, Alice, is that you?" Dad says from the couch in the front room. "Are you just getting in now?" He gets up slowly, bones creaking audibly, and punches the alarm sequence into the panel. Just then the telephone rings. I hear Mom talk to the alarm company on one of the upstairs extensions.

"Last night. I slept on the floor in my room."

"John? Is that Alice?" Mom calls from upstairs, still sounding groggy.

"She's safe," Dad hollers back.

Mom comes tromping down the stairs.

"Where were you?" she says. She pulls me into a tight hug.

"I don't know...out?" I say into her shoulder.

"*When* were you?" Dad asks.

"I don't know...umm...eleven years ago, I think?"

Mom releases me from her embrace and cups my face in both her hands. "Are you okay?" She kisses me on the forehead.

"I'm fine, Mom."

She looks me in the eyes, "Sure?"

"Yes! *God*, Mom, I'm not a child anymore, you know."

"We are aware," she says, taking a step backward and away from me.

"You dismantled my wall."

Neither of them says anything at first.

"We only have your best interests at heart, Alice, you know that, right?" This from Dad.

"What's in my best interest is to figure out what the hell is happening to me. You can't control what I do forever, you know."

"We do." Dad again. "Know." Then, more defensively, "We're not trying to control you, Alice."

"So, where is it?"

"Where's what?" Mom asks, knowing full well exactly what I mean.

"My wall."

"Gone."

"Gone! That's it? Just...gone."

"Alice," Mom says, sympathetically, but I'll have none of it. She wouldn't freak if I made a scrapbook page about my trips through time. She wouldn't freak if I decided to track my trajectory through time on the wall in my cupboard. Why can't she get it through her thick skull this is no different?

It's like all of those ghosty shows, like *Ghost Whisperer* or *Touched by an Angel*. If I find out what the problem is and fix it, I'll stop whatever it is I'm doing, I truly believe that. But I know neither of *them* does. Rather than try to explain, I just say, "You both suck," and pound each stair on the way back to my room, so hard my shin bones vibrate with each step.

Pete calls on me later in the day. "I thought we could go for a bike ride."

"Not interested," I tell him.

"We could talk," he says. "At the park?"

We sit on a blanket under a tree at the park and watch a toddler being pushed by his mom on the baby swings. The kid holds a *Hot Wheels* car in one chubby fist, and clings to the bar in front of him for dear life with the other, squealing. Those were the days. Before this stupid shit started happening. When I was still a normal kid with my entire life ahead of me.

I tell Pete about William Tibbar. "Have you ever met the guy in this timeline?"

Seen is not the same as *met*, so I shake my head, no.

"Wouldn't that just blow his mind, huh, Al? To have seen you all those years ago and then again, today, looking exactly the same. What a trip!"

"I don't know, Pete. He's a nice guy. I wouldn't want to give him a heart attack or an aneurysm or anything."

"I guess you have a point." Pete leans over and takes a lock of my hair, which he twists between his fingers as he speaks. "I've been doing some research of my own, you know."

"Research, huh?" I feign surprise; my hair falls from Pete's grasp. "Who died and made you Einstein?"

"Cut it out, Al. I love you, you know I do."

I flash a coy, sideways glance at him, and quickly look away.

"I worry about you and this time travel shit. What happens if you wind up somewhere and there's no Future Me or this Tibbar guy anywhere around to help? What if you get stuck in that alternate timeline and can't get back home?"

"That won't happen, Pete."

"How do you know?"

"Every time I go back, someone's there. I think sometime in the future I have that covered."

"So, you don't know, not for sure."

"*You* have a list. It stands to reason there may be other lists as well."

"But you don't know."

"Not for sure, no." I grab Pete's hand and intertwine his fingers in my own. "I'll make you a promise, okay? I promise that when I make your list I'll make others as well."

"Pinky swear?" Pete says. He manoeuvres our fingers so that only our pinkies are wrapped together.

"Pinky swear," I say.

Pete leans over and pecks me on the lips. I lie down on the blanket and use Pete's lap as a pillow. After a moment, Pete says, "Hey, Al?"

"Yeah?"

"Who would you give lists to?"

I shrug, my shoulders, butting up against Pete's thigh. "Well, there's you, and my parents, and I guess Bill—"

"But you said you had to call him."

"So?"

"So, if you gave him a list then wouldn't he have already been there to greet you?"

"I suppose."

"And your parents. You told me the police brought you to them that time when you were a kid. If they had a list, they'd have already been there too, wouldn't they?"

"I guess."

"So either you broke our pinkie pact—"

"Or something happens and I can't give them the list."

"See? This is why I worry."

I sit up so I can speak with him, eye-to-eye and face-to-face. "What could possibly happen?" I ask him and regret it the moment I hear the words ooze from my lips.

A million and two things could happen. Maybe I never travel far enough back in time to give them the list. Maybe I never see them when I travel back in time. Or maybe...

"You're a colossal ass-hat, you know?"

"Why now?" Pete says, actually looking a bit hurt.

"Up until you said that, I never considered..."

Pete pulls me close to him and hugs me tightly. I get a whiff of the acrid spice of his cologne. When he lets go he says, "This is why I was doing my research. I think I know how I can help you."

I push away from him and say, "Help me what?"

"Control your time shit."

46

Alice is 15

Pete's bright idea about controlling my "time shit", as he put it, is connected to research he's been doing about astral projection. His theory goes something like this: astral projection is the process by which a person develops the ability to travel outside of her body. This is usually done in a trance-like state. It's kind of like lucid dreaming, where you're half-awake and half-asleep, and still dreaming, only you can control it. If you can put yourself into that half-awake/half-asleep condition, and imagine you are going someplace, the theory is that your consciousness will actually go there, and leave your body behind.

When I try to explain that my travelling has nothing to do with sleep, trances, or dreaming, Pete says, "But it could, couldn't it? I mean, up until now you've only taken stress junkets to random times. But if you could figure out a way to do your stuff when you're relaxed, you may be able to control it a bit more, like a lucid dream."

I think about this for a minute, and I can't think of anything to refute his argument. "You are a Brainiac!" I say, and we high-five.

"So how do we do this?"

"I don't know," he says, "but stuff online says that lots of people claim to separate from their bodies after taking hallucinogens."

"People have out of body experiences when they die and are brought back to life, but I'm not about to do the whole *Flatliners* thing either."

We're in my bedroom when we have this conversation under the guise of doing homework, but little to nil of that's happened since before Pete arrived.

"All of the sources indicate there's a connection between astral projection and relaxation. What if I could find something harmless, like Gravol, or something, that would do the same thing? Do you have anything like that in the house?"

I shrug. "I don't know." Confident that Mom's in the basement doing laundry, or working on work stuff, I say, "Let's go check."

My mom is the poster child for verbal irony—saying one thing and meaning another (and wouldn't my English teacher be proud?). She preaches clean-eating, spends gobs of money on organic this and preservative-free that, all the while maintaining a veritable drugstore of remedies for whatever ails her on her bedside table. She goes to the gym and eats no processed food, but then swallows pain killers for her back or hip or head, practically every other day. She also talks about taking supplements to help her lose weight, which drives my dad bananas.

Pete and I sneak into my parents' room and catalogue each and every bottle on the table. Pete insists I should take one extra-strength Tylenol or Advil an hour until it threatens to knock me out, but then I find the bottle of melatonin, which claims to be an all-natural way to aid in a good night's sleep. We slip a few from the bottle, rather than taking the whole thing (in case Mom feels the need for a good night's sleep before our experiment's over).

"What do I do?" I ask Pete when we're back in my room.

"Take the red pill, Neo," he says and hands me a bottle of water.

After I swallow I say, "Now, what?"

"How do you feel?"

"It's going to take a while to start working, doofus."

Pete shakes his head as if to erase the previous conversation. "When you start to feel sleepy, fight it. You can close your eyes, but try to stay mentally alert. Think about where you want to go and focus. Imagine a long, dark tunnel, like a worm hole—"

"Like in that corny black and white series where they travel in time through a tunnel—"

"*Time Tunnel.* Just like that. Imagine you see where you want to go at the other end, and force yourself to jump."

"What if I astral project?"

"Astral projection takes time and practice. Seeing as you have neither, it shouldn't be that easy for your consciousness to separate from your body. What you do have experience at is jaunting through time. Your body should tap into a sort of muscle memory, and react accordingly."

"What if it works and I'm too tired to do anything but sleep whenever I wind up?"

"The adrenaline rush you feel from your trip should be enough to negate the melatonin in your system."

"But what if it's not?"

"What if it is?"

"What if I'm able to control it and I sleep through it?"

"*I'll* know it was a success because I'll see you disappear."

"Won't I be vulnerable on the other end?"

"Okay, so think of a date when I'm old enough to meet you and add that date to your list."

"To my one and only list," I say. I sigh. This is torture. I never make another list. My only lifeline to the future is Pete. There is a moment of silence, broken when I say, "Now, what?"

"I don't know, Al. Let's get some homework done."

About a half hour later the melatonin kicks in. "Relax," Pete says, coaching me through it. "Close your eyes. Imagine that time tunnel and some future version of me on the other end."

He's quiet for a long time, and then he says, "Al?"

"Yeah."

"You're still here."

"I know." I stretch "know" into two syllables, like "knoh-oh".

"Whine much?" Pete says, borrowing one of my phrases.

"Jerkwad," I whisper through what feels like a mouth of cotton.

"Stupid face," he replies.

"Really?" I try to open my eyes, but the lids are too heavy. With whatever strength I have left I say, "That's the best you can do?"

"Al?"

"What?"

"Shut-up and go into the light."

If this were any other day and any other time, I might laugh, but even that seems to take way more energy than I have left.

The last thing I remember is rolling over to my side, curling my leg toward my chest, and my hand under my chin.

Into the light...

Down the tunnel...

My clock reads just past midnight when I next open my eyes. I reach for my cell and text, *didnt work dope*, to Pete's number.

The screen is almost too bright to watch as I wait for his reply. *no shit sherlock*, says the first message. This is followed seconds later by *nite Al* and an array of three hearts.

47

Alice is 15

"You know, I've been thinking." Pete and I are in my room for one of our near daily "study" sessions. We're sitting in the corner behind my door. My back's up against the door. Pete's is up against the adjacent wall. Our legs are stretched out and touching so the line from our legs to our bodies and along the walls behind us form a rough square. Pete's been playing "2048" on his cell, and I've been going cross-eyed trying to beat one of those hidden object type games.

I give him my standard "We're in trouble now," that I say whenever he leads with "I've been thinking."

Pete flashes me a sardonic grin. "Ha, ha, very funny."

"Ha, ha," I say mockingly.

"Look, do you want to hear what I have to say or not?"

I beam at him for a moment, reading consternation in his eyes, smile and say, "Of course I do, Pete."

"My English teacher? She gave us a talking to today, all about being proactive and not reactive in our studies—"

"Why'd she do that?"

"We have these guys that sit at the back of the class that are literal dumb-asses." I decide not to tell him that since smartness—or dumbness for that matter—is a comment on one's intelligence and related to brain power and our asses don't house our brains, it's impossible for his classmates to be *literal* dumb-asses. I know what he's getting at—he means not like when he uses it as a term of endearment for me. "They do dick all and blame the teacher for everything. They're always getting in her face, and insisting their marks are her fault, when if they'd just do the stupid work...

"Anyhow, she said we need to take control of our education, anticipate what we might need, and ask for help *before* the due date rather than wait till after the work's been returned, and rely on her to give us a second chance.

"And that got me thinking,"

Here comes trouble, I don't respond. "I'm listening," I say, instead. I close my laptop and put it on the carpet beside me.

"I brought this." He rummages through his backpack and takes out a small velour hinged box, the kind you get when you buy jewellery.

"What's that?"

He opens the box. A rather large gold pocket watch on a thick gold chain is crammed inside.

"Where'd you get that?"

"It's mine. My inheritance from my grandfather. My dad gave it to me last year. One of his cousins' kids got married, and he said it completed my suit. He said his dad would be proud to know he'd passed it on to the next generation." Pete takes it from the box (he lets the box drop, still open, into his lap), presses the fob at the top, and the case pops open. He looks at it fondly for a second or two, and says, "I tried to give it back to him afterward, but he told me to keep it.

"I never knew my dad's dad," he says, pensive.

I wait a few seconds, hoping he'll continue on his own. When he doesn't, I say, "What's it for, Pete?"

"I'm going to hypnotise you."

"What? To make me bark like a dog or cluck like a chicken or something?"

"Tempting, but no. I read up on this. If you're susceptible, I can put you under. Eventually, we can figure out a way for you to hypnotise yourself."

"Why would I need to do that?"

"The lucid dream thing didn't work but that doesn't mean we have to give up on your controlling your time shit altogether.

"We were approaching it wrong. You told me the episodes of time travel occur when you're under stress. If you can control when you think about it, make yourself think about it to travel on purpose, you might be able to stop yourself from thinking about it when you *don't* want to."

"Why on God's green earth would I ever want to think about it on purpose?"

"It's your trigger, Al. Unless you can think of something else that sets you off, it's all we got."

Just the thought of thinking about that day, of *having* to think about that day, sets off my anxiety.

Anxiety is the first thing I feel before my fatal flaw rears its ugly head.

Maybe Pete's actually onto something here.

"Where do we start?"

Pete tells me to sit on my desk chair in the middle of the room. He kneels in front of me, dangling the pocket watch on the chain in front of my face. "Focus on the movement of the watch, like a pendulum. Follow it with your eyes only, not your head."

After four or five passes of the pendulum I start to feel a little seasick. Could be a good sign—nausea often accompanies me when I travel.

"You are getting sleeeeeepy," Pete says. "Veeeeeery sleeeeeepy."

"For real?"

Pete shrugs. "I don't know how to do this anymore than you do."

Seriously? After I put what may very well be my life in his hands? "Maybe you should've read up a bit before using me as a guinea pig."

"C'mon, Al, I've seen this done before."

"Yeah. By Krusty the Clown."

"No."

"Then who?"

"Zack...or was it Cody?"

"I rest my case."

"I *did* do research. Into the benefits of hypnotism."

Now it's my turn to look at *him* sardonically.

"The least you could do is try."

He looks so sincere, almost hurt that I would question his motives that I can't help but acquiesce. "Fine," I say, "what should I do?"

"Concentrate on the movement of my watch. Listen to my voice. Feel relaxed."

The pendulum swings another five or six times, and Pete says, "Now close your eyes. Think back to that day."

I swallow. Hard. The movie screen on the backs of my eyelids turns on, and I try to visualize the third-grade class, Miss Dinah's kind face, her soft voice rallying us to transition from circle time to our desks.

These days we hold regular lockdown drills. One of the admin team is supposed to announce, "Attention, attention, attention. We are in a lockdown situation," and teachers and students spring into action. We didn't do lockdowns, hold and secures (where the school is locked down due to a threat in the neighbourhood, but it's business as usual inside), or any other kind of drills, except for fire, until after that fateful day.

No lockdown procedure meant we were all sitting ducks when the shooter came into the room.

"Are you there, Al?"

I nod.

"Tell me what you see."

"Miss Dinah's shooing us to our desks."

"What else?"

"Lacey refusing to go into the cloakroom to get her shoes unless someone goes with her. She tells me, 'There's a ghost in there. In kindergarten, I saw a ghost,' but she pronounces it 'kiddiegarten' instead." Like so many kids I knew still said "sangwich" or "pisghetti".

"Go on."

"I tell her I think she's being silly, that there's no such thing as ghosts, but offer to go in with her. She takes my hand, and when we get to her cubby, we hear two shots. She screams." It gets hard to catch my breath. I feel almost like I'm drowning.

Pete must sense I'm in trouble because he says, "Focus on your breathing, Al. Try to slow it down," but I can't for the life of me.

"She screams and the doorknob rattles. She squeezes my hand so tightly she grinds the bones together. It hurts.

"The knob explodes from gunfire. Lacey lets go and runs from my side. I don't run—my feet are glued to the spot." Hyperventilating now. Feeling light-headed. White noise, like radio static between channels, begins to hum.

"His heels make a noise like Miss Dinah's do on the floor when she's walking fast. They sound almost like tap shoes. He has a gun!" I see the dull metal of the gun pointing toward the floor then arcing up until it's pointed at me. I want to scream; I try to scream, but my breath catches in my throat, and the sound that comes out is little more than a squeak.

"What do you do, Al?"

"I curl up into a ball and bring my hands to my head to protect it."

The static intensifies to a low whine. My head spins. I gag as if to vomit. There's a pop, like an air-filled paper bag exploding...

I open my eyes.

Pete's still at my bedside staring, face looking every bit like Munch's *The Scream*, mouth open so wide I think I can see his tonsils hanging at the back of his throat.

It didn't work.

I bury my face in my hands, elbows resting on my knees, and begin to weep.

Pete starts rubbing my back. "It's okay, Al," he whispers. "We'll try again," he promises, "we'll figure it out."

48

Alice is 15

Pete comes back the next day with another idea. He sets his gym bag down on my bed and unzips it. I gasp when I see what's inside. "Your grandma's metronome!" I say. He sets it on my bedside table. "Your mom's gonna kill you when she sees it's missing."

Pete shakes his head. "Mom hasn't so much as looked at the piano since her mother died. There's so much junk piled on top of it, she'll never notice." Pete's grandmother used to teach piano when his mom was young to help make ends meet in the household. Even Pete took lessons from her. In his third year of instruction, his grandmother proclaimed his fingers too short and fat to play, and she gave up teaching him. Pete had a hard time when she died. Though he loved his grandmother, he could never get over the rejection and swore one day he'd learn how to play and show her a thing or two. So far, that day hadn't come.

He sets the metronome to motion. "Lie down," he says.

"Wanna tell me why first?"

"Head out of the gutter, loser."

"Dweeb," I say as I lie on the bed. I clasp my hands together over my belly and let my elbows sink into the comforter beneath me. "Now, what?"

"One of the things I read online is that hypnosis is a good way to revert to a past traumatic state. We confirmed that with yesterday's failed experiment."

"Smart Pete's back," I tease.

"Quit it, Al." He sort of whines this, sounding a little hurt.

"I'm sorry. Continue, Dr. Flay. "

"Look, do you want me to help you out or not?"

It's sweet that he wants to help, that he's actually putting the effort in to investigate my case when all I can do is imagine what horrors I'll visit on Charles Dodgson when I find him. "I'm sorry, Pete. Let's do it." Whatever *it* is, I want to add, but don't—I've given him enough ribbing for one day.

"I'm going to hypnotise you, Al."

"That didn't work last time."

"It's different this time."

"Are you sure you know what you're doing?"

"No more than you do with what you're doing."

"Point taken."

"Ready?" He smirks at me. His eyes twinkle a bit.

"As I'll ever be, I guess," I say.

"Let's do it, then," he says.

I nod curtly and wait for my instructions.

"Close your eyes. Let your body relax into the mattress. Listen to the tick of the metronome. Hear the sound of my voice."

My mind flashes back to a sleepover party at Tina's a few years ago, when her cousin came up with the idea of levitation. We turned out the lights, and Tina lay on the ground.

"Breathe in through your nose," Pete says.

Tina's cousin told us to slip two fingers from each hand under her body.

"Out through your mouth..."

She told Tina to relax and imagine herself lighter than air.

"In through your nose..."

She talked about feathers and leaves taken on the breeze, clouds, and the air itself.

"Breathe in time to the metronome, deep belly breaths. In through your nose..."

By the time we were all chanting "Light as a feather, lighter than air," we'd lifted Tina almost three feet from the ground, just a half-dozen ten-year-olds using two fingers each. When we'd realized what we'd done, someone giggled and broke the spell. Tina went tumbling to the shag carpet, the only cushion between her backside and the concrete basement floor.

I breathe a bit on my own and then Pete starts talking again. "Imagine yourself at the end of a long tunnel."

I briefly consider reminding him that the tunnel imagery didn't work the last time, but then I see it, the tunnel, kind of like a long, dark straw, pulling me toward it.

"When you see the tunnel, go toward the light."

I think of that *Poltergeist* movie, of the small, feisty woman telling the spirits to go into the light. The tunnel in front of me wavers with my concentration. My mind squints to see it more clearly, focused only on the rim of the entrance and the light within, and the image strengthens.

"At the other end of the tunnel is the day of the shooting. That's where we're going."

I feel my breathing hitch. It shifts from measured and slow to quick and gulping. My body's reaction to the mere suggestion of returning to that day worsens the situation tenfold.

"Don't forget your breathing, Al. Slow and regular, like the metronome.

"Take a step back in your mind and find that rhythm again."

I imagine myself stepping back. What I feel is more of a slide. The image of the tunnel has changed. Instead of random light patterns at the other end, I see the grade three cloakroom, as if it were filmed in black and white and then colourized. Ethereal shapes are distorted and framed with backlit haloes.

Pete waits until I get my breathing under control and says, "You sure you want to do this, Al?"

I want to give him the thumbs up, but my body is way too heavy. I nod instead.

"Take a few steps toward the tunnel."

I see my foot lift in my mind's eye and my whole body slips forward until I'm at the mouth of the tunnel. Spectral shadows cross in front of the light at the other end.

"At the other end of the tunnel is the grade three class. When you're ready, step into the tunnel and go to the other side."

I imagine setting one foot in front of the other as I traverse the tunnel, and step out into the grade three class in my mind. Pete says, "You're still here with me, Al." He takes my hand and squeezes it. "What do you see?"

"The cloakroom," I say. My voice sounds far away and faintly echoed.

"What else?"

I blink. Everything's moving in slow motion. Kids slowly reach for jackets. Miss Dinah peeks around the corner of the cinderblock wall, arms crossed, tapping her toe in time to the metronome. "Children," she warns. The word lasts longer than its two syllables warrant. Her voice is deeper than I remember, too. I chalk this up to the time distortion I'm experiencing.

I blink again. The light fades, the haloes disappear, time speeds to normal. Children run helter skelter across the room.

"Today, please." Miss Dinah says.

"What do you see, Al?" Pete says, his voice overlapping with Miss Dinah's.

"I think it's recess time."

"Why?"

"Everyone's grabbing jackets. Miss Dinah's trying to shoo them out of the class."

"Not the day of the shooting?"

"Could be earlier that day."

"Fine. Move forward to later in the day."

I visualize the clock on the wall and advance the hands to just before two p.m. I'm in the cloakroom with Lacey when I hear the click clack of hard soles in the hall outside the class in beat with the metronome. My breathing quickens.

"What's happening, Al?"

"Footsteps," I tell him. The word comes out as a whisper.

"Where?"

"Outside." I look around and catch a glimpse of a bright pink Converse shoe, white ankle sock above that, Lacey's dark brown leg jutting from it from inside one of the cubbies. There are still kids in the class. "I have to get them out!" I say. My breath quickens further.

"Who, Al? Who do you have to get out?"

"The kids." The door knob jiggles.

"Take a breath, Al. Try to find the sound of the metronome."

I hear the wall clock tick in time to the contraption but can't get my breath to do the same.

The doorknob explodes in response to the sound of a gunshot.

The door swings open.

I open my eyes to see my reflection in the metal faceplate of the metronome.

I blink.

49

Alice is 15

A car horn blares.

I feel a draft.

The bed beneath me has been replaced with blacktop.

Wheels screech.

I open my eyes and raise my head. I'm lying in the middle of a busy six-lane street.

I pop into a crouch.

Another car whirls by, driver's heavy hand on the horn.

I stand up.

There's a car coming straight for me. A woman tenses behind the wheel, the knuckles of one hand gripping the steering wheel, the other laying on the horn. By her stance, I can tell she's practically standing on the brakes. The wheels screech, and I hear the ka-thump, ka-thump, ka-thump of the anti-lock braking system that Mom curses every time they kick in.

This is it.

I'm going to die.

I can't believe I survived the shooting only to die here and now.

I crouch into a ball again, cover my head, turn my side to the car and brace for impact.

50

Alice is 15

"That was amazingly cool, Al!"

Pete.

Carpet beneath my feet.

I'm still alive.

It worked!

Sort of.

"Ass-hat! You almost got me killed!"

"When did you go, Al?"

"I don't know. I wound up on a busy street in the middle of rush-hour traffic."

"The point is: it worked!"

"The whole point of this was to keep me safe. This little experiment of yours landed me smack dab in the middle of harm's way. In what universe did that work?"

"You tried to time travel and you did."

"But I almost got flattened by this woman I've probably scarred for life."

"The point is you were able to control when you time travelled. We tried to trigger an event and we did."

Never mind the woman I've scarred for life. *I'm* even more scarred if that's at all possible. I really thought that was it; that it was the end of me.

Though being able to control *when* I travel without being able to control *where* is still kind of lame, it's something at least.

It's progress.

At least, I think it is.

That day, we celebrate getting sick on froyo. Each of us helps ourselves to a large cup overflowing with a gazillion flavours, topped with as many toppings as we can fit in. "YOLO, Al!" Pete keeps saying until maybe it is his repetition of the tired phrase that makes me sick, rather than the froyo.

On the walk home, Pete says, "I wonder why the metronome worked and the pocket watch didn't."

I shrug.

"What did we do this time that we didn't do last time?"

I shrug again.

"Maybe it was the sound," he says. "You know, like how when they did those experiments on consciousness and zombies on *The Walking Dead*, and played the music over and over, hoping that when the guy came back as a zombie, the music would remind him of who he was."

"Music soothes the savage beast," I say.

"Huh?" Pete asks.

"Nothing."

We walk a bit without speaking. Pete breaks the silence when he says, "What's the last thing you remember before you travelled?"

"I don't know. Buzzing in my ears?"

"Not the sound of the metronome?"

I shrug and shake my head. "I remember seeing myself in the metronome."

"And then?"

"Then nothing. Then that woman freaking out when she tried not to hit me."

"Huh," Pete said.

"Huh, what?"

"Nothing. I'm just thinking out loud here, Al, but what if that's the key?"

"What if what's the key?"

He takes my hand, pulls me to the grassy boulevard between the curb of the road and the sidewalk, and motions for me to sit with him. "What's the last thing you remember seeing before you leaped on That Day?"

"I don't know," I say, hugging my knees against my chest. "The gunshot?"

"After that?"

I close my eyes. There was the tap-clack of his shoes, the blam of the gunshot, and the rattle of the doorknob. Children were screaming from all directions. The doorknob shattered. Then the woman. Then the gun click again. Then I left.

I relate this to Pete.

"Anything between the gun clicking and you leaving?"

I think. Hard. In my dreams I see my face distorted like a grotesque mask or a crazy reflection in a funhouse mirror.

When I tell this to Pete, he says, "Your reflection again? Where?"

"In the leg of the cloakroom bench."

"Boo-yah!" he says, startling me.

"Boo-yah what?" I ask.

"Boo-yah that's the missing puzzle piece. You didn't leap out of there when we tried with the pocket watch because your eyes were closed, but when you saw your reflection in the metronome, you were able to leap."

I don't want to talk about this anymore. I can appreciate this is all new to Pete, but he didn't relive the most traumatic event of his life earlier in the day. "I don't follow you," I say. "And I don't know that I want to anymore." I try to stand, but Pete grabs my wrist and pulls me down again.

"This is it, Alice! Now we have the key. It's your reflection."

"No, Einstein. It's my genetics."

"It's *in* your genetics, yes, but..." He sighs and looks off into space as if trying to think of a definitive answer for me.

"Take a car, for example. A car can go places, but not without the ignition key. A fully gassed up car is no good without the ignition key."

"So?"

"So you're like the car. When you're stressed, your genetics make you like the gassed up car, but you need the ignition key—your reflection—to make you go."

I look at him shaking my head. Could it really be that simple? Was that the reason why sometimes my time zones got jumbled and other times they didn't?

"It's like we learned in grade nine Science class: you can't have electricity flow unless you have a closed circuit. When you get stressed you turn the electricity on, but it doesn't flow until you look at yourself in a reflective surface. There's something about you looking at your reflection, and your reflection looking back at you, that completes the circuit and allows you to time travel."

There could be some validity to what he's saying. Though I can't remember if I've seen my reflection every time I travelled, it certainly made the difference this time. "So you're saying that if I want to force a trip through time, all I have to do it think about That Day and look at my reflection, and then—"

"And then boo-yah!"

Boo-yah, indeed.

51

Alice is 16

The weeks and months that follow are spent in experimentation. Pete wants to leave me his grandmother's metronome, but his mother would probably have a cow if she saw it missing. We find a metronome app to use instead (which only goes to show there really *is* an app for everything), but it isn't long before I learn to visualize the metronome and hear it in my mind's ear without any assistance.

Try as I might, I can't seem to forgo the reflection piece to the puzzle. I must learn to accept there's something about my condition necessitating that key, that completion of the circuit, in order for it to function correctly.

We practice every day after school, at first going only a few minutes back or forth in time (which entertains Pete to no end), but then expand to a few hours or a few days. We are sure to record all of the times I go to on Pete's list.

A month later I'm ready to try a few years either way. We record the future and near past dates on Pete's list, and the decade or so dates into the past on a separate list to give to my friend, Bill Tibbar. I decide not to share any of the artificially generated dates with Mom. She's firm in her belief that my malfunction is kind of like an epileptic seizure—you avoid blinking lights, and when it happens naturally, you deal with it. What Pete and I are doing is the equivalent of an epileptic setting up a whole whack of strobing lights and staring at them, daring the seizure to happen. Mom'd have a whole herd of cows if she knew.

Eventually, I'm ready.

After my mom forced me to dismantle my case wall, I reconstructed it so it was portable. I found this sort of portfolio, about the size of a binder, that unfolds until it's about three feet square, with a whole bunch of pockets inside at the As Seen On TV store at the mall. I'd even added my own flaps and extra pockets until it was five or six feet square when it lay flat. When I was done with it, the whole thing folded up and went onto my bookshelf where it hid in plain sight.

Genius!

Pete and I unfold my portfolio and sit, knee to knee, in front of it on the floor, studying. Pete says, "Hey, Al? Did you ever consider that we're all stuck in the Matrix and you've just learned to control it?"

"So I'm Neo?"

"I was thinking more along the lines of Trinity."

I punch his arm. "Why, goofus?" I'd said the word that one time when my tongue mixed the words "goof" and "doofus" and the portmanteau stuck.

"Because you're a girl."

"So who's Neo?"

Pete shrugs.

"Pete, honey? You can't be Neo. You can't go anywhere. You're stuck right here in the Matrix with everyone else."

"I can do this," he says and starts tickling me, toppling me sideways and climbing on top of me. I giggle at first, but then realize how perilously close we are to my portfolio, and say, "Okay! Okay! My case wall!"

Pete stops cold. His face hovers above mine, and our eyes lock, and we have a moment before he eventually pecks me on the lips, and climbs off of me.

It's quiet for a few minutes as we get back to studying the mind map of my case wall, and then Pete says, "So what's the plan?"

"I want to learn about Dodgson."

"How are you going to do that? I mean, wouldn't it be dangerous to make contact with him?"

"I need to do some recon first. I want to see his OSR." OSR stands for Ontario Student Record. It's a file that's opened when a child enters school in junior kindergarten and contains intelligence on the kid, collected and added to, for as long as he remains in the school system, as if the Ministry of Education were CSIS, or the FBI, or something, and we're all suspects. It's rumoured that everything there is to know about a student is kept in those files under lock and key, super-confidential, eyes only. This is probably why when I say I'm going to check out Dodgson's OSR, Pete gasps, as if I'd told him I was going to Area 51 to check out Majestic 12's top-secret UFO files.

"But those are confidential."

"I won't tell if you don't."

"But they're locked in a safe."

I shake my head. "They're locked in the back room in the guidance office."

"What if you're caught?"

"Then you'll bail me out."

"But you're going into the past."

"If I get into trouble I'll tell Bill when I get back."

"You're sure you want to do this?"

I nod.

"Then good luck and Godspeed, Al."

"I'm not flying a mission over enemy air in World War I, Pete."

"I know, but—"

"You're worried."

Pete nods.

"Fold up the portfolio in case there's air disturbance." I didn't know it, but Pete told me there's like this rush of air when I leave this timeline, as if the air around me can't wait to fill the void I've left behind.

When he's done, Pete looks at me, winks, and nods. He holds up a compact mirror I picked up at Dollarama.

I smile back and concentrate. Imagine the metronome. Breathe in time to the tick.

The buzzing begins. The chirp of cicadas.

The air is sucked from my lungs. My head starts to swim.

I close my eyes.

When I open them I see my reflection in The Dollar Store mirror.

I blink.

52

Alice is 16

There's a moment of panic when I open my eyes and see nothing but darkness. Then I realize I'm inside a small room with the lights out. I grope along the wall until I find a light switch. When I turn, I see a row of about a dozen filing cabinets, some of them so close together there's no way a person could ever get between them. On the end of each cabinet is a wheel that looks like a ship's steering wheel, and I get that the cabinets must be moved before you can get into them. Luckily, Dodgson is in the first cabinet on the right, which is fixed in place a short distance from the wall in front of it. I squeeze into the small space and search until I find his file, which is rather thick in comparison to the others. So I don't forget where it came from, I tilt the folders before and after it on the shelf so they're sticking out, and take Dodgson's folder to the table near the light switch.

Affixed to the inside of the folder are pictures of him from kindergarten through grade twelve. I had no idea they do this. I'm kind of tempted to find my own folder to see what's inside, but I'm not here for that kind of trip down memory lane.

Dodgson's educational career started quite innocuously. He was, by all accounts, an average kid with average grades.

In grade seven, he was given an in-school suspension for swearing at a teacher.

In grade nine, he sent a threatening letter to his teacher through the classroom printer. IT from the board was called. They were able to match the print job to Dodgson's computer, warranting a three-day suspension. Police were called, but because Dodgson was still a minor, he was let off with a warning.

In grade ten, he hacked into a teacher's email account and sent random pornographic pictures to everyone on the teacher's mailing list, including other students in his class. Once more, police were called, but because the evidence was circumstantial, no charges were laid. Another suspension for Dodgson, this time ten days.

After a student tipped off school administration, Dodgson was caught with a BB gun in school in grade eleven. He'd insisted he and his friends only used it for target practice, shooting cans in his basement, and that he'd only brought the gun to school on a dare. Once more, the police were involved, but because it remained hidden in his bag, they couldn't charge him. That one garnered him a twenty-day suspension and a psychological evaluation. The report for that is also in his OSR, but when I read it, there's nothing there of interest. If Dodgson were acting out for anything other than kicks and recognition, he was really good at hiding it.

In grade twelve he was arrested for contributing to the delinquency of a minor when he was found with three joints of marijuana and two grade nines, smoking up in the school parking lot, of all places. He earned another twenty-day suspension for that stunt. Because he was eighteen, he also earned a criminal record.

So Dodgson's a bad guy, I get that, but I don't know why. What happened in his grade seven year to set a relatively normal guy on a downward spiral, culminating in a shooting spree in his eighteenth year?

I need to share this information with Pete, so I replace the folder on the shelf.

Luckily, the trip home requires no reflection. Rather than complete the circuit, I need to kind of break it, so I turn out the light, close my eyes (though it's so dark in the room the difference between eyes open and eyes closed is negligible), and imagine the metronome's rhythmic tick-tick-tick...

53

Alice is 16

How does a kid go from general mischief and a misdemeanour drug charge to using a gun to make Swiss cheese out of his primary school? How deep-seated must his hate for the education system be to wake up one morning and decide to shoot up innocent teachers and students?

In the case of the Columbine High School Massacre, threats began on a website the shooters had initially created to discuss first-person shooter video games. At Sandy Hook Elementary, the perpetrator was mentally ill and obsessed with the Columbine shooting. In Montreal's École Polytechnique Massacre, 28 people were shot—mostly women. The shooter's mental illness and hatred for feminists were blamed. The thing they all had in common—besides taking place in schools in North America—was that the shooter had left behind signs something wasn't right. Because the crimes were so horrendous and people are generally trusting of friends and family members, no one even thought to look for signs pointing to the possibility of mass bloodshed in the future.

Besides his brushes with the law, no one knew Dodgson harboured such animus for the school system, let alone his elementary school.

For the time being, Dodgson is locked away in prison awaiting trial, which could take upwards of a year until its number showed up on the court docket.

More than a whole entire year!

It might as well be forever.

I've suffered most of my life because that bastard couldn't keep it under control. I mean, look at me: I was traumatised as a child, told I suffered from Post-traumatic Stress Disorder, and forced to see a shrink who hadn't a clue as to my true defect. There's no medication to help my particular condition. Instead, I'm doomed to do the Hokey Pokey through time, showing up God knows when and God knows where.

I don't go around hurting other people; why should others feel the need?

Four words: Mom, Dad, Pete, and Bill.

What if Mom and Dad had pooh-poohed my PTSD instead of insisting I get help? What if I didn't have Pete to confide in or Bill to get me out of hot water?

Rather than be comfortable in my own skin, I might blame the same school as Dodgson for my sorrows. I might eventually lash out.

I shake my head in spite of the fact I'm in my room alone and no one's there to see. No way, I tell myself. I could never do that. I wouldn't know the first thing about where to *find* a gun let alone *shoot* it. Forget about taking it to my school and shooting others—*killing* others—with it.

Chances are my time travel glitch would have manifested without Dodgson's prompting, anyway. If what Dr. Rickman says is true, and my condition *is* genetic, it would have eventually reared its ugly head, PTSD or not.

Regardless of the why, sources online agree the how of it could have been prevented if people had recognized the bread crumbs the killers had dropped in the days, weeks, months, even years before the massacres.

I'm going to look for Dodgson's.

"You're crazy, Al," Pete tells me when I share my plan with him. "You can't change the past."

"You don't know that for sure."

"Neither do you."

"How would *you* know, anyway? If I'm successful, chances are I'll be the only one who'll know what I've done."

"I'd know."

"You wouldn't. Remember that Ray Bradbury story? The one about the guy who steps on the butterfly in the past? When they return to the future, he's the only one that notices. Everyone else goes about their business as if everything's normal. And to them, it is."

"Why don't the other guys in the shuttle notice anything about the change? *They* weren't on Earth when it happened, either. I mean, logically, shouldn't *they* notice the changes, too?"

"It's written in third person limited point of view, phlegmwad. We don't know what the others are thinking because we're inside the head of the butterfly killer."

"Oh," Pete says.

"I call you a phlegmwad and that's all you have to say?"

"Oh. Fudge-nozzle."

"*That's* more like it."

Pete punches me in the arm.

We try looking Dodgson up online but come up empty. He's got a Facebook page (closed to anyone but his "friends"), a Twitter feed (also private), a few profiles on random gaming sites, but nothing condemning. He's smart enough to keep his private and public profiles separate, I'll give him that.

The media has nothing more to offer than coverage of his arrest and arraignment, and that he's being held without bail until the trial date. The police are, understandably, remaining closed-lipped about what—if anything—they've found amongst his possessions.

I have no choice but to go back in time and do a little investigation before the fact, to see if there are any signs I can report in order to get him the help and support he needs.

Pete insists on being there with me whenever I try to go back, something about him being the first line of time when I return, like I'd know just by looking at him whether or not I'd changed anything. But there are some things a girl's gotta do on her own. Going all Winchester on the ass of a demon is one of them.

I need to check out Dodgson's history on my own.

Step one in my quest is reconnaissance.

Dodgson's house is nearby, but the street's still a media circus. Police tape cordons off the house and garage, and the street's all but impassable due to the news trucks lined up along the curb. Going there on foot is pretty much out of the question—someone may recognize me—but if I look the address up on Google Street View, I can still get a pretty good look at the house.

The Dodgsons live in a two story, two garage back split. This poses a problem: because I can't see the back of the house I can't be sure how many bedrooms are in the house, or which of them is Dodgson's. What if he doesn't live in a bedroom on the second floor? What if his bedroom is in the back of the house on one of the main floors, or in the basement?

Growing up, my mom's friend had a house with a similar façade. If I assume the interior layout is similar as well, I can visualize where the downstairs bedroom may be. But if Little Charlie was planning a bloodbath, he may not do it in his bedroom where Mrs. Dodgson or the cleaning woman might find it. Chances are the evidence will probably be in a man-cave of his in the basement where, I'm guessing, few but Little Charlie ever go.

The basement: the destination of my first solo quest.

Step one: position the mirror at my bedside.

Step two: get comfortable in my bed.

Step three: imagine the tick-tick of the metronome.

Step four: breathe slowly, in through the nose and out through the mouth. Concentrate on the ticking and the breathing.

...tick...tick...

Click.

...tick...tick...

Clack.

For some reason—probably all the Dodgson talk—wires get crossed in my psyche until the tick-tick of the metronome melds with the click-clack of Dodgson's heels on the tile of the corridor outside the grade three classroom, and my breath quickens in spite of my best efforts to remain calm.

I open my eyes and blink at my reflection, and for a split second I'm back in Miss Dinah's cloakroom, shivering in fear, hugging myself, curled into a ball in the middle of the room.

Then something shifts...

54

Alice is 16

The air around me dampens and grows cold, and the bed beneath me hardens. I realize I'm lying on my back, on the concrete slab of a rather large basement.

It worked!

Pete's a genius to have devised this method of controlling my defect when even Dr. Rickman's geneticist friends and Dr. Hatfield's mental-know-it-alls couldn't. Pete should be the one writing papers on it.

Never mind all that—back to the task at hand.

First order of business: make sure I'm alone.

Outside of the furnace room and crawlspace, the basement is made up of two large rooms, connected kitty-corner to each other. There is a bathroom and closets along the back wall and more closets along the front wall. Dodgson's "man-cave" consists of a puke green throw rug in the middle of the larger room, a shit brown sectional couch, and a cabinet-style television set. The whole set-up screams seventies, and anxiety gathers in the pit of my stomach for a moment because I think I may have messed up on the calendar, but I manage to squelch those thoughts—I have a plan to execute.

Dodgson leaves nothing out in the open. The bathroom's pretty stark. The closets at the back of the basement are just that: storage closets. Boxes are stacked and labeled in one closet. Clothes hang in the next.

The boxes could have been mislabelled in a ruse by Dodgson. I'll have to come back and take a closer look if I come up empty.

Of the three "closets" at the front of the house, two are actual closets, storing more boxes, winter coats and boots, and a rolled rug or two. The third door in the far corner has been made into a small office. It smells of mothballs and farts. Along one wall is a sheet of wood propped up between two beams to create a makeshift desk. There's an overhead light, no more than a bulb with a string. I pull the string, but the light doesn't turn on, so I give the bulb a tap and it flickers. Probably just loose in the socket. I give the bulb a few turns and the light becomes blinding. When my eyes adjust, I can see more of the small, dank room.

Playboy centrefolds hang on the wall, wasted and buxom women display everything God gave them, and then some, for the world to see, and I think about my own body. The women in the posters' breasts are huge monstrosities hanging from their shoulders, which they knead and press between their hands as they pose, legs alternately splayed and spread every which way.

I don't look like that. With any luck, I'll *never* look like that.

Somehow, I manage to pull myself away from Dodgson's little shop of horrors, and take stock of what's on the desk and the shelves around it.

Books and binders populate the shelves. There are a few on video gaming—*World of Warcraft: Official Strategy Guide, Halo 2: The Official Game Guide, The Meaning and Culture of Grand Theft Auto: Critical Essays*—and a few novels—Mo Hayder's *Ritual, Misery* by Stephen King, Bret Easton Ellis's *American Psycho*—but not much else.

On the desk are notes for a *Richard III* essay.

Richard III. That's got to be senior high school or university material, which means I've pinpointed my destination much closer than I'd first thought. Unless there were *two* psychos living in the Dodgson household, one older or younger than Charles, it looks like I'm almost spot on in time.

As I rifle through the papers on the desk, I knock the chair into it, and a bulletin board propped against the wall at the back of the desk falls over to reveal that Dodgson has a case board of his very own.

Without fail, the shooters involved in each of the other massacres had penned some sort of manifesto, what the author hoped to achieve in his movement, and Dodgson is no exception. Dodgson's case board is his attempt at compiling a manifesto.

In the centre of the board is the picture of a man, vaguely familiar. I flip it over and realize the graphic's been torn from a yearbook of some kind. Maybe the guy's a teacher? But from which school, grade, or subject, I have no idea. There's also a picture of Principal Cotton. Both Mr. Cotton and the other teacher have huge red Xs across their faces.

In the corner of the board is the school logo and mascot, a buck-toothed beaver wearing a toque with a maple leaf on it, torn from the same yearbook. Bucky's also been defaced, his incisors lengthened and sharpened with a black marker until they're vampiric and dripping gouts of black blood.

A nine-and-a-half by eleven word-processed page has been pinned to the upper left-hand corner. It looks like a letter. Just as I pull the chair from under the desk and sit, I hear the crack of footsteps from the beams supporting the floor above and the slam of a door.

Someone's home.

Shit!

What I wouldn't give for my cell phone camera!

My breath freezes in my throat, and my heartbeat accelerates.

Maybe one of the Dodgson clan has forgotten his lunch.

Maybe one of them is home for lunch.

The snap-beat of the footsteps continues down what I imagine to be the front hallway, done up in ceramic (hardwood footsteps would be more muted), and then clatter down a short flight of stairs, into the lower back-split level.

I close my eyes and try to secure my breathing.

The footsteps clatter down the wooden basement stairs.

There's enough presence of mind to reach up and pull the string to turn out the light and reach out to close the door, latching it slowly so as not to make a sound.

The springs on the sectional squeak. The television turns on. There's a mixture of clipped words as whoever has arrived, presumably Charles Dodgson himself, surfs channels. He settles on what sounds like *The Flintstones*. Barney speaks in falsetto insisting he's Tillie Shimmelstone, come to collect the money Fred claims to have found. I crack the door a bit hoping to catch a glimpse of Dodgson, hoping the television's loud enough to hide any noise the latch might make, but Dodgson turns his head toward the click, and leans forward in his chair, craning his neck toward the sound—toward me!

I close my eyes and tell myself to breathe...breathe Al, or Alice, or Mabel, or whatever the hell my name should be—just breathe.

I scamper under the desk and pull the chair as much into the well beneath as will fit. Please don't find me, I pray. Please, God, no.

Breathe in...

Home.

Breathe out...
My house.
Breathe in...
My bed.
Breathe out...
I envision the cool taupe walls of my room, the antique blonde dresser on one wall, the desk along the other, the face of each Directioner and of Demi and Selena, and my breathing eases in spite of Dodgson's footsteps taking up once more as he crosses the room.

The comforter on my bed. Whirls of neon blue, pink, green, and black, circulating around the faces of each of my British boys.

Allie the Alley Cat.

Princess Pinkie Pie.

When I open my eyes, I'm still in a small, darkened room. The damp, farty smell has subsided. So have the footsteps. My eyes adjust to register a small crack of light beaming on my face through a partition in the wall.

I'm in my own closet, in my own room.

I'm safe again.

For now.

55

Alice is 16

I'm in my room with Pete. He's brought Tina with him (I told Tina about my secret a while ago. All it took was a demonstration or two to convince her). When we made our study date I told Pete to bring as many yearbooks as he could find and I guess he'd enlisted Tina for help. There are six unique yearbooks between the three of us, all from our primary years. I've just relayed the reason why I wanted the yearbooks, Dodgson's manifesto, and all.

"You what?" Pete says. "I don't know whether to kiss you or kick you."

"Kiss please," I tell him, and my face flushes.

"Holy shit, guys—get a room," Tina tells us.

"You could have been killed," Pete says.

"Dodgson's not a killer, not yet."

Tina says, "You don't know what he is, Al. He could've had a gun."

"Hey," I say to Tina, putting on a frowny face, "whose side are you on?"

"Yours, Al. That's why I think going to Dodgson's alone was a stupid move." I don't point out to her that since I needed to travel through time to go there and I couldn't take anyone with me when I went, there was no other way to go but alone.

Pete nods and points to Tina with his hand palm up, as if to endorse the statement.

"He didn't kill me," I say.

"But he could've," Pete says.

"I seriously doubt he would've shot me right in his parents' basement."

"You don't know that, Al," Tina says.

"Puh-leese," I say, rolling my eyes as I do. Taking another tack, I plaster a huge grin on my face, lean forward, hug Tina first, and then Pete, planting one on his cheek before I let go.

"I love you both," I tell them, "and I know you love me, but we really need to get on with the investigation."

"The game's afoot," Pete says.

"WTF, dude?" Tina says.

"It's what Sherlock Holmes would say."

"Weird, much?" Tina says.

"You guys are a bunch of cheese-and-a-halves. Can we get on with it?"

"Butt-munch," Pete mumbles.

"Ass-pirate," Tina mumbles back.

"Now that we know who everyone is..." I say. Though I'm quite peeved at them, and can practically hear the clock ticking down the seconds we have together, it's enough to crack me up. My outburst ignites a round of giggles lasting a few minutes. No sooner do we manage to cool our jets than someone starts laughing, which sets us off again.

Tick...tick...tick, the metronome in my head taps. I look around and see reflections in practically every surface in the room. Not now, I beg my psyche. Stay in the here and now. Please! "Can we focus, people?"

Pete nods.

Tina wipes tears from her cheek.

"Lay on, Macduff." *Macbeth*. Pete. I'm impressed.

"What are we looking for, Al?" Tina asks.

"Pics of male teachers."

"Which ones?"

I shrug. "Don't know. I'll know when I see him."

"This the guy with the X across his face?" Pete asks.

"Yeah," I say.

"Freaky."

Freaky deaky. "Tell me about it."

"Three guys in our JK year," Pete says.

"Only three male teachers in the whole school?" I ask.

Pete shrugs. "I guess."

"Let's see." He hands it over. No go. These aren't the guys.

"Our SK year," Tina says.

Still no go.

"This is interesting," Pete says.

"You got something?"

He hands me the yearbook. "Our grade three year."

"Epic Fail Year." Though Tina didn't go to our school back then, she still says this almost reverently.

"This guy." He points to a man's picture. "Dormer. He was supposed to be grade three teacher that year."

Tina grabs the yearbook from my lap. "Then why was Miss Dinah your teacher?" She flips the page. "Miss Dinah's picture isn't here."

"Maybe she was off on maternity leave," I suggest.

"But she was a miss and not a missus," Pete says.

"Wake up and smell the twenty-first century, prude," Tina says.

I shake my head. "There was no mention of Miss Dinah having any kids in the media circus after the shooting."

"She could've been sick," Pete says.

"Or laid off—like...surplused—that year," Tina says.

"Let me see." I take the book back from Tina and flip through the pages. Miss Dinah's not in the list of teachers absent on photo day either.

I flip back to the teacher photos and study the black and white of Mr. Dormer. Mr. Lewis Dormer. The hair is right. So's the nose, mouth, and angle of the chin. So I didn't get a lot of time to actually study the face on Dodgson's case wall, and quite a bit of the picture *was* obliterated by the red X drawn with a pen so fierce it gouged holes in the paper where the lines crossed, but if I had to gamble, I'd be willing to place money on it that the guy on Dodgson's wall and Mr. Dormer were one and the same.

"That's him," I say, barely more than a whisper. Suddenly, my throat has turned to sandpaper and my tongue's grown to twice its natural size. "Mr. Dormer. The guy on Dodgson's wall."

"If Mr. Dormer was our teacher that year, how come I don't remember him? And when did Miss Dinah come back?" Pete asks.

I shrug. "Maybe she was reinstated at the last minute?"

"I'm on it," Tina says. She grabs her tablet and starts flicking the touch screen. "Says here Lewis Dormer was in a car accident early September of grade three."

"I don't remember a guy teacher before Miss Dinah. Do you, Al?" Pete asks.

"Uh-uh."

"Then what gives?"

"Broke his femur, a few ribs, and cracked his head good," Tina continues.

"Dodgson's grudge was with Mr. Dormer?" Pete says.

"Seems like," I say.

"What could a primary school teacher possibly do that would warrant something like that?" Pete again. "You saw Dodgson's OSR, Al. What happened in grade three?"

I try to remember what I'd read. I shrug. "I don't remember. The first thing I remember seeing was grade seven. And it was pretty benign. Swearing at a teacher."

"And he went downhill from there?" Pete says.

"At Mach speed," I say.

Tina shakes her head and says, "The average kid takes his lumps after a mistake and learns his lesson. Maybe this guy Dodgson's a bad seed."

"Maybe," I say.

Grade three. Eight years old. How much of that year would I have remembered if Dodgson hadn't literally went ballistic on us? What I do remember of my pre-grade three schooling is in snapshots—friends in the schoolyard, sitting in story circle, dodgeball in the gym…

But if something horrendous had happened in those years?

What could have possibly happened that was so horrendous it warranted *that* kind of retaliation?

Verbal abuse?

Beating?

Molestation?

How about being made the object of target practice?

"Anything else on Dormer?" I ask Tina.

"Like what?"

"Like is he still teaching?"

"What are you thinking, Al?" Pete asks.

"I don't know. If he really is some kind of monster, surely someone would have figured it out after all these years."

"Teacher's certificate on the College of Teachers website shows he's still active," Tina says.

"Just means he's paying his dues," Pete says. I reach for his hand and squeeze. Good thinking, Pete.

"Here's a quote after the shooting in a *Star* article." She reads, "Primary school teacher, Lewis Dormer, was originally slated to teach Dinah's grade three class, but was sidetracked after his car was totalled by a drunk driver. 'I thought the accident was the worst thing that ever happened to me in my life,' he says. 'Turns out it was a blessing in disguise.'"

"Miss Dinah's tragedy is his blessing?" Tina says. "Phlegmwad."

"Colossal Phlegmwad," I agree.

"So this Dormer's not a monster?" Pete says.

"Lacking in compassion and tact, but sadly, apparently, not a monster," Tina says.

We sit in silence, pondering what we've just learned.

All I can think about is what a stupid-ass super-colossal loser Charles Dodgson is, taking out a whole class like that without even checking to make sure he had the right teacher in his sights. Then I get an idea. "*Is* he still teaching?"

"Huh?" Tina asks.

"Dormer. You never said if he was still teaching."

Tina swipes at her tablet screen a few times. "There's a teacher named Dormer at a nearby primary school."

"The same guy?" Pete asks.

"There's nothing in the school directory for 'Lewis Dormer', just 'Mr. Dormer'."

"We need to talk to him," I say.

56

Alice is 16

Mr. Dormer's in his classroom erasing the chalkboard when we knock. He turns toward us, three kids armed with Tina's tablet and a steno pad from the dollar store (Pete's idea), determined to find the truth. Pete's dad just got him the Blu-ray collection of *The X-Files* television series. He fancies himself Mulder in this scenario. "The truth is out there, Al," he says to me while waiting in line to pay for the steno pad. "The question is, do you believe?"

"We're not hunting aliens, Pete."

"But wouldn't it be cool if Dormer turned out to be one?" Tina says. "An alien, I mean. From space." I glare at Tina. "Not the kind from another country."

"Don't encourage him," I tell her.

She mutters an almost inaudible, "Sorry."

The time walking from Dollarama to the primary school is spent rehearsing our cover story. We are from our school newspaper. The editor thought it would make good copy (we had to use the word "copy" to show we were actual reporters) if kids that witnessed the shooting wrote the investigative report into Dodgson's arrest and trial.

Dormer turns his head toward us after we knock on his open classroom door. "Can I help you?" he asks. We must look strange standing there, the three of us, much older than the usual sort he might encounter knocking on his door.

"Mr. Dormer?" Pete says taking the lead.

He makes one last swipe at chalk residue on the board, puts the eraser in the tray, and brushes his hands together to rid them of chalk dust. "Yes?"

"We're here to do a story for our school paper, a retrospective of sorts, given Charles Dodgson's capture and impending trial," Pete continues, nailing the persona of investigative reporter. I wonder if he's ever considered taking Drama?

"I don't know what I can do to help. That was the year my car was t-boned by a drunk driver and I was out for most of it."

"But you *are* aware Dodgson chose the third-grade classroom because he thought you were the teacher there?"

Dormer lets out a nervous chuckle. "I know I was supposed to teach third-grade that year, but I highly doubt I was Dodgson's target."

"What if it comes out in trial that you were? His target, I mean," I ask.

"That would be unsettling, to say the least."

"Did you know Charles Dodgson before the shooting? Had you taught him before?" Pete asks.

"I did."

"Would you say he was a grudger?" Tina says.

"A what?" Dormer asks, followed by that same nervous chuckle.

"Is he the type to hold a grudge?" I clarify.

"I assure you, I wouldn't know."

The conversation is had in the doorway of Dormer's classroom, him on one side, us craning for equal space in the doorway from the hall side, like *The Three Stooges* attempting to enter a room, only to bottleneck in the doorjamb. I don't think we appeared as comic to

Dormer. Our appearance had more of a—what was the word he'd used?—unsettling effect on him than anything else.

"How would you describe Dodgson as a child?" Pete asks.

"Quiet? Introverted?"

"Can you recall any confrontations you might have had with him prior to the incident?" Tina asks.

"Just what are you implying?"

"We're not implying anything, sir." I push through Pete and Tina until they're behind me, in chevron formation. "We know Dodgson was troubled, but records show he didn't begin to act out until seventh grade," I say, trying to smooth things over before Dormer becomes unsettled to the point of shutting down. "We're just trying to fill in the blanks with respect to his behaviour prior to that day."

"I can't help you." Dormer places a hand on the side of the door as if preparing to close it in our faces. "I am prohibited from speaking about one student with another."

"But we graduated elementary school, so, technically, we're no longer your students." God, Pete! Way to alienate our only lead.

"This conversation is over." Dormer begins to swing the door closed.

I don't know what possesses me—desperation, maybe—but I stick my foot between the closing door and the jamb.

"Move your foot, now, before I call the office and have you thrown out on your asses for trespassing."

Whoa! Didn't see that one coming. Somewhere along the way one of us struck a nerve. A pretty raw nerve. Confrontations with Dodgson, that's what Tina had asked before he'd shut down.

"Sir? Please," I practically beg. "You were lucky enough to dodge that day, but we were all there. In the room when Dodgson was shooting. Our teacher died. So did a few of our friends. I was in the cloakroom with him. He pointed the gun directly at me." Tears begin to form in the corners of my eyes, which is great if I want to garner Dormer's sympathy, but if it's a warning that my DNA's about to malfunction, not so much. I find the least reflective surface I can—Dormer's suit jacket—to focus on. "I had to look down the barrel of that gun. I thought I was a goner."

"You kids are so self-centred, all you can think of is yourselves." Dormer widens the crack a bit, lessening the pressure of the door on my foot. "Have you ever heard of 'Survivor's Guilt'? It happens when someone survives a disaster—like a plane crash, or a shooting—and experiences post-traumatic stress, the same as if he'd been directly involved. You were there, and I'm sorry for that, but don't you for a minute assume that because I wasn't there, I don't suffer all the same."

Oh, boo-hoo, I want to tell him. You feel guilty because you *survived*? You suffer post-traumatic stress because you *weren't* there? Don't expect any sympathy from me, buddy. Instead, I say, "Whether you want to admit it or not, *sir*..." I say 'sir' just like that, with mock respect, because, let's face it, after claiming that his lot in life for *not* being there is worse than mine—than *ours*—for being there?

With that thought and the anger that accompanies it, the bees come out of their hive and begin to buzz in circular formation around my head, whispering in my ears to give it up before I show him how bad post-traumatic stress can really be.

"Charles Dodgson chose to shoot up the third-grade class because of some kind of altercation between the two of *you*. Now, we're not here to lay blame. We just need to know what that was. What set him off to the point of doing what he did to a bunch of *kids*—"

"Charles Dodgson did nothing," he says, and just as I think Dormer's blurted an admission of *his* culpability, he says, "literally nothing. All day. Just...sat there, at the corner desk, playing on his cell phone underneath it.

"When I called his parents and they cried to me about how they couldn't control his video game and computer use at home, I had the audacity to suggest they take his cell phone away. I even went so far as to tell them that I wouldn't recommend allowing any child the use of a computer in his bedroom. Suggested they remove it from his bedroom, and put it in a central location where they could better monitor both his time *and* the content he was viewing online.

"His parents wanted to know more about his behaviour in class, who his friends were, and I made the mistake of naming names.

"He came to school the next day and had the arrogance to tell me off for complaining to his parents about his friends, if you can imagine. This little pre-pubescent shit-for-brains has the nerve to tell me off for naming names to his parents.

"I've never hated a student before then, and never since, but I can tell you, I hated Charles Dodgson. They ought to give me the Academy Award for being able to carry on for the rest of the school year being pleasant to his ugly face after that."

Shit-for-brains? I've never heard a teacher talk that way about a student before. Raw nerve hit, indeed.

"When you asked me if he was a—what was the word you used?"

"Grudger," Tina says.

"When you asked me if he was a grudger earlier? Hell, yeah, he was. The little bastard never said another word to me for the rest of the time he was in the building.

We could be the only two people in an otherwise empty hallway and he would just as soon slit his own throat than acknowledge my presence.

"It was just as well. I'd have to admit I'd probably do the same thing, you know? Slit my throat than be nice to him when I no longer had to."

By this time the door is back to being wide open, and all three of us are in Dormer's full view. He looks at each of us in turn and adds, "All this is off the record, of course. I've been candid with you. Perhaps even a little too much so."

"Off the record?" I say. "Of course."

57

Alice is 16

We walk to a pizza place in a nearby strip mall, heads down and in relative silence. I don't know what does it, the weight of what we've learned, the way Dormer spoke about his former student, or the fact that our quest to stop Dodgson was futile at best.

We sit in a booth backed on one side by a cinderblock wall and another booth on the other to lick our wounds. Pete pops open his soda can and says, "Well *that* was a red herring,"

"Dormer's got a serious attitude problem when it comes to students," Tina says.

"Seriously," Pete echoes.

"Not all students," I remind them—Dormer was pretty okay to us. "Just Dodgson."

"This is messed up," Pete says. "I mean, what head case screws around in class and then plans revenge—"

"For like, a dozen years—" Tina says.

"On his teacher for telling his parents?"

"My English teacher?"

"Miss Proactive-Not-Reactive?" I ask Tina.

"That's the one. She says it's her job to call home when a kid's in trouble, that she'll get told off by the principal if she doesn't."

Pete picks up where Tina left off. "She also says that if we do our jobs and take advantage of the chances she gives us we'll be successful, and there's no *need* to call home, except to tell our parents what a good job we're doing."

"Yeah, except she never does."

"You don't know that," Pete defends.

Must be nice to have a teacher like that. The last teacher I wanted to defend, the last one I clung to every freaking word that came out of her mouth, was Miss Dinah.

We chew a few bites in that awkward, contemplative silence until Pete says, "So now what?"

"You can't change the past, Al," Tina reminds me.

I shake my head. "I refuse to believe that."

"The evidence shows—"

"What evidence, Pete?" I say, practically cringing at the tone; I hadn't meant to sound so harsh. "What a bunch of people with overactive imaginations make into movies?"

"Actually, yes."

I make a small sound of derision in my throat and shake my head.

"Time travel's an impossibility, Al. *You're* an impossibility. It stands to reason that if you exist in spite of that...if you have this amazing ability, then maybe other things are possible, too.

"We don't know what the deal with time travel is, whether things like paradox are even possible, or if we can change the past, or even travel to the future because it hasn't been written yet—"

"I *went* to the future, Pete. I met *you* in the future."

"The Macbeth Conundrum," Tina reminds us.

"Screw Macbeth," I say, feeling anger at my sheer rise in frustration. I'm tired of debating the facts and foibles of theoretical time travel. Pete himself said it: I exist. I'm an anomaly. I refuse to believe I'm like a residual haunting or something, bound to relive the same damn life and all of its missteps, without the power of intelligence to interact with the world around me.

"I refuse to believe I'm powerless. God, or the Powers That Be, or whomever, or whatever, didn't give me this...this...ability, as you put it, without a reason.

"There's gotta be something we can do—something *I* can do—to save Miss Dinah and prevent traumatizing all those kids. *I'm* not ready to throw the towel in yet. Anyone wanting out, now's the time to say so."

"Speaking as one of those traumatized kids? I'm in," Pete says.

"Me, too, Al," says Tina. "What do you propose?"

I shake my head. I'm at a loss. It's one thing to be spunky and passionate for a cause, it's another to know what to do about it. "I can't talk to Little Chuckie Dodgson because he's just a brat.

"I can't talk to pre-shooting Dodgson because he's too far gone.

"Talking to him after the fact, after he's already awaiting trial, is too late—"

"We want to stop him, not understand him," Pete says.

"We already have a pretty good understanding of him, right?" Tina says. "I mean, he's like, evil personified, or something, right?"

I nod at Tina with a forced smile. Then I have an idea. I punctuate it with an open-palm slap on the table in front of me. "I need to confront Dodgson."

Pete says, "Been there, done that, remember, Al? In his basement? When you found his manifesto?"

I shake my head. "I mean just before he does it. In the grade three cloakroom."

"Bad idea, Al."

"If I could just confront him, talk him down—"

"Let me get this straight," Tina says. She squirms in her seat a bit before continuing, as if settling down for the long haul. "You want to go back to the grade three cloakroom on the day of the shooting, appear to Dodgson while he's holding a gun, and quite literally, going ballistic, and...*talk*? *Bad* idea, Al. Bad, bad idea."

Pete nods his agreement.

"If he just knew Miss Dinah was the teacher and not Mr. Dormer—"

"What are you going to do to get his attention?" Pete asks.

I shrug. I have no idea.

"Like a girl suddenly appearing out of thin air in front of him won't already have his full attention?" Tina says.

"He's liable to be so surprised at seeing you materialize that he'll pull the trigger in a...what do you call it? Automatic response?"

"Auto*nomic*," I correct.

"Alice! Dude! I don't care! The point is, you'll be a goner."

Tina nods. "Yeah, Al, he'll shoot you dead."

"He won't shoot me," I say, not knowing who I'm trying to convince more, them or myself. Yes, Dodgson is dangerous, especially on that day, and I'm taking one hell of a risk trying to intervene. There *is* the possibility I won't succeed because he'll kill me. Okay, so it's a *strong* possibility. There's also the possibility I won't succeed because I can't, because the universe won't allow a paradox to occur, that I can't possibly stop Dodgson from doing what he did because the past, having already been written, is immutable. But because no one—to the knowledge of the world as we know it—has ever time travelled, we can't possibly know for sure.

"What makes you so sure?" Pete asks. His eyes have grown dewy, making his irises look like melted dark chocolate.

"You said an older version of myself gave you a list of dates when you were a kid—"

"What? You went to see *him* and not *me* in the future?" Way to make it all about you, Tina.

"If I survive this thing with Dodgson I promise to visit you in the future, Tina."

"Not cool, Al."

I shake my head at her, then turn back to Pete. "If I die when I'm a teenager, how can I possibly visit you as an adult to give you the list."

"I was nine years old, Al. What nine-year-old knows the difference between sixteen and twenty? All I know is you *looked* like an adult. You could give me the list tonight, be shot by Dodgson tomorrow, and I'd never know the difference."

"I saw you when you were thirty, maybe forty. You were talking on the phone to someone that might have been me." Or it could have been Tina. The jury's still out on whether or not Tina's a home wrecker in the future, breaking me and Pete up, or if Pete and me break up and Tina moves in. Either way, there's probably a reason I haven't visited Tina in the future. I decide not to share that peach of insight with the group.

"Did you hear me call you by name?"

"Well, no. But there's a really good chance you were talking to me."

"Or I might have been talking to my future wife."

"A future wife that would let you pick up your former girlfriend in the middle of the night?"

"If you're dead in that future, why would she care?"

"If you told her your former girlfriend time travelled then why wouldn't she have you locked up instead?"

"Children! Please," Tina says. "Our teacher always talks about letting ideas percolate when we're stuck. I vote we take a day or two to think about this and let our thoughts percolate a bit. There has to be a better solution than putting Alice's life at risk again."

"I second that motion," Pete says.

Tina holds her hand out, palm down, hovering over the table. Pete puts his hand on top of hers.

"Are you in, Al?" Tina asks.

I don't know what to do. I feel as if I've run out of options. What possible good would taking time do? Dodgson's still in jail because of what he did. I refuse to believe there isn't anything—not a single thing—I can do to change what happened. Pete called my time travelling an ability. Until I am able to put it to good use, to do something *with* it, I'd consider it more of a ginormous liability.

"Third the motion, Al," Pete tells me.

I shrug and put my hand on top of Pete's. "I'm in. I third the motion."

"So you'll wait?" Pete asks.

"I'll wait."

"Team effort?" he says.

What's that they say? That it's better to ask forgiveness than permission?

"Team effort," I say, hoping they'll forgive what I'm about to do next.

58

Alice is 16 and 9

In my room.

Ready to go.

I've spent hours going over and over it in my head.

Should I, shouldn't I?

Advantage, disadvantage.

The outcome is always the same: if I'm ever going to save Miss Dinah, there's no other way—I have to confront Charles Dodgson, in the flesh, face-to-face.

On my bed, lotus position, metronome app set. I haven't really needed it in the past, but this time my destination is precise, surgical, no room for error. It should start out slow. If I metre my breathing, it should help me relax. When it begins to speed, if I can match my breath to it, it should help agitate my psyche enough to the point where I...you know.

I prop the Dollarama mirror up on my bedside table.

The digital metronome starts the second I touch the "Start" button. Tick...tick...tick...Breathe in...breathe out...in through the nose...out through the mouth. Tick...breathe in, deep into my belly...tick...slowly hiss it out between my lips.

I am calm. I am Zen. I can do this.

The ticking speeds up a bit and I breathe in time with the new beat. Time to start thinking unhappy thoughts.

The layout of the third-grade classroom.

The orientation of the classroom with respect to the cloakroom.

The kids in the classroom transitioning from story circle to take a practice spelling test.

The tick of the metronome quickens again. It takes a beat or two, but I regulate my breath accordingly.

Practically hyperventilating, my head starts to lighten. The room gives a swoop which I feel, even with my eyes closed.

It's working.

Little Alice runs to the cloakroom to get something from her backpack, I don't remember exactly what. A pencil? My spelling book? My homework? Lacey tags behind so she can get her shoes.

I imagine myself in the cloakroom, unhooking my backpack from the wall, rummaging through it.

Breathing faster now. Tuning into the hummingbird wings beating near my ear.

It was about then I heard the crack of the gun. I thought one of the beams in the ceiling was about to give way.

Then there's another.

Children screaming.

Miss Dinah herding kids, trying to maintain control. Instructing kids to overturn their desks and use them like shields, to make themselves small and invisible behind them.

She recognized the sound for what it was.

Gunfire.

Lacey jamming herself into a cubby at the side of the cloakroom.

No desks to hide behind.

If I make myself small and crawl under the bench?

The click-click of the metronome speeds again, as if counting seconds down. I can no longer catch my breath.

My comforter is soft beneath my bum and legs. Sweat drenches my hair and neckline. My palms are dewy. I feel my mouth widen, gasping for air on its own accord.

Now's the time, Alice, I tell myself, so I open my eyes and turn my head toward the mirror. I see my reflection in the periphery of my vision, but just barely.

Then the mattress hardens. Children weep somewhere to my right. My damp skin forces a chill in the changed air. I hear heavy breathing behind me, and I blink.

I'm there. In the third-grade cloakroom, sitting on the linoleum in lotus position. I climb to my feet, grateful for the return of blood flow to my legs.

The doorknob rattles.

I take a step back and practically trip over a little girl, crouching half under the bench behind me.

She's scrunched into a ball, nearly hyperventilating, hands over her ears as if to protect her head, weeping.

Instinctively, I crouch beside her, smooth the hair at the back of her head and whisper, "It's going to be okay, sweetie, I promise," to her.

The door handle explodes, startling the two of us. It swings quickly open.

Dodgson.

"Shhh, shhh, shhh," I tell the girl one more time. "It's going to be okay." I rest my hand on the back of her head, and then stand up.

Dodgson's broad body fills the doorway, blocking the view to the corridor. He wears clothing reminiscent of combat gear, which speaks volumes as to how he sees himself. In his mind, he's a freedom fighter of sorts, a mercenary sent to smite the evil Mr. Dormer, retaliation for ruining his life. He carries a gun in his hand. Whatever make or model, it's big; that's all I see.

I take a step toward him and he kind of smiles, like I'm making his job easy for him or something, and in a way, I suppose I am.

"You're Charles, right?"

He laughs. My brain hears it in slow motion, syllables lengthening into a sort of mwah haa haa, deep and sinister. He levels the gun at my chest. "Who wants to know?"

"We don't have time for niceties, Charles. The important thing is you need to know Mr. Dormer's not here."

His eyebrows knit together and the gun lowers to about 45 degrees from the ground.

"He's out for the year. Drunk driver got him."

He looks to the ground as if considering his predicament, but then raises the gun and points it back at me. "What do you know about Dormer?"

"I know you have some sort of stupid grudge against him." Okay, so maybe calling his *raison d'etre* stupid isn't the best tactic given the situation, but in all of the scenarios I'd imagined, him letting me engage him in civil conversation wasn't one of them. "I know you're going to hurt, possibly kill, innocent teachers and students if you don't stand down now."

He presses his eyebrows together again as if thinking, and squints at me.

A cacophony of heels clack in the hallway and a few voices shout, far away at this particular moment in time, but getting closer.

Dodgson looks toward the noise and I take a step toward him. I don't know what I think I'm doing...preparing to disarm him? Yeah, like that could ever happen.

He looks back at me. His face relaxes. Then he grins, levels the gun, and pulls the trigger.

I Will Be Alice

59

Pete is 9

Alice gets up to play a game of hopscotch with one of her friends before the end of recess. I'm lying under the old oak tree, thinking about our conversation, when a woman calls to me from the other side of the schoolyard fence.

I sit up and turn toward her, kind of tilting my head as if to ask her who she is.

"Pete Flay? That you?"

I walk toward the chain-link fence enclosing the schoolyard, throwing stranger-danger to the wind. YOLO, right? Besides, I'm over here and she's over there. There's not much she can do to me through the fence, anyway. "Do I know you?" I ask.

"I know Alice," she says. "Alice Carroll?"

I shrug.

"You like Alice, don't you?"

Of course, I do. Alice is my closest and bestest friend, but I don't want to tell *her* that, so I just shrug again.

"If she were in trouble, you'd want to help her, wouldn't you?"

Stupid question. Of course, I would. I sort of nod.

"Good boy," she says. "Here." She shoves a piece of three-ringed, lined paper, rolled into a tube through one of the diamonds in the metal fence.

"What's this?" I ask. If I go to get the paper, I'd have to get closer, within touching distance, which could be bad.

"A note. Something for you."

My hands jerk, as if they intend to take the page from her without my permission. When I get back control, I fold my hands up behind my back. "I shouldn't. I'm not supposed to talk to strangers."

"I'm not a stranger, Pete, not really. Not if we both know Alice. It's like...have you ever heard of that game, Six Degrees of Separation?"

"I've heard of Six Degrees of Kevin Bacon. They played it in a movie I saw once."

"Something like that," she says. "If we both know Alice, then there's no more than two degrees of separation between us at best."

"We're practically related," I say, making a joke because I'm nervous. Games can be fun, and the message on her paper could be like a treasure map or something. The more I think about it, the more I need to know, so I ask her, "What's on the paper?"

"Take it and see for yourself."

No getting away from it now. I take a quick step forward, jerk the paper from her hand, and take a quick step back, like a great boa pouncing. When I unfold the paper, I'm kind of disappointed at what's there. "Dates?" I ask.

The woman nods. "Uh-huh."

"None of them have even happened yet."

She shrugs.

"What am I supposed to do with it?"

"Keep it. Put it somewhere safe."

"Then what?" I take another look at the dates, counting them, and then counting on my fingers, trying to figure out how many days, weeks, months, or years before the first one.

"Be ready to help Alice on those days."

"Why does Alice need help?"

"That's just it. She doesn't. Not yet."

I kick at the leaves at the bottom of the fence. I've already lost my interest in this game that doesn't seem like a game. If I can get in on the soccer game with the other kids before the bell rings...

I look over my shoulder at the guys playing and then back to the woman. "*Why* will she need help?" I ask.

"I can't tell you that."

"How am I supposed to help? I'm just a kid."

"Alice will find you when she needs you."

"How will she know where to find me?"

"I'll tell her."

One of the teachers on yard duty calls my name, so I swing my head around, trying to get it all the way around without moving my body, like an owl, so I can see her. The woman says, "Keep the list safe," in no more than a whisper. "And whatever you do, don't share it with Alice."

She walks away. I fold the paper roll into a long rectangle, fold it in half, stuff it into my back jeans pocket, and make a mental note to take it out and put it in a safe place before Mom throws it into the wash with my jeans.

60

Pete is 16

Mrs. Carroll lets me in. Tells me Alice is in her bedroom. When I get there the door's closed, so I knock, but there's no answer. I wait for a ten-count and knock again. When I hear nothing again, I call her name and press my ear to the door.

I think I hear shuffling and moaning. This can't be good.

I say, "I'm coming in," and turn the doorknob practically simultaneously.

Alice is lying on her bed. She gasps for air and I notice the blood. So much blood. "Oh my God!" I say, and rush to her side.

"Alice?" I say. I tap her cheek with an open palm like they do on television whenever someone's unconscious, and her eyelids flutter, but otherwise there's no response, so I grind my knuckle into her solar plexus. They do that, too. On television. Whenever someone's out cold. Before they try to revive them.

Still nothing.

Her bed sheets are practically saturated with blood.

There's a t-shirt on the floor. I get it, ball it up, and press it against her wound. It looks exactly like what I imagine a gunshot to look like, small and circular, with a raised ridge around the perimeter.

"Mrs. Carroll?" I call as loud as I can. "Help! Mrs. Carroll!" but I don't know if she can hear me. I have to go get her. With hands so shaky I can barely control them, I prop Alice's hand against the makeshift bandage and rush to the top of the stairs. "Mrs. Carroll!" I call as loud as I can. "Help! Call 9-1-1!" and I return to put pressure on Alice's wound.

A second or two after I re-position myself at Alice's bedside I hear Mrs. Carroll bound up the stairs.

"Oh my God!" she says after taking in the scene. She squeezes between me and the bedside table and strokes Alice's cheek.

"She's still alive." My voice wavers as I speak.

"Alice?" Mrs. Carroll says, and I realize if anyone's going to call for help it has to be me.

The EMTs arrive what seems like an eternity later, put pressure on the wound, affix an oxygen mask to Alice's face, load her onto a stretcher, and rush her out the front door. Mrs. Carroll announces she's going with Alice in the ambulance and takes off like a shot, leaving me behind to contend with the police.

When I manage to convince them I wasn't involved in the shooting, they swab my hands for gunshot residue (also like on television) and tell me not to leave town until the investigation is resolved, which is so cliché it's practically comical.

The police investigate Alice's house but they find no guns. No evidence anyone except the investigating officers has ever brought a gun into the house.

They x-ray and ultrasound Alice's body. She was shot in what you call a through-and-through. There's an entrance wound and an exit wound, and the bullet missed all internal organs, which is good because they don't have to do surgery beyond sewing her up.

In the end, even though there was no gunshot residue on Alice's hands and they never found the bullet, they dub Alice's situation a suicide attempt, claiming the wound was self inflicted. Death by committing *hari-kari* with a hot, invisible poker? That's a new one, even for me. They eventually drop the case. If Alice pulls through they will keep her on a 48-hour psych hold and get a court order demanding regular meetings with a shrink.

Mrs. Carroll wastes no time in calling Dr. Hatfield to set the appointments up.

When they let me see her, I can't bring myself to stay more than a few minutes. She looks so small lying in that bed, naked except for the white sheet covering her, machines breathing for her. They explain they've put her in a medically induced coma to expedite the healing process, but I don't know.

I sit at her bedside holding her hand, praying; at this point, it's the only thing I know to do that might actually make a difference.

61

Pete is 18

When the day arrives I check my list for the address, find the route on Google Maps, and set out to get her. What I see is Mabel, all of fourteen and practically naked in shorty pajamas in the designated alleyway. The wheels screech when I stop the car. I reach over to unlatch the passenger-side door, throw it open, hold out my hand and say, "Come with me if you want to live," in a cheesy Arnold impersonation; she doesn't appear impressed.

I throw her a blanket, tell her to stay warm, and take her to my dad's condo.

Once there I open a tin of chicken noodle soup and wait for her to change her clothes. When she comes back, she pours herself a glass of water, and my phone rings.

My Girl.

Tina.

I made it her ringtone after that stupid night when we threw that flash birthday for her at Alice's, and she got drunk, and we danced on the front lawn to the bass of that song as it played on the basement stereo. Life was good then. For that one night, Alice forgot about her problem and we partied like the kids we were meant to be.

I send the call to voicemail which, for some reason, sets Mabel off. She wants—correction: demands—to know why Tina would be calling me. When I'm evasive with my answer, she bolts out the door and down the hall. I catch her at the elevator and talk her back in.

I can't tell her why Tina's calling me. Back in our teens, back when this all began and Alice decided to try to take control of her problem, she swore me to secrecy. She knew about the list Future Alice gave Little Pete and told me she didn't want to know. I wound up sharing the burden with Tina because I had to talk to someone. If that someone couldn't be Alice, then Tina was the next best thing.

Did she really think I would...could...betray her? And with Tina, of all people?

She needs an answer—she never was one to accept a no—so I make something up. I tell her she and I drifted while Tina and I grew close.

Mabel gets up and manages to shimmy between my torso and the table and onto my lap. She hugs me, resting her head on my shoulder. Before I can protest, she pulls her head from my shoulder and kisses me on my lips.

I pull away and say her name, but she tells me to shush and tries to kiss me again. I take her hands from behind my neck and hold them together in front of her and between us. When I look at her I see glimpses of my Alice. But this one's not her. This one's jail bait. I could get into serious trouble if I don't shut this down, like, yesterday.

"This is wrong," I tell her.

Ever the hopeless romantic, Mabel says, "It's not, Pete. We were meant to be together. You know we were."

Tina chooses that precise moment to call again, probably anxious to find out if my mission was a success, if the dates on the list Future Alice gave me were actually correct.

"Impeccable timing," Mabel says. She's right. And thank heaven for that.

"Look," I tell her, "I gotta get this or she's just going to continue calling until I do." I answer the phone with a "Hey, babe."

"Babe?" Tina says on the other end. "Since when do you call me babe?

"Do you have her?"

"Of course I do," I tell her. I turn toward Mabel as if to confirm what I've just said with my own eyes, but all that's left of her is a half-eaten bowl of soup and glass of water on the kitchen table.

62

Pete is 31

I arrive just as Mabel's being swarmed by a bunch of kids in the designated alleyway clad in a humungous white sweatshirt reading "I love Toronto", but the love is a heart, and inside the heart is a Canadian flag.

Though I realize this scenario most likely ends with one or both of us dead, I push the kids out of the way and extend a hand to Mabel, which she takes without hesitation. I pull her from the epicentre of impending disaster and holler, "Run!" practically dragging her down the alley, along the adjacent street, and down the driveway leading to the employee entrance of the Royal Ontario Museum. We stop and I scope the area. When I'm sure we're okay, I lean over onto my knees and try to catch my breath. It's times like this I realize I need to hit the gym more often.

"I think we lost them," I huff out between breaths.

Feisty as ever, Mabel says, "What the hell?"

I can't explain. Not now. Not ever. We have a pact. Alice, me and Tina. And though it seems childish, I'm bound by that pact for all of eternity. Lives—our lives, Alice's life—may rest in the balance.

"No time," I tell her and pull her into the employee entrance.

While Mabel is using the washroom I call Tina to let her know everything went off as planned. Sort of.

Tina answers saying, "You got her?"

"Yeah," I tell her, "I've got her."

"How is she?"

Cold. Terrified. Curious. "She's fine," I say.

"You're sure? 'Cause I understand this one's rough."

Rough? You can say that again. The question is, who it's rougher for: me or Mabel? I say, "No, really, she's fine." I hear rustling and turn to see Mabel dressed in a grey t-shirt and black, baggy yoga pants. "Look, she's here now. I gotta go," I tell her.

"Okay. Keep me posted if anything happens."

"Okay. Same here."

Now that she's out of that hideous sweatshirt and into the light, I see that this Mabel is much younger than the last time she came to visit me. This one's pre-pubescent and full of spit, vinegar, and questions.

She insists on calling me Charming, as in Prince, and I'm reminded of the first time Snow White meets Prince James on *Once Upon A Time*. I wonder if she's thinking the same thing when, after I tell her she's incorrigible, she sarcastically confirms that dubbing me "Charming" was the right move.

Bored in the staff room, Mabel passes time putting me through the inquisition. Do I save damsels in distress for a living? How do I know her? When are we in time? Do I know her parents? How old am I? What is our relationship?

I remember Alice at that age. Only two things interested her: her British boys and food.

"Are we married?" she asks.

"Are you hungry, May?" I say, hoping to change the subject.

"I could go for food."

Bingo!

Mabel takes one of the bowls of red Jell-O and a bottle of orange juice from the tray. She opens the juice bottle, takes a sip, and resumes her game of twenty questions. Thank goodness she's tired of calling me Charming.

"Drink up," I say, hoping to divert her attention.

"Why?"

"Keeps the potassium levels high." It's getting late, nearly ten. Pretty soon security's going to start ushering us out so they can lock up for the night. I manage to stifle a yawn, taking my glasses off and rubbing my eyes instead.

"Pete?" Mabel asks.

"No." I stuff my mouth with the largest cube of Jell-O in my bowl, pull the bowl close, and focus on selecting the next piece rather than make eye contact with her again.

"Why can't you just tell me?" she asks.

I try, but can't pinpoint the year we had the discussion about contaminating timelines and creating paradoxes, about how even the fact that the two of us sitting here having this conversation might be equivalent to that butterfly in the Bradbury story, changing life as we know it for all eternity. Rather than re-hash the entire history of time travel popular culture, I say, "Because I don't want to affect the timeline. I kind of like who I am, who you are, and I don't want to change any of it, so can't we please just eat our Jell-O and wait in silence until you go back?"

Mabel sighs and says, "You were right. Time travel *is* lame."

63

Pete is 46

I come home after a late-night business dinner. It was worth the time spent schmoozing the evening away, stuffing myself with nachos and chicken wings, nursing my one and only beer of the night—we got the contract.

After escorting the client to the hotel elevator, multiple high fives from my colleagues, and repeated pats on each others' backs, it was time to go home, to get whatever sleep I could salvage before I had to report back to work in the morning and de-brief.

I let myself in, lock the door behind me, detour to the kitchen to take a swig of Pepto to settle my stomach, and tiptoe up the stairs.

The bed is unkempt and empty, just as I left it this morning. I hardly ever make the bed anymore. What's the point of making it when the house sits empty all day and you're only going to unmake it when you return later in the day?

I loosen the knot in my tie. There's a puff of air behind me, and I turn to see her standing there. Her hair is wind-whipped, damp and wild, her complexion ruddy, as if she's been caught in a storm. Her metabolism is like it was when she was a teen, helping her dodge the mid-life, mid-section bulge to which I've succumbed. Her body's all angles and curves, her skin smooth as silk, unmarred with the exception of a small, circular, spider-webbed scar just above her left hip.

She takes a step toward me, throws her arms around my neck, and squeezes her body close to mine. She smells of vanilla and pine. I take her by the shoulders, take a step back, and kiss her, long and on the lips.

"I was beginning to worry," I tell her.

"Just getting home now?" she asks.

"Client took a bit more convincing than we'd previously thought."

"I'm going to take a shower." She turns, enters the *en suite* bathroom and closes the door behind her.

"Did you do it?" I ask through the door. "Did you give me the list?"

She opens the door just enough to poke her head through. "You were so cute at that age. What happened to you?" She cocks her head to one side, smiles, and sticks her tongue out, as if I wouldn't understand she was joking otherwise.

"Ha, ha, very funny." I reach out to grab her tongue and she pulls her head back. "You're a laugh riot, Alice," I say, quoting Jackie Gleason from *The Honeymooners* repeats my dad forced me to watch growing up. I absolutely hated black and white television but thought it hilarious that Gleason's wife on the show had the same name as my best friend at the time.

She closes the door between us and I hear the lock click.

"So, you did it?" I ask again.

"Why don't you see for yourself?"

I unlock my cell phone and open my photo gallery. In the list of albums is one called "Alice". I open it, slide through the pictures of Alice as a kid, as a teen, as a young woman, until I find the one I want. When at last I see it, I can't help but let out a sigh of relief.

It's a picture of the list. Dates and locations. The one Future Alice gave me that day in the schoolyard, just as I remember it.

Reader and Reviewer

A glooming peace this ending us doth bring;
The story, it is hoped, will pleasure give:
Go, hence, to have more talk of these glad things;
Some shall be excited, and some pensive:
For never was story craved not review
Please go online and write lines but a few.

About the Author

Elise Abram is high school teacher of English and Computer Studies, former archaeologist, editor, publisher, award winning author, avid reader of literary and science fiction, and student of the human condition. Everything she does, watches, reads and hears is fodder for her writing. She is passionate about writing and language, cooking, differentiated instruction, and ABC's Once Upon A Time. In her spare time she experiments with paleo cookery, knits badly, and writes. She also bakes. Most of the time it doesn't burn. Her family doesn't seem to mind.

http://eliseabram.com

IF YOU LIKED *PHASE SHIFT*

YOU WON'T WANT TO MISS

MOLLY AND PALMER IN

THROWAWAY CHILD

The skeleton of a young girl is found beneath the cement basement floor in an abandoned Victorian in Toronto. On duty is Detective Constable Michael Crestwood who contacts forensic anthropologist Dr. Palmer Richardson to assist in the investigation. What they uncover is the story of a six year old Cree girl, stolen from her family, warehoused in a government run facility and then forgotten.

In a story with ties to current headlines, THROWAWAY CHILD explores the injustice experienced by two girls imprisoned in a mid-twentieth century residential school and the tragic fallout ensuing as a result of one girl's need to find a home.

amounts to nothing but a huge cosmic mistake, she finds purpose in her abilities when she is recruited to help Zulu and Morgan complete their missions.

Malchus is Morgan's long dead twin brother. A powerful necromancer, Malchus manages to find a way to return to the living, and he has a score to settle with Morgan. Believing Morgan responsible for his death and out to seek revenge, Malchus begins to raise an army of undead minions and use them to hunt Morgan down. As Malchus closes in on Morgan and his charges, the trio soon realizes the people most in need of saving are themselves.

www.ingramcontent.com/pod-product-compliance
Lightning Source LLC
Chambersburg PA
CBHW060947120726
47910CB00002B/529